SUTTON'S SECRETS
THE SINFUL SUTTONS
BOOK SEVEN

SCARLETT SCOTT

Sutton's Secrets

The Sinful Suttons Book 7

All rights reserved.

Copyright © 2023 by Scarlett Scott

Published by Happily Ever After Books, LLC

Edited by Grace Bradley

Developmental Editing by Emerald Edits

Cover Design by Wicked Smart Designs

This book or any portion thereof may not be reproduced or used in any manner whatsoever without the express written permission of the publisher except for the use of brief quotations in a book review.

The unauthorized reproduction or distribution of this copyrighted work is illegal. No part of this book may be scanned, uploaded, or distributed via the Internet or any other means, electronic or print, without the publisher's permission. Criminal copyright infringement, including infringement without monetary gain, is punishable by law.

This book is a work of fiction and any resemblance to persons, living or dead, or places, events, or locales, is purely coincidental. The characters are productions of the author's imagination and used fictitiously.

For more information, contact author Scarlett Scott.

https://scarlettscottauthor.com

For my readers, with everlasting gratitude for your support, kind words, and love for my books. I'll never be able to thank you enough.

AUTHOR'S NOTE

Some events within this book happen concurrently with events which happened in previous books in The Sinful Suttons series. If you haven't read those books, don't worry. This is stand-alone. But if you have, you'll be seeing these events from Logan's perspective.

CHAPTER 1

Logan took a puff of his cheroot, watching everyone, trusting no one. Smoke hung in the air, a silver shroud providing him with a momentary screen as he surveyed the chamber. Willowby's was a stunningly plummy establishment. A place where sinners congregated to partake in any vice they chose, assured of their privacy.

The walls were hung with scarlet damask, offset by elaborate French curtains draped over the windows to create an illusion of seclusion from the outside world. Even the chairs, Grecian affairs fashioned of mahogany with inlaid ebony and red Morocco leather, were a marvel. The matching card tables were enhanced by scrollwork and gilt.

One had to merely step one foot inside to know it was for the well-equipped. Only culls flush with coin would be able to afford the games being played within this lair. And aye, by comparison, it made his own family's gaming hell, The Sinner's Palace, look like a tumbledown, second-rate den for vagabonds and filching coves.

But it had been some time since he'd last been within those once-familiar walls, and he wasn't here to fret over the competition. Nor to gamble or sample the fine swill or attract the even finer quim.

Rather, he was here on deadly important business, awaiting the arrival of a man known only as *the Major*. The exchange—information about the next secret meeting amongst the remaining members of the London Reform Society in return for two hundred pounds—had been arranged by Logan's superior at the Guild, Archer Tierney.

The group of revolutionaries behind the Society were as depraved as they were brazen. They were willing to commit any crime, regardless of the victims, in the name of their proposed revolution. Attacks on the Tower of London, plots to murder prominent members of the government. And that was just the start. All of which necessitated a great deal of care in the negotiations which would ensue this evening.

Nothing had been left to chance.

The Major was to meet Logan here, sit at the table, and tell him that he heard the port at Willowby's was particularly fine. The Major had been previously informed concerning the details of Logan's appearance; the color of his hair, the coat and cravat he would be wearing, the table at which he would be seated.

Logan and his informant would share a glass of port. At some point during the course of their interview, a missive would be passed to Logan from the Major. Logan would pay the man the agreed-upon sum. He was to linger at Willowby's, to avoid drawing undue attention to himself and his mission, lose a game of *vingt-et-un*, and subsequently depart. He would then take the communication immediately to Archer.

But the appointed hour for the Major's arrival had already come and gone. The fellow had either been waylaid or had experienced a change of heart. It wouldn't be the first time an informant failed to appear since Logan had begun his covert work for the Guild. And he knew it wouldn't be the last.

Feigning *ennui*, he extracted his pocket watch and consulted the time.

The Major was one quarter hour late. Logan reached for his port, taking another slow, small sip.

And that was when he saw her.

She was not the only woman in the club's main room. Nor was she the only beauty. There were petticoats aplenty to distract, for Willowby's was a place where men and women mingled freely.

But this woman was different from all the rest in a way that was indefinably alluring. It was an enchanting combination, he thought, of the way she carried herself and the way she dressed. She simmered with intelligence and boldness, and a glance at the other coves proved he was not the only one captivated by her.

But inevitably, his gaze returned to her. She moved through the throng of gents with grace and poise. She wore a gown of vibrant, red velvet that showed her figure to perfection, her pale breasts on display above a bodice bedecked with silver rosettes. Her shoulders were bare, her arms concealed in white lace sleeves that hugged her wrists, and a necklace of triple pearls with gold ornamented her throat. Rubies glimmered from her ears, her hair a profusion of glossy jet curls framing her face and caught at her crown to trail in further ringlets down her nape.

From across the chamber, her gold-brown gaze collided with his.

Logan felt the intensity of that stare—that marrow-deep connection—to his soul. It was as if he were looking at the other half of himself, someone who was meant for him. The acknowledgment was tacit, but he swore she felt it too, simmering between them, as tangible as a touch.

But as longing arose, he suppressed it with force. He was not here at Willowby's tonight to be distracted by a woman, regardless of how enticing she was. He was here to meet with the Major. To gain information that could ultimately prove priceless.

It was imperative that he remain clearheaded and calm. He could not afford for lust to addle his wits. When he had first become part of the Guild—a clandestine group of mercenaries who reported directly to Whitehall—he had never imagined how deep London's secrets ran. Nor how entrenched in them he would become.

His former life had been his family, the Suttons. His boisterous brothers and sisters and The Sinner's Palace. Until he'd chosen to join the Guild, leaving them all behind without a word of where he'd gone or why. Abandoning them had been as devastating as it had been necessary. He could no longer call himself a Sutton now; instead, he'd taken on the surname Martin. Yet another disguise. One more way to keep his identity secret and the family he'd left safe. It was the least he could do; he owed them far, far more.

His fingers tightened on his glass. His eldest brother Jasper would no doubt have had his hide for inviting such peril upon himself. And Logan couldn't blame him. Their hell had been growing stronger and more profitable every day. They'd each had a role, a hand in its success.

But Logan couldn't deny the draw to take on something beyond their little world. To do something important. To make a difference. To weed out the traitors amongst them and bring them to justice.

His gaze slid back to the woman in red. She was sweeping toward him, the light of the wall sconces and chandelier overhead dancing in the glint of her earrings and the silver threads adorning her gown. She was nothing short of dazzling, and he, who had dallied with any number of fine morts, had never seen anyone quite like her.

Damn it.

If she distracted him and kept him from the Major…

She approached his table, near enough to touch now, bringing with her the divine scent of something floral and decadent. *Violets.* He drew on his cheroot to distract himself, relishing the burn in his lungs, and exhaled, chasing her perfume with smoke.

"Good evening, sir," she greeted in a voice as sweet and thick as honey.

And his first thought, dicked in the nob as he was, was that he wanted to hear that voice moaning his name. *Floating hell*, what was wrong with him? He wasn't here to bring a woman back to his rooms. He was here on behalf of the Guild.

"Good evening," he returned, not rising as a gentleman likely would. Just as well. Logan Sutton wasn't a bleeding gentry cove.

"You are not here to play?" she asked softly, her gold-brown gaze still holding him captive.

Her eyes were wide and expressive, framed with lush, dark lashes. He realized belatedly that she carried a brisé fan, only after she opened it and fluttered the painted ivory before her.

"I'm currently here to sit in this chair," he told her, raising a brow, keeping his countenance blank.

It was a polite way of telling her to shift her bob without uttering the words *go away*. But she didn't leave. Instead, she pressed the fan to her lips, as if she were enjoying a game of her own, keeping a secret. If the corners of her eyes were any indication, she was shielding a smile that he very much wanted to see.

"And partake of the port, presumably," she said, her gaze dipping to his hand, curled around his glass.

His fingers tightened. Little sparks of lust lit like a hundred small, agonizing fires, burning him from the inside out. Fortunately, he was too strong to succumb.

"Forgive me, milady," he drawled, "but I'm waiting for a friend."

She drew the fan away, revealing her mouth, which was the same dark red as her velvet gown, and looked every bit as soft and inviting. He wondered if it was an effect. Had she painted her lips? Or were they naturally so dark and lush?

He didn't have long to consider the nonsensical questions.

For that mouth opened and, quite impossibly, uttered the words he had been waiting all evening to hear.

"I have heard that the port here at Willowby's is especially fine."

∼

SHE HAD BEEN TOLD that the man she was to meet would have striking red-brown hair and that he would be wearing a coat of midnight with a black cravat. Arianna had not been warned, however, that he would be so handsome that he stole her breath. That his eyes, neither blue nor green, but instead a rare and mysterious shade of hazel with hints of other hues, would burn into hers as if he could see her every secret. That his jaw would possess the sharp angle of a blade, his cheekbones high, his entire being sizzling with an intensity that made her knees go weak.

But then, it was not as if Father would have relayed any of that most pertinent information. All he had told her was where to be and when, along with what she was meant to do with the missive tucked safely within her stays.

As she offered the observation Father had told her she must to the stranger—a means of proving to him that she was the Major—the man's demeanor shifted. His eyes sharpened, his entire bearing tightening, shoulders going taut. And his gaze swept down her body in a way that made forbidden awareness wash over her.

"You have, madam?" he asked, his voice gruff and low as he dragged a hand along his tensed jaw.

He didn't trust her.

It came as no surprise. He was likely hardened and experienced, while she was naïve and raw. Nervous and new to this game she was being forced to play, hands trembling as worry coiled in her belly like a serpent ready to strike.

She was doing this for Juliet's sake, she reminded herself sternly, thinking of the sister she loved beyond measure. Anything to give Juliet the chance at the happiness she deserved. The happiness which had been denied Arianna, through circumstances beyond her control.

She fluttered her fan in coquettish fashion, hoping that anyone in the room who looked upon them would see what she wanted and nothing more. A widow who had come here to gamble, to flirt. That they would have no notion of how quickly her heart raced, nor how damp her palms were beneath her gloves.

"May I sit?" she asked the alluring stranger.

He nodded. "Reckon so."

It was hardly an invitation. His tone, like his countenance, was forbidding. Grim.

Arianna summoned her bravado and gave him a slow, forced smile, closing her fan. "Were you not expecting me?"

His nostrils flared. "Don't know what I was expecting. Sit."

With his booted foot, he gave the leg of the chair nearest her an indelicate shove.

Not one for manners, then. He seemed vexed with her, his mood an abrupt shift from the sparkling connection that had been simmering from the moment their stares had met and held. She'd never felt anything like it, that searing bond, as if he had reached out and clasped her hand in his, an invisible force pulling her toward him.

It had only been belatedly that she had taken note of his appearance and realized he was the man from the Guild that she was meant to meet.

Arianna drew back the chair a bit more and seated herself primly, aware of her proximity to his tall, lean form. Of how he was near enough to touch, the heat emanating from his big body almost palpable.

"Thank you," she said demurely. "Perhaps I ought to taste the port for myself."

Father had been clear on what she was meant to do. The missive secreted in her stays felt like a leaden weight. She found herself wishing that she could be herself with the man watching her. That she did not have the burden of Juliet's future and her father's welfare weighing upon her conscience.

But then she reminded herself sternly that she was the only one who could be here at Willowby's. Juliet would be ruined if she stepped one foot inside such an establishment, all hopes for a future match—already made dismally slim by virtue of their father losing his entire fortune—banished in the blink of an eye. And given Father's association with the London Reform Society, he could never be seen meeting in public with a member of the Guild. The risks were far too great.

The gentleman opposite her signaled for one of the attendants to produce another glass. It was placed before her, filled too full for her liking. She wished to remain as lucid as possible.

She waited for the servant to move away before bringing the glass to her lips, holding the gaze of the man opposite her as she did so, taking care to leave a lone drop lingering. With her tongue, she slowly licked it away, gratified when his expression changed, a new, carnal flare of awareness burning in the depths of his eyes as his gaze slipped to her mouth.

"You are here to meet the Major, are you not?" she asked now that she had his attention where she wanted it.

"You know I am," he said. "But you ain't a cove."

She gave him a smile, taking her fan and dragging it slowly along the edge of her bodice. "How observant you are, sir."

Arianna wondered what his name was. It shouldn't matter, but she wanted to know it just the same. In her mind, if not on her lips.

"Do you 'ave it?" he asked suddenly, the absence of the *h* drawing her attention to the coarseness in his accent, a hint of the rookeries he seemed to do his utmost to hide.

But something was nettling him enough to draw out that tiny, revealing hint.

Excellent. She wanted his guard lowered. Wanted him to desire her. And it startled her to realize that it was not merely because of the role she was playing, the duty she performed on behalf of her father and her sister. Instead, it was because of the man watching her with that glinting gray-green gaze.

"Do I have what?" she teased him, the missive burning from its careful position just between her breasts.

"What you're meant to give me," he said, lifting his own glass of port slowly to his lips.

She watched, captivated by the sight, forgetting herself for a heartbeat. How alarmingly easy it was to do so in this man's presence. To disregard the carefully planned series of events she was meant to orchestrate. There was danger in her reaction to him, for if she lowered her own defenses, she made herself vulnerable to discovery. And, in turn, she made her father vulnerable as well.

This is a matter of life and death, he had warned her grimly, just before she had departed earlier that evening. *Yours as well as ours. We are relying upon you. If the London Reform Society should ever discover my involvement...*

He hadn't finished his thoughts. He hadn't needed to.

She jolted herself from the spell the handsome stranger had seemingly cast over her, reminding herself she was the one who possessed all the power in this exchange of theirs. "And what is it that I am meant to give you?"

He raised his glass to her in mock salute. "You know, *Major*."

The way he said *Major*—slowly and with deliberate, sensual intent—rolled down her spine. Sent longing winging through her like lightning through the sky, shocking her with her own response. Her marriage to Edgar had been cold and passionless. She'd surrendered all hope she would ever experience desire.

She suddenly wanted to be alone with this man.

To be anywhere other than here.

But that was not how she was supposed to handle this situation, and she knew it. She was supposed to flirt. To proceed slowly. And above all, she was to never reveal the truth of who she was, what she was doing, or why.

"There is a private room," she told him quietly, for all the plans had already been laid, nothing left to chance. "Through the door over my shoulder. Down the hall. Second on the right. Meet me there, and I will give you what you have come for. I will go first." She paused, drawing the cool ivory of her closed fan over her bare flesh, casting a surreptitious glance around to make certain no one else was watching them. "Wait a few moments and join me."

She rose, intending to seek the chamber she had been told would be readied and awaiting her use. But he stayed her, his hand circling her wrist beneath the lace of her sleeve.

"Wait."

Arianna froze, trapped not so much by his grasp, which was firm yet not painful, but by the sensation of his touch. Her heart hammered hard. Every part of her became intensely aware of him. It was as if her body were enshrouded in hot silk.

She was a widow. She had been touched before.

But no one had ever affected her the way this man did.

"Unhand me," she demanded, careful to keep her tone quiet.

"I'll go first," he said, his hand still on her wrist.

She had not expected him to take command. Nor that she would *like* it.

Arianna raised her chin, studying him. "Do you want what you've come for, or do you not, sir?"

Taking another meditative puff of his cheroot before abandoning it, he slowly stood, unfolding his body from the chair until he towered over her. He was even taller than she had supposed, his long legs hidden beneath the table. And as he stretched to his full height, he seemed much larger as well. Stronger.

More dangerous.

Sinful, too.

Tempting.

He held her wrist as if it were delicate, but she also sensed he would stop her if she chose to flee.

He leaned nearer. "Your true name. Tell me."

Confiding in him, trusting him, revealing anything about herself...all these things were against the very strict rules Father had set in place for her. One false step, and she could ruin everything. And yet, she could not look away from the drugging power of his gaze. She found herself swaying toward him, drawn to him. Feverish with longing.

"Arianna," she whispered, the lone revelation all she would allow him to know.

It was reckless, making any admission, and she knew it. But everything about this man felt somehow different.

He released her wrist and then took her fan, shielding her from the other men and women in the large gaming room. But then, she doubted they would take note, consumed as they all were in their next wager, their next hint of vice. It was one of the reasons why Willowby's was an excellent choice for such assignations.

"What is your name?" she dared, knowing the man would likely not give her a truthful reply.

For all he knew, she had lied as well.

He could tell her anything, and she would have no way of knowing whether or not he was being honest.

"My name is Logan," the man said then, shocking her by using her own fan against her, trailing it along her breasts, dipping slightly to travel down her bodice. To the place where the missive was hidden. And much to her shame, her nipples tightened into painful points beneath her stays. "I could take it now, you know. But I don't want others to see."

It shocked her to realize he was speaking of the missive.

How had he known where it was hidden?

He must have understood the flash of surprise within her, for he smiled slowly, knowingly. "Come and find me."

With that, he strode away, taking her fan with him as if it were his to claim. She had to steady herself with a hand on the back of his vacated chair as she watched him go, his words echoing in her mind, one half dare, one half threat.

Come and find me.

She lingered for a few moments, attempting to collect herself, sipping far too much port in a futile bid to calm her frayed nerves. She had never supposed the man she was supposed to meet would be so wickedly handsome. That he would cause stirrings of hunger within her she had thought long dormant. But he was. And he did.

Oh, how he did.

Arianna finished the port, and then, she went in search of him.

CHAPTER 2

Logan waited in the shadows of the room Arianna had specified.

Not merely Arianna, he thought, *the Major.*

It was still almost impossible to believe that the beautiful goddess who had so entranced him and what he had presumed had been the cove he was meant to meet were one and the same. He'd never expected the Major to be a mort. But then, the façade was stupidly clever. Likely, no one expected a female, and most definitely not one so hauntingly beautiful. How better to hide?

He took stock of his surroundings, ever cognizant of the pistol secreted in his coat. Growing up in the rookeries had been bleeding perilous, and one never knew what to expect. In his old life, he had often armed himself as he was this evening. But since he had become a member of the Guild, he almost never traveled without gun and blade both. Nor did he fail to take note of any imminent danger, even when he was distracted by a beauty.

The chamber was small, a private sitting room of sorts. Stuffed chairs, a Gothic sofa table, and a fireplace dominated the room. He had taken note of the latch on the door, one on the outside and another within. The chamber was, he would wager, used often and for possibly nefarious purposes. Revealing his name to her had likely been a misstep, but lying to her had felt wrong, despite everything he'd been trained to do as a member of the Guild.

He wondered how often Arianna found herself within. Supposing Arianna was indeed her true name. Wondered how she was connected to the London Reform Society. She was involved in something deadly. Something damned dangerous. He told himself it didn't matter. That he was meeting with her to obtain the document secreted somewhere on her luscious person.

He had not missed the surprise in her eyes when he had used her fan against her, dragging it across the tempting tops of her breasts, lingering over the place where he suspected her missive was hidden. The cool ivory felt hot in his palm now as he clutched it, thinking of her.

It was wrong to be so damned drawn to a woman he could not trust.

But before he could consider his inconvenient lust any further, the door opened.

She crossed the threshold hastily, in a swirl of ruby and silver and raven curls, snapping the portal closed at her back and sliding the latch into place. She hesitated for a moment, her back presented to him, her head bent. It was the first hint of vulnerability he had spied in her since she had approached him.

Logan took the opportunity to admire the elegance of her neck, the dainty swells of her shoulders, creamy and begging to be touched. The fullness of her hips beneath the carefully draped velvet.

And then she turned to him, head held as high as any queen's. "You have my fan."

He could not contain his half grin as he sauntered toward her, drawn as surely as if there were a rope between them, and she pulled it taut with inhuman strength, luring him in. "And you have my missive."

If it was where he suspected it was hidden, it would still carry the warmth from her skin when she relinquished it to him.

"I suppose you expect an even trade," she said, meeting him halfway across the small chamber.

He was near enough to be tempted to touch her, but he denied himself the pleasure with stoic insistence. Instead, he dragged the closed fan over his open palm, watching her closely. "You failed to appear at the appointed hour. One could argue you owe me something aside from the letter."

She raised a brow, her countenance turning defiant. "And why should I owe you anything beyond what I have promised to provide?"

Her fire was intoxicating. He almost forgot, in that moment, that she was somehow in league with traitors who intended to destroy everything he risked his life to preserve. In league with them enough to know some of their secrets. To offer them for sale.

Logan leaned closer to her, stooping low so that his lips nearly grazed her ear when he spoke. "Because my time is very valuable, *Major.*"

He rose to his full height then, his grip on the fan tighter than ever to keep himself from touching her. Because he knew that if he did, remembering the clear boundaries he had to maintain would grow all but impossible.

She frowned at him, a pout on lips that were deuced kissable. "Don't call me that."

Her voice was soft. A whisper of sound. But it may as well have been a caress for the effect it had upon him.

"Don't call you Major?" he taunted, enjoying their

repartee despite himself. "Why not? It *is* your name, is it not? The name you gave to the Guild when you decided to sell the secrets of your treasonous friends."

Her nostrils flared, another indication of her distress. "They are not my friends."

Her words softened something inside him, which had previously been hard and pointed, all harsh, angry angles.

"You do not agree with them, then?" he couldn't resist asking.

He didn't know what the devil was wrong with him. He'd never taken an interest in any of the covert sources he'd met with in the past. And there had been many. A bleeding waterfall of them. But then, none of those culls had ever possessed honey-brown eyes that seared him to his soul, glossy curls, or curves that made him want to trace them with his lips and tongue.

And yet, he awaited her answer, tense as ever. Because it mattered to him.

"It is immaterial whether or not I am sympathetic to their cause," she said quietly.

Disappointment skewered him.

"Their cause is treason," he pointed out. "You do know what they've been plotting, do you not?"

She shook her head, her countenance going pale. "I have no wish to know. The less I know, the better."

It rankled that she would associate herself with such violent cutthroats. Some of the lust for her had abated, but much to his chagrin, not all.

"You prefer to live in ignorance, then?" he queried. "How are you connected to them, hmm? A brother? A father?"

"No." Some unknown emotion flashed in her expressive eyes.

"A husband or a lover?" he guessed again.

"Neither." Her lips tightened. "I'm a widow."

"Ah." Something inside him shifted. He would not say it was pity that he felt, but he understood what it was like to lose the ones he loved. Only, his family wasn't dead, but very much alive. It was Logan who had become a ghost to them. "My condolences, madam."

"Thank you," she said quietly.

Her flirtatious air had dissipated, leaving her instead looking pale and drawn. It had been bravado that had given her such boldness at their first meeting, he realized now. She was not the accomplished flirt she had pretended to be, dragging the ivory of her fan along the edge of her bodice, drawing his attention to her succulent breasts.

Breasts he must not notice now.

Or ever.

His gaze dipped.

Fuck.

What a cad he was, learning of her widowhood and then gaping at her breasts as if he'd never seen a finer pair. Although, in the interest of honesty, he was reasonably certain he hadn't.

"The information, then," he forced himself to say, his voice thick and husky, even to his own ears. "Let's have it."

The bleeding mort was seducing him without trying. He was going to have to surrender his post in the Guild if he didn't cease ogling her and get back to the business at hand. And he damn well hadn't surrendered his family and the life he'd known merely to walk away from the Guild as well. Not for a set of petticoats, regardless of how alluring she was.

"Would you be a gentleman and turn about so I can retrieve it?" she asked, her tongue wetting those dark-red lips and leaving them glistening.

Floating hell.

What he wouldn't give to kiss them.

And that was a problem. She was dangerous, this woman. To his position, to his sanity. To his restraint.

"I ain't a gentleman, love," he said, giving her a conspiratorial wink. "And I ain't a fool. I'll be watching."

It wouldn't surprise him if the London Reform Society had sent such a beautiful vixen with the promise of information, knowing every cove who saw her would give his left arm to bed her. And once the cove turned around for her to retrieve the information, she gave him a blade or a bullet to the back instead.

"Very well." Her tone was cool, but her eyes flashed fire at him. "I will turn about for my own modesty's sake if you are not willing to exercise some manners."

He shrugged. "As you please."

She made a low sound of disapproval, as if she had expected to shame him into playing the part of a noble swain and respecting her *modesty*. Ha! Rich, that was. Where he hailed from, modesty didn't even bleeding exist.

Was she a lady then? For the first time, he wondered who she truly was, beyond the woman who had come to pass off information to him. Her accent was educated enough. She carried herself well. And that velvet gown—it was fine. *Interesting.*

She turned, velvet skirts flying in her haste and revealing a hint of trim ankle encased in silk stockings. And he noticed, bastard that he was, as she presented him with her back. He noticed, too, the curve of her rump beneath the gown, the sleek curls captured in a neat chignon above her nape. She fussed with her bodice, extracting the missive from its hiding place just as he had suspected.

The devil in him thought about stalking to her, clamping his hands on her waist, and spinning her about. Hauling her lithe curves into his body and then taking her lips with his.

But he wasn't entirely touched in the head, so he

remained where he was, telling himself to think about everything that would make his cock shrivel instead. The scent of a chamber pot emptied out a window into the street. The feeling of a rat brushing up against him in the darkness. The time he'd nearly been shot...

His cock finally decided to comply and then she was facing him, extending a slender arm toward him, the sealed missive in her gloved fingers. "The information, sir."

He took the offering from her, their fingers brushing, and wild heat coursed through him, even with the barrier of kidskin separating them. And damn, but just as he had predicted, the letter was warm from the heat of her body. He would wager if he held it to his nose, the sweet violet scent of her could be detected.

Later, he thought, tucking it into his coat instead of giving in to the temptation. He extracted her payment and presented her with the exchange.

"Thank you." Her voice was quiet as she accepted the two hundred pounds.

He wanted to say more to her. To warn her of the dangers of being involved with the London Reform Society. So close to traitors and violent men. But he supposed it would have to be enough that she was willing to sell their secrets. A crisis of conscience? Or was it something else? What reason had prompted her to betray them?

His mind teemed with questions, but that would have to be where it ended, and he knew it. The rules of the Guild were unbreakable, and his duty was to his country, not to himself and his own selfish desires.

"If you have more information, you know how to reach us, I trust?" he asked, reminded of that responsibility, stronger and larger than himself.

"I do," she confirmed, before turning again.

He watched her grimly, fighting to keep from noticing

her lush, feminine form, and hoped for his own sake that there would be no further meetings between them and he would never see her again after this night.

∿

Arianna slid the payment into her bodice for safekeeping, guilt lodged heavy as a stone in her chest. She did not like what she had been reduced to—selling the London Reform Society secrets on Father's behalf. Logan's words echoed in her mind, a warning she could not shake. *Their cause is treason.*

And her father consorted with them. Sympathized with them. *Betrayed* them.

If they discovered he was behind the information being provided to the Guild…

A shiver swept over her. But no, she must not think of the consequences now. The payment—two hundred pounds that was desperately needed to pay off some of their creditors—was secured in her stays. She hoped it would be sufficient to hold everyone at bay for a time. There was some relief in knowing she had done her part in keeping them from imminent ruin for just a bit longer.

"Cold, *Major*?"

The low rumble of Logan's voice, just over her shoulder, reminded her that their meeting had yet to conclude. The same irresistible surge of awareness that had washed over her when their eyes had first met across the room earlier returned. She spun about to find him watching her with a hooded gaze that made her wonder what he was thinking. He was mocking her again, she thought, his stare cool and assessing and yet heated, too.

"I am perfectly warm," she said, "and please, do cease calling me that."

"Why? You don't like it?" he drawled, his tone deceptively lazy.

There was nothing indolent about the man before her. She had no doubt that he emerged the victor in every battle in which he engaged. He was rather reminiscent of a lion she had once seen at the Royal Menagerie. Powerful, fierce, and almost frightening.

"I've already told you my given name," she countered. "You may as well use that instead."

"Uncomfortable with your little foray into being an informant, hmm?" He raised a brow, studying her intently. "I can't say I blame you. The London Reform Society is bleeding dangerous. If they catch wind you're the one who squeaked, you'll pay for it dearly."

Father had always been a reformer, but his actions in the last few years had grown increasingly hazardous. He had aligned himself with a group of men whose actions were insupportable, and the danger was more than apparent. She'd read of the foiled plot against the Tower of London in the papers, along with accounts of the search for the men responsible.

"I'll take my chances," she told him calmly, although within, she was anything but composed. "However, I do thank you for your worry on my behalf."

Was he truly concerned for her? She couldn't tell, but then, it hardly signified. She would never see him again when she left this room and Willowby's behind. The sooner, the better.

But he was not finished, it would seem. "You're playing a treacherous game, love. I've seen what they do to their enemies before, and it ain't pretty. You'd be well-served to stay far away from them and from the Guild, too."

Fear crept into her heart, making her hands clench into impotent fists at her sides. "You are supposing I have a choice, sir. Sometimes, there are games we are forced to play."

To protect and save the ones we love, she thought to herself.

Oh, Father. How did you land us in this horrid mess?

"Forced?" he asked.

Her admission had been a mistake. She saw that now. A poorly calculated revelation which had, rather than staving off Logan's attention as she had intended, only served to heighten it instead.

"You needn't fret over me," she said, taking note that he still held her fan captive. "My fan, if you please. I shouldn't think you've any use for it."

His expression grew contemplative. "Mayhap I ought to require an even exchange for the fan as well. You tell me who's forcing you to sell information about the London Reform Society, and you can have it back, eh?"

She shook her head instantly. "No."

His jaw hardened. "Is someone threatening you, Arianna?"

His use of her given name told her that he was serious now, no more mocking taunts. There was almost a protective air about him suddenly, as if he intended to defend her against whomever had obliged her to meet with him today as the Major. Something inside her softened. Warmed. It was ludicrous, of course. This man was a stranger to her. Their paths would never again cross. And yet, she felt a deep connection so strong that it was visceral.

"You don't know me," she said. "You hardly need burden yourself with my problems."

He strode nearer, towering over her with his superior height and broad form. "Tell me something about yourself."

She frowned, tamping down the impulse to take a step in retreat so that she was not so tempted by his proximity. "There's no need."

"There's every need. Tell me something true. Something that only you know. Something you've never told another."

She ought to ignore his challenge, she knew. To step around him, leave this room and Willowby's altogether. To never again think of him or this moment of heady awareness, their bodies so close. She did not think she had ever been so attracted to another, so keenly drawn to any man. And it was not just Logan's handsome face or lean, muscled strength. It was simply *him*.

"I was never in love with my husband," she confided, shocking herself with the raw honesty of her response.

But there was something about this place, their solitude, that made her feel as if they were suspended from the outside world. As if anything were possible. There were no repercussions here. He did not know Edgar. He did not know Arianna. She was at liberty to say almost anything.

"There," Logan said calmly. "Now I do know you. You've just told me something you've never confided to another. How did it feel?"

"Freeing," she admitted.

"You must have kept that secret locked inside yourself for some time," he observed. "How long did you know your husband for?"

"Two years," she said.

Their first year had been spent in courtship; Arianna had not been drawn to Lord Edgar Stewart, the quiet, scholarly second son of the Duke of Marlton. But her Father had been eager for her to make a match. The pressure for her to wed had, in the end, won out. Her mistake had been apparent from the onset of their wedding, when Edgar had proven so inattentive a new husband that he had inadvertently left her behind at a coaching inn on their way to Brighton for their honeymoon.

"And how many of those years were spent married?"

Logan persisted, toying with the fan still captured in his long fingers as he watched her, awaiting her response.

"One," she said, thinking of how quickly that year felt now in retrospect and yet how dismally it had passed at the time, with painful torpor.

"Did he make provisions for you after his death?"

There hadn't been sufficient time for further consideration, aside from the meager widow's portion which was not enough to support even the smallest and most modest of households. Young and naïve at the time of her marriage, she hadn't considered the full implications of being left at the mercy of her husband's cold, uncaring family should something befall her husband. And Edgar, always of a weaker constitution, had nonetheless seemed far too young to succumb when he'd become ill with a lung infection. Ultimately, however, it had killed him, and his family had promptly turned her out without a ha'penny more than her portion.

"I have found a home with my family once more," she said primly, knowing the strain her return to Father's household had caused, though she attempted to ameliorate it every way she knew how.

"And does your family know what you are doing?"

Logan was disturbingly close to the truth. She had already revealed far too much. What a fool she was. But then, she was not accustomed to involving herself in such matters. She had only done so after Father's desperate plea, knowing he would never have come to her for aid unless he had been faced with no other choice.

"Does *your* family know what *you* are doing?" she countered, curious about him and wanting to know more now that she had revealed a part of herself.

He passed a hand over his jaw, his expression hardening. "No, they don't."

She thought she detected an undercurrent of sadness in his voice. "Are you close to them?"

"Not any longer." His voice was clipped, cool. "This ain't the profession for a man with a family."

But of course, it was not. The Guild was shrouded in secrecy and mystery, but she knew enough to understand that Logan was a spy. The men of the Guild reported to Whitehall, but they were mercenaries involved in dangerous missions.

"I don't suppose it is," she said, searching his gaze for hints of more. "You aren't married, then?"

She told herself that whether or not he had a wife was no concern of hers. This mad attraction she felt for him could never be acted upon. And yet, she couldn't help but to wonder.

He shook his head. "No."

His answer was succinct. Stern. He didn't like being the one to answer questions about himself, that much was apparent. And he was not very forthcoming with answers. But that didn't stop her, and nor did it stay the relief rising, knowing he wasn't wed.

"You've had your secret from me," she pressed. "It's only fair that you give me one of yours in return. Tell me something that only you know. Something you've never told another."

He watched her with such intensity that she longed to look away, to break the connection, and she was persuaded he would not answer until at last, he spoke.

"It's been my greatest regret to leave my family without a word." His voice was hoarse with suppressed emotion. "As it is, they think I'm dead, and they're better off believing it."

Her heart ached for him at the revelation. How lonesome he must be. And how terrible the choice—the Guild over his family.

"Surely they're not better off believing you dead," she said quietly. "Don't you think they would wish to know what has become of you?"

He shrugged, a muscle ticking in his jaw. "They're safer this way."

"But you've decided for them," she pointed out. "Perhaps you should have allowed them to choose the risks they were willing to take."

Because no one knew better than Arianna the willingness to take risks on behalf of those she loved. She was here, in this room, because of it.

"What of you?" he countered. "Did you allow your family to choose the risks you've taken in coming to me tonight?"

How neatly he had turned the tables.

"My fan, if you please," she said instead of answering Logan's probing question for fear that if she revealed too much, she would give her father's involvement away.

She had no notion what would happen to him if word of his connection to the London Reform Society became known to Whitehall. Two of its leaders had prices upon their heads, with rumors swirling that they had managed to secure passage to America and had disappeared.

"You ain't the sort who ordinarily squeaks," he persisted. "Was this the first time?"

She heaved a frustrated sigh. "Why do you care?"

And furthermore, why was he so perceptive, so dogged in his determination to wrest the truth from her?

His hazel gaze settled on her lips before flitting away. "Because someone *ought* to bleeding care, and the fact that you're standing here alone with a strange cove, selling secrets of culls who would as soon hush their enemies as blink, suggests to me that no one does."

She opened her mouth to defend Father, but then realized

she didn't dare. Once more, Logan was pressing her to reveal far too much.

"I look after myself," she told him stubbornly. "Now, my fan, sir. I don't dare linger any longer."

"You shouldn't have to look after yourself," he told her, before relinquishing the fan. "You should have a man willing to throw himself onto the fire so you can walk across the bleeding flames without getting burned. Not a man who tosses you into it to save himself."

He was speaking of her father without knowing it. But speaking, too, to a deep and dark part of herself where the pain of the past dwelled. Edgar would have consigned her to the flame to save himself, and Father was no better.

But still, Arianna held Logan's gaze, unflinching. "I'm not afraid to walk through the fire alone. Nor to get burned."

Especially if it meant saving her sister and her father. She loved them, and she would do anything to protect them. Even if it meant putting herself in danger.

Gripping her fan so tightly that the ivory cut painfully into her palm, she dipped into a curtsy and then fled from the chamber before he could stop her.

CHAPTER 3

"You didn't tell me the Major was a bleeding mort," Logan grumbled as he passed the sealed missive he had received from Arianna to Archer Tierney.

They were seated in Tierney's office at their current headquarters, a rather tumbledown affair not far from the East End where Logan had cut his teeth as a babe. The Guild regularly moved to avoid too much scrutiny.

Dark-haired, green-eyed, and ruthless, Tierney had built his fortune as a moneylender before finding his way into a far more lucrative pursuit as a member of the Guild. Logan reported to Tierney directly, and it was Tierney who had sent him on the mission to receive the information about a future meeting of the London Reform Society from the Major. But while their work was rooted in financial gain for them all, it was also steeped in duty and loyalty.

Tierney accepted the missive Arianna had provided now, his lips twitching in ill-concealed mirth. "You didn't ask."

Logan tried not to think of just how beautiful a mort she was, or how drawn he was to her. Nor to think of the sadness haunting her honey-brown eyes. Or how his lust for her had quickly grown into something deeper, concern for her circumstances taking precedence over even his mission as he had sought and won more revelations from her.

He scrubbed a hand along his jaw. "You might've warned me."

Aye, and he also might have warned Logan how stunningly beautiful she was.

Tierney shrugged. "Didn't know she was one until you told me just now. The Major contacted me with a missive, no sign of it having been delivered by anyone. I came into the shop one morning to find it waiting for me beneath the door. I gather she's a dimber mort, then?"

A sudden streak of possessiveness reared up within Logan at Tierney's query, so fierce it made his stomach tighten.

"You shouldn't be speaking of 'er that way," he growled before he could stop himself.

Tierney arched a brow, a look of speculation overtaking his stern features. "You smitten?"

"Of course I'm not," he bit out, for such an admission would do him no bleeding good.

Even if it were true.

And it wasn't true.

Liar, accused a voice within. A voice he promptly silenced and ignored.

"Of course not," Tierney agreed mildly, before extracting a cheroot and holding it to one of the lit tapers on his desk and lighting it. Smoke puffed into the air. "And the grass also isn't green."

Damn it to hell. Tierney was a hard, unforgiving cove and trusted no one. It wouldn't be be beneficial for him to think Logan vulnerable, especially where Arianna was concerned. Even if a part of him was. Their meeting had affected him.

He couldn't lie to himself. But regardless of the odd sense of connection he felt to her, he had sworn his loyalty to the Guild.

"I'm not," he repeated firmly. "My loyalty is to the Guild. I've already sworn that."

But he was also a man.

One who was very much aware of Arianna. Tempted by her. Drawn to her as he'd never been to another. It was dangerous, and he knew it. Reckless and he knew it. Bleeding stupid, and aye, he knew that too.

Didn't stop him from feeling the way he did about her.

"If you are, it could be used to our advantage," Tierney said, appearing to be mulling the notion and mining it for ways to benefit the Guild. "Our informants aren't often women. If she's pleasing to the old peepers—"

"She ain't," he cut in, lying.

Tierney stroked his jaw, puffing on his cheroot in deep contemplation. "If she writes me again, I could always have one of the others approach her and attempt to seduce some additional information from her. Ridgely should do nicely. He's never met a set of petticoats he hasn't wanted to tup."

The Duke of Ridgely was a conscienceless rakehell. He was a fearless spy, it was true. But the notion of Arianna being paired with such a rogue set Logan on edge. The mere thought of another man touching her, claiming her, set him on edge. He couldn't bear it.

"No," he bit out. "Not Ridgely."

"Then perhaps—"

"I'll do it," Logan interrupted. "If she contacts the Guild again, I'll be the man to do what must be done."

He could not bring himself to utter the forbidden words *seduce her* aloud for fear of the effect it would have on him. But he would be damned if he allowed any other member of the Guild near her.

Tierney flashed him a rare half grin. "There's a lad. I knew you were up to the task."

Seducing Arianna would hardly prove a *task* should it come to that, but Logan kept his mouth firmly shut on the matter. His mind traveled instead to the bold, defiant beauty with the sad eyes and the many secrets he sensed she hid. He'd not use her in such cruel fashion. She deserved far better.

But he nodded instead of confiding in his superior, or questioning him. "You know where my loyalty lies, sir."

"I'll be getting this to Whitehall." Tierney tucked the still-sealed missive into his coat. "When we have need of you again, I'll send word to one of your little birds, same as before."

Logan had scamps who told him whatever he wanted for a price scattered all over London. They were an invaluable resource. It was through his little birds that he'd learned of danger at his family's gaming hell and his eldest brother's home a few months before. He'd managed to save his brother's wife's life that day, solely because of them. Of course, none of his siblings knew of his involvement. They *couldn't* know. His world was the Guild now.

Logan jerked his head in another nod, knowing he'd been dismissed. "Until then."

He could only hope that Arianna didn't have need to sell further secrets from the London Reform Society, and that she would heed his warning, keeping herself far from their dangerous clutches.

∽

ARIANNA INSTANTLY TOOK note of the rectangle of vividly dark, chaise-longue-shaped wool in the drawing room as she crossed the threshold in search of her sister. The sun had done its work on the faded carpet surrounding it, but beneath the place where the chaise longue had formerly dwelled, the Axminster looked new and rich.

The moment she spied the evidence of more of Father's frantic selling off of household assets, her heart sank.

Juliet was within, elegantly poised at a carved window seat, her embroidery in her lap as her needle passed rhythmically in and out of the handkerchief she was working upon. Her younger sister, three years Arianna's junior, was either blissfully ignorant of the latest missing piece of furniture, or feigning it was not gone. But then, knowing Juliet, it was the former rather than the latter.

She glanced up at Arianna's entrance with her customary bright, cheerful smile, looking like an angel with the sunlight catching in her golden curls. "Good morning, Arianna dearest. Where were you at breakfast?"

"I overslept," she answered, which was partially true.

No need to mention the reasons why. A certain handsome, auburn-haired stranger had haunted her dreams. She had tossed and turned through a fitful night of rest, thinking about him, recalling the fiery connection they'd shared, wishing their meeting had occurred in a different fashion. That she would see him again.

"It's most unlike you to oversleep," Juliet commented, putting her sewing aside in its basket and rising.

The comment was not a condemnation, but it was a reminder that her actions were noted by the household. She would have to take greater care.

"We are all due for an aberration, every once in a while, I suppose," Arianna answered, crossing the room to greet her sister in truth with a buss on the cheek. "Where has the Grecian chaise longue gone, darling?"

"Oh, Father said it needed to be repaired," Juliet answered

earnestly, naiveté sparkling in her eyes. "He had it packed away and sent off."

"Along with Mother's secretaire and circular bookcase, half the chairs in the dining room, and the French window curtains in the library?" she commented, frowning as she paced the length of the drawing room and noted a vase missing as well.

It had been their mother's favorite for a daily showing of hothouse flowers. After their mother's unexpected death, their father had never been the same man. He had descended into the very depths of a gambling addiction from which there had yet to be proven a return.

"There was also Mother's sapphire parure that he asked to have from me, wishing to have it placed in a different setting that was more suited to a lady of my age," Juliet explained blithely, following her across the chamber. "I do so think it would look lovely at the Marquess and Marchioness of Searle's ball with the gown I plan to wear. Madame Fournier has created a ballgown for me that is simply divine. I vow that if I am not able to win myself a husband wearing it, I shall be forever doomed to remain on the shelf."

Because of their mother's death, Juliet's presentation in court had been delayed to observe the period of mourning. As a result, at two-and-twenty, she was already a bit older than some of her competitors on the marriage mart. And her notably diminished dowry was also a matter of some concern amongst prospective suitors.

Arianna winced at her sister's unknowing confession that their father had asked her for the sapphire parure so that he might use it also to alleviate some of the tremendous weight of his debts. Since her own reduced circumstances had forced her to return to their father's home, she had offered up her widow's portion as assistance, as well as all the jewelry in her possession of value, aside from a few gowns of value, her mother's triple-strand pearl necklace and ruby earrings. Unfortunately, it had not been nearly enough. And although she had done her utmost to hide the truth of their reduced circumstances from Juliet to keep her sister from fretting, Father's actions were growing more dire, which was worrisome indeed.

"You did not give it to him yet, did you, dear?" she asked her sister carefully, taking stock of the mantel and discovering an ormolu clock and twin matching braces of candles missing as well.

"I was going to fetch it for him this afternoon," Juliet said brightly, still persuaded of their father's generosity.

Oh, to be so trusting and certain that everyone around her was acting in her best interest. That all would be well. That she would dance at the Searle ball and find a love match. But Arianna was determined that her sister's fragile hope not be crushed.

She patted Juliet's arm. "Why do you not give the parure to me for safekeeping? Just until the ball, at least."

Her sister's brow furrowed. "But Father said—"

"I know what he said," Arianna interrupted. "And it is quite...considerate of him to wish to see it reset. However, I fear there isn't nearly sufficient time. I'll keep it for you until the ball, and if he wishes to have it altered afterward, he may feel free."

It had been a miracle that Father had scoured enough funds for Juliet to have the gowns she required for her Season. Arianna had been too fearful to ask him how he had managed it when they were rationing candles and reducing the servants in the household. Regardless of how, this was Juliet's chance to find a future for herself that didn't involve being at the mercy of their father's poor choices. Arianna was not going to allow him to sully it by selling off Mother's parure and lying to Juliet.

"Very well," Juliet allowed, still looking concerned. "If you think it wise."

"I think it most wise," Arianna said, linking her arm through her sister's. "Now come, and let us fetch it."

∽

Logan approached the rear door of Guild headquarters and offered the customary series of raps.

Knock-knock. Pause. *Knock-knock-knock.*

"Wot you want?" came the familiar growl of Lucky, Tierney's guard and right-hand man, through the closed portal.

"It's Mr. Martin," he called, carefully checking the alley around him for signs he was being watched or followed, for one of the little birds had recently warned them that there were those on the street who had begun to suspect Tierney was involved in more than mere moneylending within these walls.

And they couldn't afford for the truth to be revealed.

Logan had been summoned this evening unexpectedly, which likely didn't bode well. The premonition of danger coiled in his gut, and he couldn't shake the notion it was somehow related to Arianna and the information she'd provided. All had been silent from Tierney following his delivery of the missive.

Logan had been partially relieved, for the lack of further communication from Arianna meant that he wouldn't have to subject himself to further temptation where she was concerned. But another part of him had been disappointed at the notion their paths would never cross again.

The door wrenched open, and Lucky glared at him. Not unusual, that. A tall, dark-haired man with a long blade of a nose and a perpetual scowl, Lucky was foul tempered and ruthless.

"Yer late," Lucky pronounced, disapproval lacing his voice.

The feral guard didn't concern him, however. They'd butted heads on numerous occasions in the past. Lucky protected Tierney at all costs. It was understood. Everyone else could go straight to bleeding hell in a runaway hack as far as Lucky was concerned. And that was the way of it.

"Came as quickly as I could." Logan shrugged. "You know what they say, Lucky. Better late than never, eh?"

Lucky's lip curled into a sneer, but he cast a glance about the alley past Logan's shoulder before jerking his head. "In with ye, then."

Logan bit his tongue to avoid offering a retort. He was in a rather foul mood himself after his thoughts had been haunted by one raven-haired temptress ever since he'd seen her at Willowby's. He crossed the threshold and waited for Lucky to bar the door at his back before following the guard down the main hall, which led to Tierney's office.

Lucky knocked at the closed door. "Mr. Martin's 'ere, sir." He cast a disapproving scowl over his shoulder in Logan's direction. "One quarter hour late."

It was perhaps the politest fashion in which the guard had ever introduced Logan. He would have laughed if he weren't so bleeding worried about the reason for his summons.

"Come," Tierney barked from within.

With another pointed stare and a matching frown, Lucky swung the door open for Logan, but not without muttering something rude beneath his breath. Logan swore he caught the word *arsehole*, but chose to ignore it.

Tierney was standing by the small hearth, a glass of what looked to be jackey in hand, a cheroot clamped between his teeth.

He plucked the cheroot from his mouth and exhaled a cloud of smoke. "That'll be all for now, Lucky."

The guard grunted but took his leave, the door closing with more force than necessary at his back.

"Sir." Logan removed his hat and offered an informal bow in a show of respect to his superior. "I came as quickly as I could."

Tierney took a lengthy swig from his glass before setting it on the mantel. "Never mind Lucky. He's always crabbed, that one. It isn't a matter of life and death. Yet."

The ominous lone word had Logan's spine stiffening. "Why did you summon me this evening? Is it the Major?"

He'd almost slipped and called her *Arianna*. A fool's mistake. What was it about her that haunted him, that held him so thoroughly in her thrall and wouldn't let him go?

"It's about the information the Major provided," Tierney answered, before taking a calm puff of his cheroot. "It was either false, or whoever gave it to the Major also warned the Society. Our men arrived at the appointed hour and place, but there were no Society men. Nor did a meeting take place."

Disappointment mingled with relief, curdling his stomach. Relief that the news wasn't of something ill having befallen Arianna. Disappointment at the prospect that she had willingly sold false intelligence.

"I'm inclined to believe the Society was warned," Logan offered, thinking of his lengthy interactions with Arianna at Willowby's.

He had always been an excellent judge of character, with an innate ability to know whether or not a cove was a liar or a cheat, which came from his days at his family's gaming hell. He didn't think he was wrong about Arianna, that she was trustworthy and honest. That she had somehow been forced into the dangerous world of the Society, whether because she was desperate for the funds, or because someone else had coerced her.

Tierney raised a brow. "Are you thinking with your knowledge box or with your tackle?"

A possessive surge rose within Logan, the urge to protect Arianna overwhelming even his vow of duty to the Guild. It made no sense, the fierceness of his reaction to her. He'd given up everything for the Guild, even his precious family, just to keep them safe. And yet, after one meeting with Arianna, he was willing to sacrifice everything in her name.

He raked a hand through his hair, frustrated with himself and the circumstances as much as with Tierney for his crude question. "I always think with my knowledge box."

And sometimes with his tackle. But no need to admit as much aloud. He could think very well with both, curse the bastard.

"Hmm," Tierney said, taking another contemplative puff of his cheroot.

"I've met with any number of informants," he pointed out, feeling the need to redeem himself and chase away some of his guilt. "Most of them ain't any more trustworthy than a kitchen rat. But there's something different about her."

"Something different, yes," Tierney drawled. "You want to shag her."

Aye, to his shame, Logan did.

"No, I bleeding don't," he denied just the same.

Tierney grinned. "As you say. But if you do get her into your bed, don't turn your back on the wench. And make sure you find out everything you can, even if it's whilst you're—"

"Christ," Logan interrupted, not wishing to hear any more of Tierney's taunts. "Stubble it. I've promised to discover what I can, but I'll do it through honorable means."

Tierney laughed. "The Guild isn't the place for honor, Loge. I expected you would have discovered that by now."

The use of the shortened version of Logan's name brought with it a sudden flash of pain. His siblings had always referred to him as Loge. Although he daily tamped down the anguish at removing himself from their lives, and despite knowing he'd had no choice, he still missed them all terribly. One day, when he left the Guild, he would return. He just hoped they wouldn't despise him for the lengths he'd gone to and the way he'd disappeared.

His grip on his hat was almost painful as he fought the rising regrets. "I know we're all of us rogues. But there's still honor amongst thieves, no?"

Tierney looked amused as he finished his cheroot and calmly tossed it into the grate. "If it comforts you to think so."

Logan wasn't sure what could provide him comfort these days. Likely, nothing.

"Have you heard from her again?" he asked instead of responding to Tierney's jibe.

"As it happens, yes." The levity fled Tierney's countenance. "I received another note this afternoon. The Major claims to possess knowledge of where Charles Mace and his brother Clifford have been hiding. We exchanged several messages. I let her know we weren't happy with the first set of information proving fruitless, and that if she didn't provide us with something accurate and substantial, we won't be paying for her services any longer."

That meant Tierney had doubts about Arianna and the veracity of her communications. But there was something even more troubling than that knowledge making Logan's guts twist into knots.

"Mace?" he repeated, unease unfurling at the mention of the leader in the foiled plot to attack the Tower of London.

The bastard had narrowly escaped arrest in the wake of the failed uprising he and other Society members had plotted. While some of the conspirators had been captured, a handful had not. Mace, the most dangerous of all, was rumored to have taken passage to America. But Whitehall had reason to believe he was still hiding in London with his brother. The Guild had been charged with finding him, though all their leads had thus far been fruitless.

And if Arianna knew where Mace was, that could also mean she was involved far more deeply in the Society than he'd supposed. He damned well didn't like the idea of that.

"The five-hundred-pound reward being offered for his capture apparently proved a suitable lure, just as Whitehall hoped," Tierney said, shaking Logan from his troubled thoughts. "The meeting with the Major is tomorrow evening. That's why I called you here. I'd like you to attend, supposing you're amenable to the task. If not, Ridgely would likely be more than pleased to go in your stead."

Over his dead and rotted corpse.

"To the devil with Ridgely," Logan bit out. "I'll meet with her. Only tell me when and where."

Tierney smiled. "That's what I hoped you'd say."

∼

"I'VE ARRANGED another meeting with the Guild for tomorrow evening."

Her father's pronouncement made the heavy weight of dread sink like a stone in Arianna's stomach. And yet, along with the dread there was another emotion intermingled. Vexing and persistent. Troubling, too.

Eagerness. For she was thinking of Logan, wondering whether or not doing her father's bidding would mean that she would see him again.

She was seated opposite her father in his study, where the air was redolent with the scent of spirits. It was only afternoon. His thinning, dark hair was scraped to his pate, oily and slightly mussed, suggesting that it had been far too long since he had last bathed. The grooves about his deep-set blue eyes had been carved by years of worry, sadness, and responsibility.

She frowned. "Father, have you been tippling?"

"Of course I haven't," he denied, just as he always did.

Father's disavowals always meant one thing. He was lying.

"Brandy, then?" she guessed, wrinkling her nose as she took another discreet sniff of the air.

He slid a sealed missive across the polished surface of his desk toward her. "As I told you, I haven't been imbribing today...ahem, *imbibing*. But I do thank you for your daughterly concern. You are too good to me. I'm very proud of you for the help you've been providing me."

Oh dear. It would seem that he had consumed more brandy than she had initially supposed. Whenever he consumed spirits in heavy amounts, Father grew maudlin. And whilst she appreciated his sentiments—she loved him, despite his many faults—she could not help but to wish such accolades were offered when he was not in his cups or requiring favors.

She shifted on her chair, uneasiness making her restless as she eyed the missive and then her father, thinking again of the warning Logan had issued.

The London Reform Society is bleeding dangerous, he'd said. *If they catch wind you're the one who squeaked, you'll pay for it dearly.*

"Father, I am concerned about the danger you are placing yourself in, selling these secrets," she said, allowing the missive to remain where it was, enshrouded in mystery, temptation, and trepidation all at once.

Accepting it meant the possibility of seeing Logan again, and she could not deny the appeal, despite every inner sense of self-preservation warning her against involvement with a spy. But it also meant inviting further danger and ruin into their lives. One more opportunity for the London Reform Society to discover they'd been betrayed. One more reason for them to begin searching for the culprit. It was a risk she could not think it prudent to take.

"There is no danger, dearesht daughter," Father assured her, slurring the endearment as he did so. "I've taken all the proper precautions to ensure no one will know I'm responsible."

But what about me? She longed to ask. *Will anyone discover I am responsible? And if they do, what shall become of me?*

Instead, she said, "I was hoping the two hundred pounds would suffice. You promised me it would only be once."

"They are offering five hundred pounds for Charles and Clifford Mace, the lead conspirators in the plot against the Tower," her father said. "With five hundred pounds, I could settle a great deal of my debts, including the positively ruinous bill from that blasted modiste your sister insisted upon visiting."

Well, then. That certainly explained how Father had managed to pay Madame Fournier. He hadn't.

Her heart sank at this fresh evidence that no amount of selling off household goods was sufficient to assuage Father's debt. And the knowledge he was so deeply connected to the men who had planned an attack on the Tower of London, just as she had feared, made her stomach cramp in a painful knot.

"Father," she said quietly, cognizant of the ever-depleted ranks of servants yet roaming the halls beyond the closed study door, "pray tell me that you are not so thoroughly involved with the London Reform Society that you have knowledge of where they are hiding. They are dangerous cutthroats."

"They are men who wish for changesh," Father countered,

still slurring. "I will acknowledge the means of obtaining it, as they imagined, was faulty."

Her father had always been an ardent supporter of reform, despite the fact that he was a peer. A champion of the lower classes. But he had never been a revolutionary. Then again, he had not been a drunkard or a gambler either before Mother's death. She stared at his familiar, weathered features now, thinking she scarcely recognized him.

"It was not just faulty, but treasonous," she hissed. "This is dangerous business, and I cannot like it."

"It's perfectly safe, Arianna dear," her father said, using the same condescending tone he acquired whenever he was determined to have his way. "The Guild reportsh to Whitehall, and Home Office ishn't about to reveal their sources to the very men they've been charged with apprehending."

His logic, despite the telling overlap in his speech, was sound enough, she supposed. As she understood it, the Guild was working alongside Home Office to find and uncover all the members of the London Reform Society. Both organizations would wish to keep their informants safe, lest they lose their access to the information being provided. However, she could not shake the premonition that her father's continued close involvement with the men, coupled with his decision to sell their secrets, would come back to haunt them all.

"Do you believe I would knowingly place you in danger?" Father pressed, frowning at her, as if he found the very notion an insult.

"Not knowingly, perhaps," she allowed reluctantly. "But you cannot truly believe that these men will not discover you were the one responsible, particularly if they are discovered and arrested. Even if you give the name of only one man, should he be captured, the rest will come for you."

She did not know what information had been in the missive she had sold to Logan. She had not asked, and she'd deemed it best never to discover its contents. The less she knew of her father's dealings with the Society, the better.

"Trust me, daughter," Father said. "This is the only way to keep a roof over our heads and give your sister a Season. I know of no other. And I promise you, it will be the last time. No more, after thish—*this*."

It was on the tip of her tongue to reprimand him. To tell him that if perhaps he spent less time wallowing in his brandy and the gaming tables, they would not have found themselves in such desperate straits. But in the end, she swallowed any harsh words she had for him. She loved her father, and she knew that losing Mother had cut him so very deeply that it had changed the fabric of his being. He had never recovered.

Her only hope was that one day, in time, he would.

Until then, she had no other choice. She would have to do as he had asked.

And mayhap, whispered an insidious voice inside her, *see Logan again.*

"Very well." She took the missive. "Tell me where to be and when, and I shall do it."

CHAPTER 4

Logan stood in the small, private chamber of The Velvet Slipper, passing the time by smoking a cheroot as he awaited *her*.

Arianna.

Her name had not strayed far from his thoughts ever since that night at Willowby's. Nor had the memory of her flashing honey-gold eyes and midnight hair. From the moment Tierney had informed him that another meeting had been arranged, the location changed this time to the den of iniquity owned by the Duke of Ridgely, he had been able to think of nothing else. Before he and Tierney had parted ways the night before, he had reminded Logan that he was to seduce any additional information out of her that he could glean.

And although the premise of such a seduction was distasteful, Logan couldn't deny that he wanted her. Wanted her badly.

A knock sounded on the door, then another in quick succession. It was the signal that she had arrived.

He took one last puff of his cheroot and then tossed the remnants into the fire.

"Come," he called.

The door opened, and in she swept. She was wearing a handsome blue gown this evening, her face discreetly obscured by a veil. He couldn't find fault for her discretion—unlike Willowby's, which was devoted exclusively to gambling, The Velvet Slipper's clientele came in search of a far more prurient vice. If she was the sort of woman who gave a care for her reputation at all, she would not wish to be recognized within. Men and women alike sought out the club for carnal diversion of all forms, some of them more depraved than others.

Logan told himself it was a coincidence that Tierney had arranged the meeting at The Velvet Slipper and not an implied command.

She closed the door at her back and moved forward with the same grace and fluidity of movement he recalled from Willowby's. For a wild moment, he wondered how she must look when she danced, all sleek, elegant feminine curves spinning and whirling. Having been born and raised in the rookeries, he'd never been to a ball. Never had a desire to attend one either, even if he'd been the sort of cull to obtain an invite. Not that he was. But for the first time in his life, he understood the allure of such pageantry.

Hellfire, he truly was dicked in the nob, he thought wryly, before striding to meet her halfway.

He sketched a courtly bow, making a mockery of the seriousness of the moment and his own foolish thoughts both. "Major."

"Sir." Her voice was throaty but hesitant as she dipped into a curtsy.

Logan could not help but to think it was likely the only occasion upon which two people had met with such polite civility within The Velvet Slipper. Christ knew what manner of sins carried on within these walls. Ridgely gave the word *rakehell* a bad name.

"I see you did not heed my advice to avoid associating yourself with dangerous men," he observed, allowing his gaze to roam over her form in a fashion that was far from well-mannered.

He'd scarcely slept last night, plagued by thoughts of her that mingled between erotic fantasies and worry over her involvement with the Society. He intended to discover just how deep her ties ran before they parted ways again.

"If I had, I would not be finding myself here with you, would I?" she countered with impudent defiance, removing her hat and veil to reveal the loveliness hidden within.

For a moment, it was like receiving a punch to the gut.

How was it possible he'd forgotten just how beautiful she was, the full effect she had on him?

"I'm not dangerous, love," he found the presence of mind to drawl, seizing upon just a bit of his charm, all the while thinking that *she* was far more dangerous to him than he could ever be to her.

She raised a dark brow, the epitome of refinement. "How am I to trust that you aren't?"

The same pearl necklace adorned her creamy throat this evening as it had on the first occasion he had seen her. He could not help but to imagine kissing her there, just above the ivory strands. Finding her pulse with his lips to see if it raced as fast as his.

Because it was his duty, he reminded himself sternly. Not because he wanted her.

By all the saints, who was he trying to fool?

"Because I say I'm not," he answered, "and I'm a damned trustworthy cove."

"I do think I shall reserve my judgment," she said primly,

and then moved past him to settle her hat and veil upon a nearby chair, which had not been fashioned merely for the purpose of sitting, if the design of it was any indication.

If she took note of the unusual construction however, she said not a word.

"Wise of you," he agreed, following her movement so that he was just near enough to torment himself with the fresh scent of her—rain mingled with violets. "Perhaps you ought to have applied that same logic to your treasonous chums, hmm?"

She was still, staring down at her hat and veil before removing her pelisse and carefully placing it over the arm, then plucking off her gloves and draping them atop it. Her silence was a remonstration, he thought. And curse it, he was supposed to be seducing her, not antagonizing her. But beneath his desire for her there simmered something else. Some strong, unidentifiable urge to look after her.

The plotters were damned dangerous. There were a great deal of reforms which needed to be made in England, and no one agreed more with that than he, but violence wasn't the way to achieve change. Not in Logan's estimation. And he'd been charged with doing everything in his power to stop it.

"I never said they were my friends." Her words were soft and husky as she turned the full force of that honey-brown stare back upon him. "If they were indeed friends of mine, I would hardly be offering them up to Home Office, now, would I?"

As she spoke, she trailed her hand lightly over the polished mahogany frame, hovering at the split between the chair's tufted blue velvet and sleek wood. Back and forth, the movements mesmerizing. He would be an utter liar if he said he did not imagine what that touch would feel like on him instead.

Logan clasped his hands behind his back to keep his

temptation in check. "Excellent point. However, if you ain't their friend, then how would you know where to find them or when they might next be meeting? It stands to reason that these are details only those closest to them would know. Details only those in their most-trusted confidences would possess."

Her lips parted, and for a moment, his gaze caught on them, and he thought about how lovely it would be to claim their dark-red succulence with his. "I suppose that makes me a dreadful keeper of confidences, then. Does it not?"

"Perhaps," he agreed. "Or it makes you a wise woman who has seen the error of her ways."

That was what he wanted to believe. What every part of him hoped was the truth.

Her mouth quirked into a sad smile. "I'm a great many things, but I can't claim wisdom among them."

"Then a desperate woman, perhaps," he guessed next, determined to get to the heart of her reason for carrying on as she was, putting herself in danger.

Decidedly not the mission he'd been tasked with.

Tierney had been clear as a window pane about his expectations. His final words of warning returned to Logan now, an echo in his mind. *No tender feelings. No romantic entanglements of any sort. Above all, don't bloody well trust her. Never forget who she is and why she's come to you.*

And yet, here Logan was, drawn to Arianna as a woman rather than someone in league with the enemy. Her reaction, a subtle shifting in her countenance and the tightening of her fingers over the back of the chair, told him he'd hit his mark.

"Hardly desperate," she denied, but there was a lack of conviction in her tone he did not miss.

"So you're not desperate, you're not friends with the revolutionaries, and you're not wise." He stroked his jaw thoughtfully, studying her. "Tell me, Arianna, what *are* you? Tell me one true thing about yourself."

She heaved a frustrated-sounding sigh. "You seek to play a game when I have come to provide you with your information and have done with it."

"Sell," he corrected. "You've come to *sell* me your information."

"Home Office itself has placed a price upon the information I give," she countered. "You can hardly blame others for accepting the offer. Particularly when it is necessary."

In her vexation, she'd made another small revelation. Logan seized upon it.

"The reward is necessary for you, then?" His gaze swept over her form, taking in the elegant gown and fine jewelry.

She wore no earrings this evening, but the gold-and-pearl necklace at her throat had to be worth a fair amount of coin. She certainly did not look like someone drastically in need of funds. But then, she had admitted on their previous meeting that she was living with her family. And she had ignored his query about whether or not her husband had provided for her in his death.

She turned away from him then, retreating to the opposite end of the chamber as she rubbed her upper arms as if she'd taken a sudden chill. "It is necessary. That is all which need concern you. And why should you care? I imagine that you meet desperate souls every day, doing what you do."

He did, but none of them had ever been her.

And, *bloody ballocks*, that was a problem. A distinct, unique problem.

He *cared*.

Christ, what an idiot. He'd dashed Tierney's orders to bits in less than one quarter hour.

Logan's resolve renewed, he stalked toward her, determined to ply her with seduction instead of questions. He stopped near enough to touch her, and this time he surrendered to the need. Reaching out, he tipped up her chin with his forefinger. The gentlest of touches, nothing more. Her skin was silken and warm, so warm. The same addlepated notion which had entered his mind the last time their paths had crossed arose. He never wanted to stop touching her.

He wanted to believe in her integrity. To know that she'd sold him the previous information in good confidence and that the Society had somehow learned their meeting had been revealed to the Guild. Wanted to hear her tell him that she did not sympathize with the cutthroat revolutionaries whose secrets she sold.

"Why should I care?" he repeated gently, holding her stare. "Because I *do*, Arianna. I care about what happens to you."

"You do?" her brow furrowed, her gaze searching his as if seeking the veracity of his words.

He didn't flinch, didn't look away. Because it was true, bleeding cod's head that he was.

He cupped her cheek, allowing himself that connection. Telling himself he was doing his duty. Knowing it for a lie.

"Aye," he said. "I shouldn't. I scarcely know you, but from the moment I first saw you at Willowby's, there's been a deep and abiding connection between us that I can't deny. You feel it too, don't you?"

He knew she did before her response, because her hand moved atop his, holding it to her face. "I do," she admitted, voice low and sultry. "God help me, I shouldn't. But I feel it, too."

The worst of it was, he meant every word he said. He wasn't, in this moment, touching her, telling her he cared, for any other reason than that he wanted to and it was the truth.

"What would you do if I kissed you?" he rasped, the very

idea of setting his mouth upon hers burning him up from the inside.

He'd never wanted to know a woman's lips beneath his more.

As he asked the question, he traced the curve of her lower lip with his thumb, just brushing against the delectable swell enough to make a sharp pang of lust rip through him.

"I'd kiss you back," she whispered, the confession sounding torn from her.

Ah, God. How was he to resist? But then, it was likely not the Lord afoot but a decidedly more sinister foe, tempting Logan with what he could not have.

Either way, his body was moving of its own volition, closing that final step separating them. And Arianna was every bit as complicit, looping her arms around his neck, bringing their bodies flush.

The crush of her breasts against him had his cock going hard in his trousers. He expected she could feel him swelling and thickening by the second. He was not a rakehell, but neither was he an innocent. He had flirted, kissed, and more with women. Sometimes to distract himself from the darkness of the world. Other times, for release. And still, he could not recall ever wanting a mort this bleeding much.

More than he wanted anything.

Even the latest bit of information she had arrived with, the mysterious missive hidden somewhere on her luscious person.

Floating hell, the effect she had on him was bleeding dangerous.

He should step away, exchange the five hundred pounds for the missive, and then take his leave. Curse Tierney's plans of seduction to the devil where they belonged. Forget he'd ever been tempted by those ruby lips. Banish the memory of the fullness of her generous curves inciting him to madness. Aye, he ought to retreat.

He kissed her instead.

Kissed her even though it was pure recklessness. Although allowing himself to feel anything for her could damn well prove ruinous. Although having her lips beneath his would mean risking the both of them. And certainly risking Tierney's trust in him. After weeks of doing their damnedest to ferret out information concerning those conspiring against the government, the Guild was finally on the cusp of information that could lead them to Charles and Clifford Mace.

But the moment her soft lips moved against his in sweet welcome, he knew.

The risk was worth it. *Heaven and all the saints*, the risk was worth having her soft mouth beneath his. Of having his free hand anchored to her waist, the supple give of her curves beneath her stays and gown nothing short of miraculous. His other hand was at liberty to travel higher still, his palm flattening on the small of her back to draw her even more flush against him, his hand navigating the hollow there. How secretive, that space, perfect for aligning their bodies together.

He deepened the kiss, his tongue swiping over the seam of her lips and dipping inside, learning the wet, silken recesses of her mouth. She tasted like tea, and although he had never particularly cared for the beverage, he knew he would never taste it again without the return of this desperate need. She nipped hungrily at his lower lip, the action—so carnal and raw—sending a renewed arrow of lust straight to his cockstand.

Desperate for more, Logan moved them, kissing her all the while. They bumped into an overstuffed armchair, and he tore his lips from hers for a moment to fall artlessly into it, pulling Arianna atop him with ease. She landed on her knees astride him, her soft, blue gown pooling in his lap, with wide eyes and a sweet exhalation of breath that feathered over his lips.

"We can stop this now, or we can proceed," he told her, breathless from the mad desire rushing through him, stronger than the fiercest storm. "The choice is yours."

If she did not want him, he would take the latest missive she had brought him and go. He had already forgotten Tierney's demand that he seduce her altogether; that was not the reason for what was happening now. Because seducing her in the name of duty felt like a betrayal to the both of them. But he needed to know that she wanted to take this risk every bit as much as he did.

The world be damned.

She was silent for a few heartbeats, watching him, lips tauntingly close. "I don't want to stop."

"Good," he growled. "Neither do I."

And then, he pulled her lips down to his for another deep and drugging kiss. Her fingers sank into his hair, tugging and holding him close, her breathy sigh of surrender urging him on. He kissed her harder, showing her how much he wanted her with the slant of his mouth, the thrust of his tongue. Nothing could have prepared him for her, for the way she made him feel. He was aflame, happy to burn in her searing heat.

To hell with the consequences from Tierney and the Guild, he thought even as warning clamored in his mind. Sanity warred with lust. He was meant to be fulfilling a duty. The edicts Tierney had issued were a muted cacophony in his mind, however. Obliterated by the rising tide of desire.

Never forget who she is and why she's come to you.

But everything else paled in comparison to the delicious weight of Arianna in his lap, the exquisitely feminine curve of her thigh beneath his hand, the welcoming blossom of warmth radiating from between her legs.

His other hand traveled with a mind of its own, caressing every part of her he could reach, sweeping from her waist to her spine, his eager fingers tracing the delicate indentation all the way to her nape. There, he could not resist finding pins hidden within her coiffure, pulling them free until her heavy hair unwound from its careful chignon. A riot of warm, silken tresses spilled over his hand.

Logan gathered his wits enough to break the kiss so that he could assess his handiwork. Her lips were parted, swollen from their kisses. They were not painted after all, he realized, answering the question that had haunted him. There was no smear to reveal her artifice as there had been with others he had kissed in the past. The deep, seductive shade was natural.

And as he drank in the sight of her, on his lap with her skirt up around her waist, her jet-black curls framing her face and falling around her shoulders, he hadn't a thought for others.

All he knew was this moment, this woman, this hunger.

"You are so bleeding beautiful," he said, running his fingers through her hair, testing the softness of her curls.

"You've ruined my chignon," she accused without sting.

Her breathing was ragged, her full breasts rising and falling over the silver-threaded edge of her bodice. She was not just beautiful.

She was magnificent.

"I wanted to see your hair unbound," he confessed, as if it were a suitable excuse.

As if he went about every day pulling pins from the hair of the morts he admired.

He didn't. But there was something about the woman in his lap that was different from every other. He could not shake the deep-seated sense that she was his. That this was meant to be.

Even as he knew how wrong it was. He scarcely knew her, and she had come to him with information no innocent would possess. Unless…

Perhaps it was not just desperation that had led to her selling secrets. Her conscience had spurred her into action, offering the information in exchange for the small fortunes she'd been promised. Surely that was the explanation.

She cupped his jaw, her thumb tracing over his bottom lip, her gaze glittering into his. "We shouldn't be doing this."

"No," he agreed, loving her touch, the way her thumb dipped into the seam of his lips. "We shouldn't."

He sucked her thumb into his mouth, nipping the pad gently with his teeth before soothing it with his tongue. Her skin tasted salty and sweet. He wanted to lick her everywhere, to savor all the new tastes of her he could discover.

It astounded him to realize that nothing mattered more than *her*.

Her, here and now. This moment. The two of them, the desire burning hot and bright.

He saw it clearly, understood it to his marrow, as their lips moved together. He would pitch himself into the flames of Hades just to have her. And it was very likely that was exactly what he was doing. He'd set out to be the seducer. But instead, he'd been quite thoroughly seduced.

CHAPTER 5

Arianna knew it was wrong, what she was doing. Not just wrong, but dangerous and scandalous, too.

But wrong and dangerous and scandalous had never felt more right.

Logan's tongue was in her mouth, and he tasted like smoke and sin and temptation. He had awakened her, made her feel alive in a way she hadn't known possible. A great, pulsing need had begun between her thighs, a desperate hunger. As if Logan sensed it, his hand moved, separated from her by the barrier of her gown and petticoats.

He found the apex of her thighs and slowly, hand splayed flat over her most intimate place, he applied maddening pressure. She arched into his touch as he used the heel of his palm to circle over her sensitive flesh in a teasing motion that had her tearing her mouth from his on a gasp. Her marriage bed had been perfunctory rather than passionate; Edgar had never touched her so intimately. This was new and wondrous, an utter revelation, for Logan to not just understand her pleasure, but give it so freely.

It was delightfully good, his big hand rotating over her sex, and she wanted more of it.

Needed more of it

More of *him*.

Conscience threatened to rain down on her, reminding her she had come here not to be debauched, but rather to secure the five-hundred-pound reward Father so desperately needed. Yet some wild part of her thrust the reminders of obligation and familial duty aside. For years, she had put everyone before herself. Accepting a marriage she had not wanted, playing the role of the dutiful wife whilst her husband neglected her, giving Father every last pound to her name so Juliet might find the happiness Arianna herself had been denied…

It was enough. She would not think of the reasons why she should not seize these frantic moments of pleasure with Logan now. Instead, she would concentrate upon the reasons why she *should*. She reached for her gown, bunching up the fabric, hauling it and her petticoats and chemise to her waist, removing the unwanted barrier to his skin directly on hers.

"Touch me," she said, half command, half plea. "Please."

She had never been burning from within at the prospect of a mere caress. But she swore she would combust for the lack of this man's hands on her.

Logan cursed beneath his breath, and then he did as she asked, his long fingers gliding over her. His caress was gentle at first, nothing more than a teasing glance as he slicked her dew over her seam, tantalizing her with the promise of more. Tenderness wasn't what she wanted from him, for that was a lie. It wasn't something she could afford to have. Not now, not with him, not ever.

Instead, she could harness her passion. Seize what she wanted. Take something for herself. Her life was not hers, her every action dictated by duty to her sister, to her father.

But the heavy weight of responsibility was momentarily shucked from her shoulders. In this stolen moment, alone with Logan, she could forget.

She could pretend to be someone else.

Someone who was free. Wonderfully, deliriously *free*.

"What do you want?" Logan asked, his voice hoarse with desire.

His eyes were still fastened upon the place where their bodies connected, his hand on her as he gently strummed as if she were an instrument to be played. It surprised her to realize she enjoyed watching him as he watched her. Reveled in the naked look of unabashed desire on his handsome face. In the way his eyes had darkened to a mysterious shade.

"I want *you*," she said.

Forbidden words. Words she never would have uttered. Not even when she had been a married woman. Was it the hedonism in the air at this wicked place? The man in her arms driving her to the edge of restraint? The desperation of her circumstances?

She could not be certain. All Arianna did know was that there was a terrible, aching agony within her. A hollowness which could only be filled in one way. She bit her lip as his fingers continued to move, parting her folds, slipping deeper to find the hidden knot of her desire, stoking the fires of her need. *Oh*, he knew how to touch her. Knew how to give her what she craved, his fingers flying ever faster, taking her higher.

"You want me here?" he asked.

"Yes," she gasped, rolling her hips into that knowing touch.

"Like this?"

She didn't answer him. Couldn't form coherent thought. Her entire being was centered upon the place where he touched her, the wicked sensations he elicited. But then, his fingers gentled, slowing. Making her realize he was awaiting her response, teasing it out of her by denying her what she wanted so desperately.

Could she seize the moment, the man? Did she dare take this fleeting offer of pleasure for herself and face the consequences later?

Yes, said her body.

No, said her conscience.

But the steady throbbing deep in her core won the battle over the rest of her.

"Like this, yes." She rubbed herself shamelessly over Logan's questing fingers. "I want you desperately. We haven't much time. If I'm never to see you again—"

"We'll see each other again," he interrupted, his voice low and sure.

He did not know that. Could not possibly be certain. And nor could she. Father had promised this would be the last secret she would have to sell. But the cynical part of her that was familiar with her father's broken promises knew that for the likely lie it was. Still…

"Even if we don't ever see each other again," she countered, stopping to gasp as he worked her pearl. "I still want this. I still want you."

"I want you, too." He slid his finger lower, leaving her throbbing as he moved to her entrance.

He teased her with light dips into the place where she wanted him most, using her own readiness against her. Making her weak. She was embarrassingly slick, his finger gliding over her with a wet noise that rose above their mingled breaths.

She lowered her head, sealing her mouth to his, because she swore she would perish if she did not have his kiss in the next heartbeat. He gave her what she needed, kissing her back with a groan, his finger sinking inside her to the knuckle. The invasion was thrilling. She gasped, then gave in to her body's need to grind against him, seeking more. Her lips worked over his with a heightened frenzy as his finger went deeper inside her, touching a place she had never known existed. And it was such exquisite agony and ecstasy all at once.

He stilled then, his mouth leaving hers as he tipped his head against the back of the chair to watch her beneath a heavy-lidded stare. "You feel like bleedin' paradise."

"I like the way you feel too," she confessed softly, breathlessly.

Although they were hidden away in a den of sin teeming with dozens of others just beyond the closed door, she felt inexplicably as if they were the only two people who existed. They were Arianna and Logan, and all the desperation and pain of her circumstances fell away.

"I've never..." his words trailed off, and he cursed beneath his breath. "Not with a lady like you before. Am I being too rough?"

How did he know she was a lady? Had she revealed too much? For a moment, worry shot through her, rivaling the pleasure, but then a second finger joined the first, and her fears faded to a dull ebb.

"I like the way you touch me," she reassured him. "I like everything you do to me."

"Floating hell," he cursed. "This wasn't what I intended tonight."

"Nor I."

His thumb fluttered over her pearl, and his fingers moved, gliding in and out of her passage. She thought something inside her would break, so potent was the sensation. She was on the edge. Painfully aware of everything, her senses on fire.

All she saw was the riddle of his eyes, their ever-changing

colors, the arresting masculine beauty of his face. She felt his body beneath hers, so powerful and muscled, yet his touch so gentle and knowing. The wet sounds of her body's need filled her ears, and the scent of smoke and musk and man surrounded her. The taste of him was yet upon her lips.

Up until this evening, she had been a respectable widow. But then, up until a few days ago, she had never sold the secrets of men wanted by the Crown, either. She'd been catapulted into unfamiliar territory, and it only served to make sense that if she must risk herself, at least she could have this one reward.

She could allow herself this pleasure with Logan.

Only this once, she told herself firmly. And never again.

"Come for me, love," he urged, his voice low and commanding, gliding over her senses like butter melting on a hot pan. "I want to watch you take your pleasure."

As he spoke, he worked her body as if he knew it better than she did herself. It was wicked and wanton, what he was saying to her, what he was doing to her. She didn't even know his surname. Their paths had only crossed on two occasions. She was selling him secrets. He was a spy. But none of that mattered.

Because he thrust his long fingers deep, curling them in a way that made her lose control. Her body seized up, bliss exploding and washing over her, making her go weak. She gasped out her pleasure, limp and mindless as she collapsed against him, burying her face in his too-long auburn locks as she rode his fingers until the last bit of pleasure had been wrung from her.

Arianna was breathless, clinging to him, her heart hammering against her chest. Her sex was throbbing with the aftereffects of her release, and it took her a moment to find the presence of mind to realize she had trapped his hand between their bodies. Still trying to gather her wits and catch her breath, she raised her head and rose to her knees again. But instead of withdrawing from her and replacing his fingers with his manhood as she had supposed he would, Logan continued to move in and out of her in slow thrusts, stoking the flames higher.

"That was bleeding lovely." He gave her a wicked smile that seared her to her soul. "Again, beautiful."

Had he called her beautiful?

"Again? I've never...I couldn't possibly...*oh*." Her protests died as his thumb once more teased the bud of her sex.

Apparently, she could.

And he intended to prove it to her. She was already worked into a heightened state, and it didn't take much for him to have her on the edge again.

"Just like that," he crooned, fingers pumping into her in a rhythm that had her moving with him, rocking on his hand as she sought the seemingly impossible. "Come again for me."

She did, faster and harder than the first time. Arianna seized his lips with hers, kissing him fiercely as she rode those knowing fingers. His tongue slipped between her lips, the kiss voracious and greedy as she cried out into his mouth. He didn't stop until the last quivers of her pleasure rippled through her.

And then on a growl, he broke the kiss, removing his fingers from her but not withdrawing entirely, slicking over her folds in tantalizing caresses.

His hazel gaze was hot and commanding, burning into hers. "You still want more?"

She knew what he was asking. Here was her chance to change her mind. To leave this meeting with a shred of her honor intact. But what was honor? She'd lived with the cold comfort of it for years, and to what avail? When would she ever have this opportunity again?

She nodded, her decision made even more firmly than it had already been. "Desperately."

His jaw hardened, eyes darkening. "Touch me."

Permission.

Her hand slid between their bodies, where she found his hardness barely contained beneath the placket of his trousers. The knowledge that he wanted her set off an answering blossom of heat in her core. She cupped him, fingers seeking, stroking over his impressive length. Good heavens, it would seem he was much larger than Edgar had been. *Everywhere.*

Logan made a low sound of approval, his stare intent upon her. "Go on. Find the buttons. Open them. Do as you wish."

Do as you wish.

So much power in those four little words. Words which no one else had ever uttered to her before. And she recognized the strength of them, the heady power he gave her. Free rein over him. Over his body, his pleasure. She had never known such unfettered relations existed. With Edgar, everything had been measured and polite. He'd never brought her to her pinnacle once, let alone twice in a row, and nor had he told her to open the fall of his trousers.

It surprised her to realize how much she wanted to touch Logan. To bring him the same bliss he had given her. Tentatively, her trembling fingers pulled the buttons from their moorings. One by one, they gave way. She was breathless from anticipation and her madly racing heart as her gaze slipped from his, dipping to where he rose, stiff and thick and ruddy from the opened flap on his trousers.

She took him in hand gently, wrapping her fingers around him. His skin was hot and smooth, and he hissed out a breath.

"God yes, beautiful," he murmured, hips rolling beneath her, seeking more of her touch. "Harder. I'll not break."

She gripped him a bit more firmly, growing bolder as she examined him. Freed of the constraint of his trousers, he was even more massive than she had supposed. The head of him was broad, a bead of his seed seeping from a slit in the tip. Guided by instinct, she stroked, her thumb swirling and slicking the moisture over him.

He groaned. "I'm not going to last if you keep doing that, love."

She paused, tearing her enthralled gaze away from the rousing sight of her hand on him. His expression was pained, that hazel gaze almost the steel of a storm-drenched sky, his sculpted lips parted to emit a ragged breath.

"Am I not doing it properly?" she wondered.

His head tipped back, resting against the chair, revealing the masculine protrusion of his Adam's apple above his simply tied cravat. He swallowed hard, and she tracked the motion of his throat, intensely interested in this mysterious, complex man and the effect she had upon him. She'd never before longed to set her lips there upon any gentleman's skin, but when she looked at Logan, there suddenly seemed no more ideal place, save his mouth.

"You're doing it better than properly," he reassured her, his voice husky and deep. "But I want to give you the pleasure you deserve."

Pleasure in the act? She'd certainly never experienced it. Vague discomfort at best. Uncomfortable stinging at worst until she had learned to better prepare herself on the nights Edgar visited her.

"You've already given me pleasure," she countered, not wishing to speak of past experience, nor to think of it.

Instead, she surrendered to the mad desire to dip her head and set her mouth on his neck, just above his cravat.

Still straddling him, on her knees on the oversized chair, his rigid manhood in her hand, she kissed the skin of his throat.

He groaned as his fingers sifted through her hair. "Ah, sweet Christ, you'll be the death of me."

She liked the edge in his voice, the way his hips moved again, thrusting, making him glide against her palm in pleasant friction. He was heavy and hot, and his scent surrounded her, musk and man. She could not stop kissing him now that she had begun. Her mouth traveled with a will of its own, feasting over his exposed skin, finding her way to his jaw. There, she rubbed her cheek against his, the abrasion of his whiskers making her nipples go hard and tight in her stays.

How she wished the both of them were utterly nude, free to explore each other. But that was not the nature of this frantic coupling. And so she settled for what she could have, kissing a path to his ear. It was as if she became a different person entirely when her lips grazed the whorl there, and she traced it with her tongue.

And it was that person who whispered in his ear, not the Arianna she had been forced to become, the demure widow who sacrificed herself for her family. Here, tonight, she was a veiled enigma. A wanton who could seize what she wanted and bask in the hedonism of the night.

"I want you inside me," said this bold stranger, this Arianna she did not recognize, as she stroked his manhood and guided him toward her.

His hips bucked beneath her, bringing the tip of him into contact with her throbbing sex. The hand on her waist flexed, fingers digging in as he issued a vile curse to the ceiling before grasping a fistful of her hair and gently tugging her head back so their eyes met and held.

"This ain't what I do with my informants, Arianna," he said. "And if I shag you now, it ain't going to be about anything other than me wanting you, and you wanting me. The rest of it—the Guild, the Society, the rewards—can all go to bloody fucking hell. This is about you and me. Logan and Arianna. Yes?"

She was grateful for the distinction he'd made, for she wanted him to know that giving him her body had nothing to do with the secret she was selling to the Guild and everything to do with wanting him. She had no other motive, save desire. And giving in to that desire was taking a tremendous risk. One that challenged everything she had believed about herself, the proper and chaste widowhood she had lived.

"Yes," she answered, unhesitating.

"Then I'm all yours," he told her.

His words sent new, decadent heat cascading over her, making the ache between her thighs almost unbearable. And yet, she did not know what to do. It seemed he meant for her to take charge, but despite being a widow, she was apparently woefully inexperienced. For she had no inkling of what to do next.

"In…a chair?" she asked.

She knew the mechanics, of course. But whenever Edgar had come to her, it had been in a bed. Beneath a counterpane. He had been atop her.

Logan's lips quirked into a rakish grin. "There ain't a bed in this room, love. Some of the chambers at the Slipper don't 'ave them. Didn't reckon we'd need one. Do you want to find another chamber?"

"No." She faltered, torn between embarrassment and her need for him. "It is merely that I don't know what to do."

"Ah," he said, a wealth of meaning in that lone word.

Her boldness disintegrated.

She bit her lip, a rush of disappointment hitting her. What had she been thinking? Logan was handsome and dashing and bold. He had a face and a physique that would make any lady in her acquaintance's knees go weak. He could have any woman he liked, and she had no doubt they had all been far more beautiful and adept at seduction than she was.

"You're probably accustomed to women who know how to please a man." She released his manhood, her hand grasping her skirt and petticoat, ready to drag them back into place. "Perhaps this was a mistake."

"No." His grip on her waist tightened as he kept her there in his lap, his expression softening, becoming almost tender. "Doesn't matter what I've known in the past. The past is where it belongs. All that matters now is the present. *You.* And you please me greatly. Do you still want me?"

"Yes," she whispered.

She was navigating new territory, giving in to herself, to what she wanted. Taking risks. Being reckless. Attempting to seduce a man when she didn't know how. And yet, Logan didn't make her feel foolish. He made her feel desired. Wanted.

Beautiful.

"And do I please you?" he asked.

Her cheeks went hot beneath the memory of just how thoroughly he had pleased her. Twice over. "Of course."

"Good." He smiled, his eyes burning into hers. "We'll do this together."

"Together," she repeated. "What happens next?"

His fingers, still tangled in her hair, moved to her nape, cupping her head. "You kiss me."

That could be accommodated. With ease and great enjoyment.

"And then?" she ventured.

He winked. "And then, I'll show you how you can ride me. In a chair."

Oh sweet, merciful heavens. If she'd been standing, she was certain her knees would have betrayed her. But she was still comfortably astride him in the oversized chair…

Suddenly, the odd nature of the furniture in the room made sense to Arianna. And her cheeks went hotter still. An answering fire burned through her. A need to know more. To have everything. If she had but one night of abandon, then this was the one she chose. And Logan was the man.

"Shall I kiss you now?" she asked, breathless again.

His smile deepened, his eyes glinting with untold promise of more. "Aye."

She didn't hesitate, lowering her head until her lips settled over his. Her eyes fluttered closed as she surrendered to the sensations buffeting her. His big hand cupped her head gently, angling her so that he could devour her. The kiss deepened instantly, tongues tangling, teeth nipping.

It was wet and needy and carnal, bruising and luscious all at once, as they battled each other for control. All the while, his other hand was free to roam, leaving her waist to glide beneath her skirts yet again. He stroked her inner thighs in smooth, sweeping motions. And then, he caressed her mound, cupping her fully in his hot hand as if claiming her.

She cried out into the kiss, hips bucking, loving the sensation of his hand engulfing her most intimate flesh. Her hips jolted, seeking of their own accord. More friction, more pleasure, more Logan.

And then, as his tongue played with hers, his touch receding. The hand cupping her head fled as well, moving to her hip. She kissed him as if her next breath depended upon the sensation of his lips beneath hers. And in a sense, it did. Because nothing had ever felt so real, nor so right, before Logan. Before now, this moment, this desire.

She understood the absence of his touch on her sex when the rigid tip of him brushed over her folds again and again, up and down her seam until he was slicked in her wetness.

And then he brought himself to her aching nub and rubbed over her, the sensation so exquisite that her thighs trembled, her muscles, already strained from her unnatural position, nearly betraying her.

"Sit on my cock now," he crooned against her lips.

Crude words. An indecent command. She should have been horrified.

But she wasn't.

Arianna lowered herself slowly, grateful for the shift in position, initially for the break it provided to her taxed thigh muscles. But then, the broad head of his cock touched her. Gripping himself, he brought the tip of his cock back to where she wanted him most. His hand on her hip guided her the rest of the way down. There was pressure at her entrance, and she knew a moment of worry that he wouldn't possibly fit, and then…

"Oh," she gasped.

Her body accommodated him with a glide as he guided her hips and slid deep inside her. So wonderfully deep. The sensation of him, thick and hard and filling her, was intensely pleasurable. She hadn't been prepared for just how good it would feel, how right. Arianna clutched his shoulders, astounded at the closeness, the connection.

"Good?" he asked, watching her with a hooded stare, looking like sin personified, so handsome and masculine, smoldering with desire.

She found the presence of mind to nod. "Better than good." Instinct made her rock against him, the small movement so pleasurable that she had to do it again. And again.

His hands clasped her hips in a possessive hold she couldn't help but love.

"That's it, beautiful. Ride me. Take your pleasure."

At his urging, she allowed her instinct to take control. She was not an innocent, after all. She knew what happened between a man and a woman. And now that they were fitted perfectly together, her body understood what she needed better than her mind did. Up and down she moved, rising to her knees, his shaft almost slipping from her, before she sank down upon his thick length. Faster. Harder.

"More," he growled.

And she gave them both more, riding him, her inner muscles clenching to the point of exquisite agony. Her breaths tore from her in gasps, her heart galloping to rival a runaway mare. She was on the edge of another release that she chased with each frantic thrust of her hips.

But she wasn't alone in her quest. After allowing her to set the rhythm and take control, Logan moved beneath her, surging upward, filling her aching channel again and again. The sounds of their lovemaking filled the room, wetness and bodies slamming together, rustling fabric and ragged breaths, punctuated by mutual moans as the flames of their desire burned recklessly higher.

One of his hands fled her hips to catch the edge of her bodice and drag it low. Her breast popped free, and his head dipped. As his hips pumped into her, he took her nipple into his mouth and sucked hard. She faltered, a rush of wetness slipping from her sex in time to the wicked suction of his lips on her breast. The sight of his handsome face against her bare skin, in a place where she'd never previously been touched, was unbearably erotic. She'd never realized how gloriously sensitive she was there. Nor how wondrous it would feel for a man to put his lips upon her.

"Logan," she murmured, half moan, half plea.

He released her nipple, then flicked his tongue over it before glancing up at her. "Yes, love?"

"Don't stop," she gasped, resuming her pace, rocking into him with frenzied need as she sought her next release. "Don't ever stop."

She knew he would have to, of course. The words leaving her lips were nonsensical. She was no longer herself, but someone she scarcely recognized. A woman seeking her own pleasure, unashamedly and without hesitation.

"As my lady commands," he murmured, and then he gave her bodice another tug so that her other breast was freed as well.

How wondrous, to suppose this big, powerful man was willing to do whatever she wished. That he was hers to command.

His head lowered, and he took the aching peak into his mouth. Arianna threaded her fingers through his long, auburn hair, holding him there as he sucked and licked and bit, and she rode him harder and faster as a new mindlessness overtook her. One fierce roll of her hips, and the explosion was upon her, taking her by surprise. Everything inside her tightened, her body bowing forward as the force of her release overwhelmed her. Tiny bursts of light like stars danced around the edges of her vision as she flew apart.

Arianna moaned helplessly, her inner walls clamping on his cock. She thrust down on him greedily, wanting to wring every last drop of pleasure from this encounter. Not just for this moment, but for later, when she could savor it. When she could think of him while alone in her bed and recall the intensity of the passion they'd shared. The pleasure washed over her, bathing her in a sensual haze, and she fell into him, wrapping her arms around his neck to keep from toppling over the side of the chair in her sated delirium.

"Floating hell," he was saying. "You're so hot and wet and… Fuck, love. I'm going to spend."

Dimly, she realized what that meant. Although she had been married for a year without issue, she couldn't be certain she was unable to conceive. And if she *could* conceive, she could most certainly not afford to become with child now.

Not when she had been a widow for far too long, her time of mourning well passed. Not when her father could scarcely sustain the household with all his mounting gambling debts. These realizations were like cold water to her senses. Alarming and unwanted intrusions upon their idyll, yet obligatory.

With a burst of energy spurred by necessity, Arianna shifted, allowing him to slide free of her with ease. And just in time, too, as he gripped his cock and spent on her inner thigh instead of inside her. The warm spurt of his seed painted her skin, and heaven help her, but she *liked* it. Liked wearing this small part of him on her, as if it marked her as his.

"My God," he said hoarsely, kissing the curve of her breast before relaxing against the back of the spacious chair. "That was…"

His words trailed off, as if he couldn't find any worthy of articulation.

But Arianna had plenty. For making love with Logan had been nothing short of wonderful. More wonderful than she could have ever imagined. But she could not linger here and she knew it. She had far too many responsibilities. And there remained the missive Father had provided for this evening, its contents revealing where Charles and Clifford Mace could be found. The reason for her journey to this house of wickedness, she thought as guilt slowly supplanted the heady passions that had banished all other concerns.

"Wrong," she finished for him, for it was true. Even if her heart did not feel as if it were. "We never should have done this."

Logan caught her jaw in a tender grip, forcing her to hold his gaze. "Look me in the eye and tell me again. Tell me how wrong it was."

She fell into his hazel stare, and she saw in those mysterious depths so much passion, such gentleness, such caring and concern, that she couldn't. Couldn't force the lie to her lips again.

"Logan," she began, then stopped, not knowing what to say.

She had most certainly not intended to allow herself to get so carried away. To lose herself with him. To forget the world.

"Don't," he said, shaking his head as he caressed her cheek. "It wasn't wrong. *We* ain't wrong. And you know it. You feel it, the same way that I do." His hand moved then, the loss of his touch leaving her bereft until his palm settled over her still madly racing heart. "Here. You feel it here."

He was right, heaven help her.

She did feel it. She felt *him*. Felt the way he brought her to life. Everything about him was so different from her past experience with her husband. Where Edgar had been aloof and inattentive, Logan blazed with intensity. When he looked at her, touched her, spoke to her, she felt *seen*. And not just seen, but cherished, too.

How was it that a man she had only met on two occasions had made her feel far more valued and desired than the man she had been married to for an entire year? It seemed impossible, and yet, it was true.

"I…" she faltered, attempting to tell him a lie and failing utterly. Her lips would not form the words. Her mind would not betray her heart. And her heart said she had somehow fallen beneath this man's spell, despite all the reasons why she should not. "I do," she admitted. "I feel it, too."

Logan's touch was a hot, reassuring weight on her chest. Until he withdrew it.

"Thank Christ." He discreetly shifted the fall of his trousers, covering himself as he hooked buttons back into their moorings.

Then, he reached into his coat, extracting a handkerchief. Using the linen square, he wiped her inner thigh clean, tending to her with such care that she hated herself for ever calling what had happened wrong. It had been her own fears which had made her blurt out the foolishness. Fears and worry and doubt. Because she was a widow and had an unmarried sister to fret over. And because her father was engaged in the reckless sale of the secrets of revolutionaries. And because one misplaced word, one whispered secret, would send their tower of carefully built deceptions crashing down.

So much was at stake.

Only everything.

It had not been wrong, but even so, it could never happen again.

Logan tucked the handkerchief away and then went about repairing the damage he had done to her bodice, chemise, and stays.

"I must go," she said, slipping from his lap with the greatest of reluctance. Her skirts fell into place, but her hair was hopeless, unbound and falling heavy past her shoulders and down her back. She glanced down to find the pins which had been plucked free and tossed away, studding the Axminster.

But Logan rose from the chair as well and suddenly was there, bending down to retrieve them all, before handing them to her. "Hold these."

She accepted them, cupping the cool pieces of metal in her palm. "You cannot intend to repair my hair."

"I did the damage. 'Tis only fair that I fix it."

His calm insistence had a strange effect upon her. Arianna found herself standing before him, awaiting his ministrations. He coiled her hair with ease, tucking pins into place. And though some scraped her scalp and caused her to wince, she was shocked to realize he had made a fair effort.

"You have had practice, then," she said, wondering at how and whom.

His hands fell softly on her shoulders, and he spun her about so that she faced him. "I've sisters I helped raise. I know my way about a lady's hair."

His explanation soothed the jagged parts inside her. Jagged parts that made no sense. It wasn't as if she had been an innocent. She was a widow. Why should she care if Logan had bedded dozens of beauties before her, which he doubtlessly had?

An uncomfortable twinge of jealousy lodged itself between her rib bones. She knew it had no place, and yet, she could not seem to shake it. Somehow, she felt as if this man were hers. She longed to claim all his future kisses, to be the only woman he made love to, futile as she knew such a yearning was.

Arianna bit her lip, wishing they had more time. Wishing everything was different. "Thank you."

"For tending to your hair or for everything else that happened between us tonight?" he asked softly.

He was teasing her, she realized then, a small, almost boyish grin curving his lips. That he could find levity when danger was so desperately near made something inside her chest seize and tighten. They had just made love, and they were strangers cast in a play of desperation. She was selling information that wasn't hers to sell, against her better judgment, and he was a spy, engaging in secretive operations to bring dangerous men to justice. Seeking those who would easily kill him to save themselves. Or kill her, though the thought had not crossed her mind until now.

She tamped down all the misgivings, concerning herself with Logan's question instead.

"For both," she said quietly, a pang in her heart at the realization that this must be their farewell.

Father had promised there would be no more meetings after this one. The five hundred pounds, in addition to the previous two hundred, coupled with all the sale of household goods, would have to suffice. She could not bear to carry on in this fashion. Not so much because of the danger it posed to her welfare, but because of the peril to her heart.

Crossing the room to the chair where she had draped her pelisse, she extracted the missive which contained the information her father had recorded.

She turned back to Logan. "Here is what you've come for, an even exchange."

He reached into his coat, extracting a small fold of notes and offering them to her, his stare holding her in its fathomless thrall. "I begin to think I've come here for far more."

But there could be no more for them, and she knew it. She took his notes and relinquished the missive, her heart heavier than ever.

She shook her head. "This can't be repeated."

"The devil it can't." Logan surprised her then by snaking an arm around her waist and pulling her nearer yet again. His gaze traveled over her face as if he sought to commit it to memory. "I want to see you again."

She wanted to see him again too. More than she could possibly express.

Emotion made her throat go thick, threatening to choke.

"I can't see you again." Arianna rose on her toes and pressed a kiss to his jaw, then another to his lips. "The risk is far too great. This must be farewell."

His jaw hardened. "It doesn't have to be this way."

But she held firm, not allowing herself to be swayed.

"It does." She extricated herself and turned away, busying

herself by pulling on her pelisse, veil, and gloves. "Thank you for tonight. I'll never forget it. Take care of yourself, Logan."

He watched her with an inscrutable expression. "And who will take care of you, hmm?"

She didn't answer. Because they both already knew. No one would. But that was the way of it for her. She'd made her choices, and now she had to live with them. Without another word, Arianna fled the chamber, telling herself it was for the best. She could never have more than this one stolen night of passion.

CHAPTER 6

He was one of eight siblings, which meant Logan had a great deal of experience in the art of patience. However, the hour was growing late, the night air was getting colder by the moment, and the obliging branch outside Arianna's bedchamber window was bleeding hard and uncomfortable. He'd been alternating between crouching and sitting for what felt like an eternity as he waited for a sign she was within her room. First, his arse had fallen asleep.

And then, his right foot.

He had to admit, hiding in a tree until well past midnight hadn't been how he had intended to spend the evening. He must have been mad to suppose this plan of his would bear fruit. But then, when he had first followed her last night at a safe distance after she'd fled The Velvet Slipper, he hadn't initially supposed he'd need to hide about like a house cracksman. Or that he would only manage to learn which chamber was hers by bribing a maid.

He also hadn't supposed Arianna was truly a lady. Nor that she was the daughter of a viscount, the widow of a duke's son. That when she had told him she'd found a home with her family in her widowhood, she'd meant her father and her unwed sister. That she was a proper lady with a father who sat in the house of bleeding lords. He'd known she was educated, had recognized the quality of her garments. But he'd never reckoned he was dealing with a nob.

Then again, he wasn't sure he'd been thinking clearly at all when he'd decided to pay a visit to her this evening under the cover of darkness. From the moment he'd made love to her the night before, his thoughts had ceased to be rational, and he knew it. He could contemplate nothing beyond the frantic need to see her again. It had eclipsed all else.

Even the need to stay on the right side of the Guild and keep his head firmly attached to his body. Duty had become a distant second to her welfare and, he'd not lie, to having her in his bed. He'd done right by the Guild, of course. He had delivered the missive to Tierney the night before and lied through his teeth when he'd sworn there'd been no seduction, that the lady was cold as ice.

But he wouldn't use the intimacy he'd shared with Arianna against her, not for the Guild's gain and nor for his own. He felt sick at the deception, at being torn between duty and his deepening feelings for her, but he didn't have a choice. Not truly.

As it was, Whitehall would likely act on the information they'd received with all haste. Charles and Clifford Mace would, he hoped, be captured, vindicating Arianna. And that would leave Logan free to pursue her as he wished, without the need for hiding in bleeding trees at midnight.

Ah, Arianna.

What a terrible coil she had him in, the sort he'd never experienced with a mort before her, and the kind he knew he'd never again experience after her. The fiery passion they'd shared had been nothing short of exquisite. But then, she'd run from him with nothing save a farewell and the warning they could never have another night together.

Never see her again? Never touch her again? Never make love to her again? Not bloody well happening as far as Logan was concerned. Aye, even if it made him the greatest fool in all the land. He couldn't help the way she made him feel.

He sighed then, wishing he had brought a cheroot with him. And that was when a light at long last glowed in the window about the curtains. *Bleeding finally.* She was within. Or, at least, someone was.

Holding his breath, Logan scooted nearer to the window.

He had already decided that if the maid who had told him which window to concern himself with had been lying, he would drop to the lowest branch and run into the night. By the time anyone was able to follow, he'd be long gone.

If it was indeed Arianna who appeared at the window, however...

Well, that changed things mightily.

Leveraging himself into a standing position required some muscle and determination, but nothing was going to stand between Logan and the chance to speak with the woman who had haunted his lurid dreams the night before and every waking second since. He simply had to see her again.

At last, he was standing, balanced on the branch, holding another limb overhead with his left hand as he leaned toward the window and tapped the pane. He heard movement within the room, saw the flutter of curtains, and prayed to any god who would listen that he had found the right room.

And then, the curtains parted, and Arianna's lovely face appeared, illuminated by the glow of a brace of candles. She gasped, a hand going to her mouth as if to conceal her startlement.

"Are you alone?" he asked quietly.

She shook her head slightly.

He pressed a finger to his lips, indicating she should keep quiet. And, he hoped, remain calm, showing no hint of upset to whomever was in the chamber with her.

Arianna nodded, and then the curtains fell closed again. The faint murmur of feminine voices reached him, and he waited what seemed an impossibly long span of time before she returned to the window, snatching the curtains to each side before thrusting open the sash window.

"Logan?"

Her voice was incredulous.

But then, he couldn't blame her. Likely it wasn't every day that she found a man sitting in the branches outside her bed chamber window. At least, he hoped it wasn't. If he had competitors, he would be damned glad to chase them off. With his fists, if need be.

"Say something," she demanded of him, her voice low.

Sultry.

He still felt the full effect of it, even standing in a damned uncomfortable tree.

"You weren't expecting me?" he asked, clinging to his charm, which had always stood him in good stead with the ladies.

Her brows snapped together in a ferocious scowl. "In the tree outside my window? Of course I wasn't. This is madness. You cannot be here."

Logan flashed her a wry grin. "And yet, here I am."

Her eyes sparked with brown-gold fire, and he wished for more light so he might see her fully; as it was, the candelabra cast much of her expression in shadows.

"How did you find me?" she wanted to know.

"Excellent question." He glanced down at the tree

branches holding him. "I'll be pleased to answer if you let me in."

"Let you in? Are you mad?"

With the lengths he had gone to just for the chance to see her again? Aye, it was likely that he was.

"Mad enough to find my way to you," he admitted, his levity fleeing, raw emotion and wild desire taking the reins now. "I 'ad to see you. I couldn't let it end last night."

"I don't live on my own," she said, a note of hesitation creeping into her tone. "I must take care with my reputation, for others as much as for myself."

Some of the vigor had fled her.

He was not too proud to press his suit. "I know. You live with your father, Lord Inglesby, and your sister, Miss Juliet Hargreave."

She gasped. "You've been spying on me."

"I followed you last night," he countered, not liking the accusation, even if it did hit a trifle close to the mark. "You should've taken better care. The driver of the hack you hired was drunk as David's sow. Anyone could have greased his palms and he'd have delivered you to them on a silver salver."

Truly, it was a miracle nothing ill had befallen her in all her late-night misadventures. It was clear that someone had to look after her, to keep her safe. Her father was not doing the damned job.

Arianna was frowning at him now. "You should not have followed me. It was a betrayal of my trust."

"I never promised I wouldn't find out who you are," he pointed out. "After what happened between us last night, I made it my mission. And if you think I'm the sort of cove who can bed a woman and not give a damn about her afterward, you're wrong. Now let me in, Arianna. It's damned cold out 'ere."

Still frowning, she held her hand out to him with a

defeated sigh. "Come in, then. The night is far too cold for me to keep this window open any longer. But you must promise to be quiet."

"Promise."

Biting back a grin of triumph, Logan ignored the hand she offered and grasped the window ledge instead, hauling himself into the chamber with ease. She stepped past him, closing the window, which made rather a lot more noise than it had originally. Arianna swept the curtains closed and turned back to him.

"What do you intend to do, now that you know who I am?" she asked, rubbing her arms as if she had taken a chill.

And perhaps she had.

He had to admit, now that the warmth of her chamber had embraced him, he realized just how cold he'd been, waiting in the tree branches and the darkness for Christ knew how long.

"I'm not certain yet," Logan admitted, unable to keep himself from drinking in the sight of her, the glow of the candles bathing her lovely features in light.

He had told himself that his recollections were wrong. That no woman could be so tempting. So damned beautiful. That her hair had not been as midnight black as he recalled, that her lashes had not been so sultry and thick, that her mouth had not been plump and kiss-worthy, that her form had not been as womanly and lush as he remembered.

And he'd been wrong.

Because she was.

She was everything he had recalled and more. So much more.

She was also vexed with him, judging from the expression on her countenance. "But how did you follow me so quickly? I left The Velvet Slipper through the—"

"Rear door into the alley," he interrupted, finishing for her. "Just behind The Duke's Bastard."

Her nostrils flared. "How did you know that?"

He always had one of his most trusted little birds, Geoffrey, watching whenever he was within an establishment. If Logan failed to emerge, the lad was to run straight to Tierney with the knowledge and the expectation that they'd been betrayed. But last night, the boy had served a far more important duty. He'd told Logan precisely where Arianna had fled. Trailing her from there hadn't been difficult.

But he wasn't squeaking just yet.

He'd come here for her, not to reveal everything he knew.

Logan shrugged. "Not many secrets in London when I'm about."

Her brow furrowed. "Is it money you want, then? A price in exchange for your silence?"

Her question stung, reminding him of where he'd come from, a place so vastly different from the Mayfair splendor in which she dwelled. And of his position even now, a mercenary, even if the work he performed was at the order of the Crown.

He shook his head, disappointment roiling in his gut along with wounded pride. "That ain't the way of it."

"Then what *is* the way of it? I confess, I cannot tell at the moment." Her voice was cool and clipped.

Indeed, the prim, outraged widow facing him bore precious little resemblance to the wicked Siren who had torn his world apart by shagging him senseless the night before.

"I had to see you again," he admitted, his voice low, thickened with emotion and desire. "I couldn't leave things between us as they were."

He was in her chamber. In her private space. Surrounded by her things and the scent of her. Violets had never smelled so inviting. Being in the mere presence of a woman had never been this intoxicating. And *floating hell*, there was her bed. Upon it was the pillow where she laid those inky tresses each night. He imagined them spilling like tendrils of darkness about her lovely face as they had when she'd ridden him. Thought about how her hair had felt, when he had plucked all her pins free. Pure, silken seduction.

"It is dangerous for you to be here," she told him, her expression still severe, her voice steeped in warning, though hushed.

"Surely not any more dangerous than going about London in the dead of night alone," he countered. "Do your sister and father know what you've entangled yourself in?"

The question had kept him awake through the night. When he had involved himself in the Guild, he had understood the risks. Had shouldered them gladly, even when the risks had become too great and he'd been forced to leave his family behind. But Arianna, whisking about London in the night, selling treasonous secrets before returning to her gilded cage as if none of it had ever happened… It was even more reckless.

"What they know or do not know is not any of your concern," she said firmly.

That was where she was wrong. It *was* his concern, damn it. Ever since last night, he had felt as if something in his world had inexplicably shifted into place.

"I don't suppose a loving family would wish for their daughter and sister to mingle with traitors, thieves, and Christ knows what else," he observed, studying her intently.

It bothered him to think of her gadding about alone in the world, interacting with dangerous men, riding in a hack whilst the drunkard driving swerved all over the bleeding roads. Inviting peril. He'd seen firsthand the damage which could be done to morts at the mercy of brutal men.

"And I can't recall asking for your opinion on the matter,"

she countered, her tone still frosty. "I gave you the information you wanted, and we parted ways. There is nothing more for us to say to each other."

He noted that she'd neatly avoided referring to the passion they'd shared at The Velvet Slipper. Convenient, that. She was stubborn. Logan knew that about her from their previous interactions. His concern for her welfare did not sit well, that much was apparent. And aye, he could well understand it. Any woman accustomed to slinking about in the dark of night, doing as she wished, would likely not welcome someone gainsaying her. Arianna was a mystery. She was a lady. The town house in which she lived was in a plummy part of the city, well-appointed and elegant enough. And yet, she was involved in something murky and treacherous.

None of it made sense.

But then, the world was far darker and more sinister than he had ever supposed. The Guild had taught him never to underestimate the evil lurking in the shadows, and even for a man who had been born to the rookeries, the revelation of how depraved and dangerous London truly was had been astonishing.

"Do you truly believe we've nothing to say to each other?" he asked, holding her gaze and daring her to repeat those words.

The awareness that had been burning from the moment their eyes had first met at Willowby's remained, hot and bright and tempting. He had never been so drawn to a woman the way he was to Arianna. Making love to her hadn't dimmed the fiery longing for her burning within him; it had only made him want her more.

She swayed toward him, and he knew she felt the same, marrow-deep connection.

"Logan," she protested, his name a breathy sigh on her lips. "We can't."

He stepped nearer to her, sensing his advantage and shamelessly exploiting it. "Why can't we?"

"Because my father—" she began, and then faltered. "If anyone were to find you in my chamber, it would go very poorly for the both of us."

She was concerned about her father making the discovery, that much was apparent.

"Is he cruel or unkind to you?" he demanded, that same protective urge surging.

Her gaze slipped from his, lingering on a point somewhere over his shoulder before returning. "No, not that it is any concern of yours."

"Everything about you is my concern after last night," he told her. "How can you think otherwise?"

Her sweet lips parted, taunting him with the agonizing memory of how they had felt beneath his. "Last night cannot happen again."

"The devil it can't," he denied, reaching for her hand. Her fingers were pliant, and she made no effort to pull away. He settled her palm on his chest as he had the day before, over his thumping heart. "There's something between us. Do you deny it?"

"Logan," she protested softly.

But she did not move her hand.

He kept it trapped lightly over his heart, forcing her to hold his gaze. "Tell me you feel nothing for me. That what we shared didn't mean anything to you."

Her fingers curled ever so slightly, the half-moons of her nails biting into him through the layers of fabric separating them. "You shouldn't have come here."

"You didn't answer me," he pressed.

"You know I can't," she whispered. "I felt it, too."

That was all the concession he needed from her.

Logan looped an arm gently around her waist and pulled

her snug against him, so their bodies were pressed together from hip to breast. "I've been thinking of nothing but you since the moment we parted. Thinking of nothing but kissing you again."

Her free hand came up to cup his jaw, caressing him in a touch that was as potent as it was featherlight. "This is reckless."

He moved his head, finding the center of her palm and pressing his lips there. "And dangerous."

"You undo me."

Her murmured confession made heat blossom within him, banishing the last of the cold. His head dipped, and he found her mouth with his. Their lips chased each other, the kiss hungry and demanding. She made a sultry sound of need low in her throat, and it made his ballocks tighten, his cock going rigid as her tongue slipped into his mouth to boldly tangle with his.

He undid her?

Floating hell, she *ruined* him.

Destroyed him in the best possible way. He wanted nothing more than to bask in her. Lose himself in her. To surrender to the delirious lust coursing through his veins. But he was also keenly aware of their surroundings. Nor did he have any wish to cause problems for her. Her allusion to her father troubled him.

There was something wrong there, unless he missed his guess.

Logan ended the kiss, reminded of their circumstances, and lifted his head to stare down at her, loving the way her lips glistened in the flickering glow of the candles. "I want to see you again. Not here. Somewhere we can be free to speak and do as we wish."

She shook her head, her countenance turning sad. "We can't. I don't dare."

But he hadn't spent the better portion of the night freezing his arse off in a tree to simply walk away from her. Nor had he risked inciting the anger of Tierney and the Guild, just to never see her again. He was willing to jeopardize everything for this woman.

"I'll make certain you're protected," he vowed. "No harm will come to you. Nor will anyone be the wiser."

Arianna's expression was torn. "I must think of my sister. She's seeking a husband, and I've invited enough scandal to ruin all her prospects as it is."

He reckoned she was speaking of her forays into Willowby's and The Velvet Slipper. And there was another element of the mystery that didn't make sense. Why would she have invited ruin at all? Where had she received her information? It seemed damned unlikely that a proper Mayfair widow was secretly meeting with revolutionaries. He had to know.

"Your sister won't be affected," he said. "That I promise you."

"Logan," she protested.

"Don't say no," he said, not above begging her. "Only tell me where to be and when, and I'll come to you. I'll make certain no one sees us. You can trust me."

She shook her head. "You can't be certain. I had no notion you followed me here last night. Nor that you somehow found out which chamber was mine."

He winked, trying to lighten the grim mood. "Ah, but you see, beautiful? The one you needed to fret over is on your side. I found you, but your secret is as safe with me as you are."

He sensed her relenting, some of the tension seeping from her shoulders. "You are sure?"

He grinned. "Utterly."

"It is reckless and foolish to agree to your mad whims," she said, worrying her lower lip. "I scarcely even know you."

"You know me well enough," he reminded her, desire thrumming in his veins as he recalled just how well-acquainted they were.

"But *you* don't know *me*," Arianna pointed out wryly, raising a brow.

His head dipped, and he pressed his forehead to hers for a moment. "I want to get to know you better."

"You make it difficult to say no," she said quietly, her honey-brown gaze burning into his.

He was winning this battle. Slowly, but surely.

"Then don't say no," he told her.

She sighed, and he sensed her faltering before she spoke again. "Very well. But I will come to you."

Reluctantly, he released her, for if he lingered, he would only be tempted to carry her to the bed across the chamber and bury himself inside her. "You'll not regret it, I promise you." He reached into his coat and extracted the calling card bearing his assumed name and the direction of the rooms he was currently keeping. "If you need anything before then, this is where you can find me."

It was a risk, allowing her to know where he lived, and he knew it. But if he wanted to dig deeper into why she was selling information about the London Reform Society and how she'd obtained it, he had to entrust her with the knowledge. He'd been tasked with a mission, after all. Even if that mission had long since ceased to be the motivation propelling him.

Even if the motivation had become his need to be with her instead.

Arianna took the card. "I'll come to you two nights from now."

"I don't like the notion of you gadding about on your own," he growled.

Her smile was sad. "It's the only way."

Blast her.

He inclined his head, capitulating. "Fair enough."

But he'd set some of his little birds on her, watching from afar just as they did with his siblings and The Sinner's Palace. If anything went awry, he'd be there for her in a heartbeat.

Logan sketched a bow as if he were a fine gentleman in a ballroom and then moved to the window.

"You can't mean to climb the tree again," Arianna said, her tone doubtful.

"Don't fret, love. Going down is far easier than up." He parted the curtains and hefted the window open, allowing a gust of cold air to enter the chamber.

He was about to clamber out the window when she surprised him by catching his cravat and tugging him to her.

"You forgot this," she said breathlessly.

Her lips met his, soft and greedy, and they kissed until another burst of wind interrupted, making her shiver. He tore his mouth from hers with great reluctance.

"I'd best go before you catch a lung infection from this bleeding cold." He paused to study her, committing those hauntingly lovely features to memory. "Until we meet again."

She nodded. "Until then."

Logan climbed through the window and into the night.

CHAPTER 7

"It was a wonderful evening, was it not?" Juliet asked with a breathy sigh of contentment as the carriage rumbled over familiar roads, carrying them home from a musicale which had been held by Lord and Lady Rayne.

Although the music had been lovely—professional players demonstrating their talents on the pianoforte and harp—Arianna had been too distracted to enjoy herself. Her thoughts had been whirling with remembrance of her nighttime visitor the evening before. And with the sure knowledge that she would be tempted to see him not just one night from now as she had promised.

But again.

And again and *again*.

"Arianna?" her sister prodded, jolting Arianna from her musings. "Are you woolgathering?"

"Forgive me, I fear that I was," Arianna said, her gaze upon her gloved fingers as they plucked at the drapery of her pelisse. "The evening was delightful, truly."

She could scarcely believe she had agreed to go to Logan.

To see him again. The risks were greater than ever, tumbling over each other in her mind. There was the fear that Father would take note of her absence, or that someone would recognize her and tongues would wag, and yet another still that her father would ask her to sell more London Reform Society information…

"I do so adore the harp," Juliet continued, blissfully unaware of Arianna's inner turmoil.

"Yes," she agreed with far less enthusiasm. "It's a lovely instrument."

"Lord Newbury was quite keen to escort me to the terrace for some fresh air in all the crush," Juliet went on. "Well over one hundred people in attendance. Can you imagine? Father would never dream of hosting on so grand a scale. But then, I suppose Lord and Lady Rayne are a great deal wealthier than Father is. Do you not agree?"

In truth, Arianna had never compared the earl and countess's wealth to their father's. Because Father had no wealth to speak of. Every ha'penny to his name had been obtained by selling something dear, whether it was Mother's jewels or the London Reform Society's secrets.

"Hmm," she murmured noncommittally, already overwrought and tired from having spent the night before tossing in her bed, unable to sleep. Having to play chaperone to her sister had not rendered her any less weary. If anything, it had served to heighten her exhaustion.

"Why are you so frightfully quiet?" her sister demanded suddenly, sounding cross. "Do you not think Lord Newbury a good suitor?"

The young Earl of Newbury had newly inherited his title and possessed the soft, almost infantile face of a child. At two-and-twenty, he was practically still in leading strings. But he was polite and kind. He doted upon Juliet. And of the crop of suitors interested in Juliet's hand, he appeared the least likely to concern himself with her nonexistent dowry and the most likely to treat her well. Whilst it was clear to Arianna that her sister was not nearly as enamored of him as she was the dashing Lord Willingham, Newbury remained an excellent candidate.

"He has been a most concerted suitor," she observed, casting an assessing glance in her sister's direction. In the absence of their mother, the duty of counseling Juliet in matters of the heart fell to Arianna, and she felt woefully unprepared for the task. Her own marriage had been anything but happy. "I daresay he is quite smitten with you."

Juliet's posture straightened, her head going high. "Do you think so?"

Apparently, the notion of the golden-haired earl harboring a *tendre* for Juliet pleased her.

"How can you doubt it?" Arianna asked. "The way he watched you this evening made it apparent that he regards you highly."

Juliet sighed, biting her lip. "But Lord Willingham is also attentive, and I have always found him ever so handsome. He's an elegant dancer, and the way he seats a horse is nothing short of splendid."

Of the two, Willingham was certainly more handsome and polished, his charm ever at the ready. He was also, if rumors were to be believed, a great deal more experienced. And in need of a bride with a plump dowry. She had no wish to stomp upon Juliet's hopes, but it was likely that Willingham was the sort of suitor who would flirt and ply a lady with easy smiles—perhaps even maneuver her into a quiet alcove for a stolen kiss—but save his marriage proposal for an heiress.

She frowned as she contemplated how best to relay her suspicions to her sister without being overly harsh. "I have heard whispers that Lord Willingham requires a bride with a large dowry."

"I've a dowry, have I not?" Juliet returned. "Mother was an heiress in her own right, after all."

Arianna winced, for she found herself in an untenable situation. Father wished for Juliet to be kept from all matters concerning the depleted family fortune. He had expressly asked Arianna to refrain from mentioning the troubles in which he had found himself. *Juliet is just a girl*, he'd argued. *I have no wish for her to be burdened with my financial affairs. I promise you, Arianna, I shall have this all sorted, and it shall be a moot point...*

Only, Father hadn't sorted his financial woes. Since Mother's death, he had spiraled deeper and deeper into the depths of hopelessness. And now, to save Juliet, Arianna was sacrificing herself. She could not hold that against her sister. It was hardly Juliet's fault that her own marriage had ended so abruptly, and with scarcely any widow's portion to support her own household. Marrying Edgar had been Arianna's choice. And protecting her sister now was much the same.

"Your dowry is not as significant as it may have once been," Arianna answered her sister hesitantly, uncertain how much she should reveal. "Indeed, it's been quite reduced."

Juliet's brows snapped together. "Reduced?"

Arianna swallowed against a rising lump of guilt. "Yes."

"*How* reduced?" Juliet asked, her voice high, her expression pinched with worry.

"You'll have to ask Father."

"I don't want to ask Father. He isn't here. You are, and I'm asking you now. How reduced is my dowry, and why?"

For the first time, she thought grimly. And only because she was concerned over how the loss of a fat dowry might impact her ability to land Lord Willingham.

Arianna tore her gaze from her sister's, staring unseeing out the window at the darkness passing by, interrupted as it was by the intermittent glow of a street lamp. "I am not privy to the details of your marriage settlement."

That much was true. But because she was privy to all the rest, Arianna had no doubt that Juliet's dowry had been equally affected through their father's inability to keep away from the green baize.

"But you knew the details of yours," Juliet pressed. "What was settled upon you? I assume it was considerable, or Lord Edgar never would have married you."

Arianna winced, for her sister's observation pricked hard at her pride. Contrary to Logan's assertion that she was beautiful, she had never been considered a diamond of the first water in Society. Her Season had been awkward and fraught with missteps. She'd never possessed the undeniable loveliness that Juliet radiated, with her golden hair and bright-blue eyes and rosebud lips. Arianna was keenly aware of the disparity between them now, though she'd tried her utmost to disregard it, and above all never allow resentment toward her sister to dwell within her.

"I supposed Lord Edgar married me for reasons other than my dowry," she said tightly, unable to keep the hurt from her voice as old wounds reopened. "I should like to think I have at least a few qualities to recommend me."

"Forgive me," Juliet said hastily. "Of course, you have many, many qualities to recommend you. Just as I'm sure there were a host of reasons for Lord Edgar to wish to wed you. You're kind and lovely and ever so accomplished. I never wished to suggest—"

"Enough," Arianna bit out, having had quite all she could sustain of her sister's awkward apology. "I don't wish to speak of it any longer."

She could not fault Juliet for her honesty. And it was

apparent from her younger sister's countenance that she had always believed Edgar had married Arianna because of her dowry, and not due to any other merit. Arianna knew she was no beauty, but she had never supposed her own sister would believe a man would have only wed her for the coin she would bring to his coffers. To say it was insulting would be a vast understatement.

And this, from a sister she had spent these last few months protecting from the ugly truths surrounding them, risking her own reputation, her very life to see that she could have the opportunity to find her own happiness. To allow Juliet to secure a husband, to be young and naïve and unburdened by the worries of the world.

The carriage ambled on in uncomfortable silence for a few minutes more until Juliet broke the hush by speaking.

"Do you know how reduced my dowry is?" Juliet asked again, her voice small.

Arianna's tenuous grasp on her patience snapped. "What do you think, Juliet? Have you not taken note of the smaller number of servants in the household? Have you not witnessed the disappearance of countless paintings and pieces of furniture? Did you truly think Father intended to have our mother's sapphire parure reset in a new fashion for you, when he cannot afford to pay a proper housekeeper?"

Her voice was sharp, even to her own ears, bearing the lash of a whip.

She had been harsh. Too harsh, perhaps. But she'd been driven to the edge, first by the maelstrom of emotions churning within her, and then by Juliet's own words. For the first time, she could acknowledge that beyond the selfless sacrifice she waged on behalf of her sister, she was resentful, deeply so, of Juliet's carefree existence whilst she was forced to help Father pay back his debts.

If not for Logan, she would have been well and truly

miserable. Adrift in a sea of hopelessness. Thank heavens she had found him. Because without him, she would have nothing.

The realization hit her with stunning intensity, rather like a blow.

He was all she had.

Except, she didn't have him, did she? He was a secret she kept. A man who could never truly be hers. The heavy weight of sadness rose within her, making her throat go tight.

A small cry, much like the sound of a wounded animal, pierced the quiet of the carriage then. Juliet was in tears, Arianna realized, as guilt assailed her. She never should have been so stern with her younger sister. So honest. She knew Juliet could not bear the weight of the truth.

"Juliet," she said, regret acid on her tongue, bile rising in her throat. How she hated this position in which she'd found herself! "Don't weep. Please."

"H-how c-can I not?" her sister asked, swiftly venturing into hysterics. "We are pockets to l-let. How am I ever to f-find a husband if we are...*poor*?"

Her sister uttered the last word as if it were a vile epithet.

Perhaps she had coddled Juliet far too much in her efforts to keep her from worrying over their diminished circumstances.

Arianna leaned across the carriage, offering her sister's shoulder a reassuring pat. "Hush now, you mustn't get yourself so upset. Do you require some hartshorn?"

"No." Juliet shook her head vehemently, golden curls swaying in the low light of the carriage lamp. "Of course I am upset. You have just told me that Father is selling off everything of value we possess. We were not nearly in such straits when you married Lord Edgar. If your dowry was more than mine, then I shall *never* manage to attract a husband."

Juliet issued the last statement with a howl of misery.

Arianna sighed. Her sister had been contented with her suitors and her evening of harp and pianoforte and her ignorance to their plight. She ought to have left it at that instead of allowing her pride to intervene.

"Forgive me for speaking plainly to you," she said. "But I cannot recall the truth, now that it has been spoken. Mother's death affected Father deeply, and since then, he has been spending unwisely." That was a rather mild way of saying he had bankrupted himself on frivolous gambling. "Our circumstances are vastly different from what they once were."

"But Mother's fortune," Juliet protested weakly.

"It's gone," Arianna said gently. "Father spent it all, and then some. The reason he wanted the parure was so that he could sell it. That is why I told you to give it to me."

Juliet pressed a gloved hand to her mouth, as if she feared she would be ill. "Spending unwisely."

"Gambling," Arianna elaborated. "Wagering everything he possessed, eventually, in the hope he could recoup his losses. But he could not."

"Gambling." Juliet's shock was palpable. "I had no notion. I feel so foolish."

"Father didn't wish for you to know," she explained. "I am trying to help him in every way conceivable. Any income owed to me from my marriage is his, and I've already sold off a number of my gowns and most of my jewelry to help."

But it hadn't been enough. And she still very much feared that nothing would be enough. No amount of sacrifice would do. No matter how many prized household goods her father sold, the price was always insufficient. Arianna kept the most foolish gesture of all which she had made—turning into an informant for a group of spies so she could sell knowledge about revolutionaries on their father's behalf—to herself.

"I must marry soon, then," Juliet said as the carriage came

to a halt. "I don't want to end up like you, dependent upon Father."

Her sister's words stung, for Arianna had sacrificed so much of herself—her happiness, her pitiful widow's portion, even her own welfare—to give Juliet a chance at the future she'd been denied. It was becoming increasingly apparent that her sister selfishly didn't appreciate Arianna's actions. But her observation was also true. Arianna *was* dependent upon their father. She had made a grave mistake in marrying Edgar, and now she was paying the price.

"I wouldn't wish to end up like me either," she said grimly as they prepared to leave the carriage. "Sacrificing yourself for the people you love sometimes leads to bitter disappointment."

And no one knew that better than Arianna.

Which was why seizing the happiness she found in Logan's arms was more important than ever, even as fragile and temporary as it may be.

⁓

Logan was compiling reports from the spies he was charged with overseeing when a knock sounded at the door of the small room he used as his office. He looked up from the code he was working on deciphering to find Chapman, his aide, standing on the threshold. Born to the East End rookeries just as Logan had been, the elder man was loyal and fearsome. He was a big, burly cove with a head of hoary hair that was sprinkled with a few strands of gray. Still strong as an ox, and no man Logan would sooner have at his back in a fight.

"What is it, Chapman?" he asked, rubbing his temples before rising from his chair.

He'd been seated for far too long, caught up in the work

before him. A glance at the mantel clock revealed more time had passed than he realized. Arianna ought to be arriving soon. His heart beat harder at the notion.

"There's a mort 'ere to see you, sir," Chapman announced. "Waiting for you in the parlor. Lovely, if you don't mind me saying. Prettiest set of petticoats I've seen in—"

"The bleeding *last* set of petticoats you'll ever see if you don't stubble it," Logan interrupted on a growl. "You ain't to be feasting your peepers on her."

She's mine.

The words were unspoken, but his intention was clear.

Chapman nodded jerkily. "Begging your pardon, sir. Didn't mean nothing by it."

Perhaps he had been a bit harsh, he thought. Chapman wasn't accustomed to having women about. Logan had never had any morts to his private rooms before.

"No 'arm done," he told his aide, irritated with himself for the rush of feeling which led to him dropping his *h* in speech.

It was telling, the effect she had upon him.

Unwanted.

And yet, so very, very wanted all at the same time.

"You're through with your duties for the evening," he added to Chapman, trying to stifle the sheer elation rising within him. "Go and get some rest. I'll see to the lady."

Chapman tugged at his forelock and disappeared, leaving Logan to scramble from the office in search of her.

She had come. He hadn't been certain, when he'd left her chamber that night, whether or not she would. There had been the shadow of fear in her eyes. And so much hung in the balance for the both of them.

Logan exhaled the breath he hadn't realized he had been holding as he stalked through the hall to the parlor. Arianna was *here*. In his space, beneath his roof. He could not shake the feeling that she was some manner of mystical creature. A fairy who would flit away before he had his chance to touch her again. Long strides took him to the parlor. The door was closed when he reached it, and he thrust it open with too much force, half-terrified he would find the chamber empty.

She whirled about with a start, holding a hand over her heart as if he had given her a fright with his unannounced—and admittedly rude—entrée to the room.

"Logan," she said softly, her voice as lilting and mellifluous as he had recalled.

"Arianna." Her name slipped from him, and he had the sudden, addlepated thought that her name was not nearly grand enough for her.

He bowed, feeling a childish lurch of excitement in his chest. It was, quite inexplicably, as if he could breathe again.

She curtsied, elegant and beautiful, bearing the grace of a bleeding queen. Their gazes held. He realized that he was standing at the threshold gawking at her as if he hadn't seen a mort in his life.

"You came," he said stupidly, and then could have kicked himself in the arse for saying something so damned idiotic.

So obvious.

"I couldn't stay away." Her tone was almost tender as she swept toward him.

She was still wearing her pelisse, and it fluttered about her as she moved nearer. He disliked the sign that she would perhaps attempt to flee imminently, for he had no intention of letting her go now that he had her here with him.

He closed the last few steps, bringing their bodies flush. Her hands settled on his shoulders tentatively, and his landed on her waist. The pose felt right. Natural.

In his arms was where she belonged.

Logan lowered his head and he filled his lungs with the scent of her—the freshness of rain mingling with violets. "Did you have any trouble finding me?"

She shook her head, her expression turning almost shy. "No."

He understood that seeking lovers wasn't the ordinary way of it for Arianna, though as a beautiful widow, she could likely have had her pick of any damned man in London. It was new territory for him as well. He'd never known a woman he couldn't resist. One who filled his every waking and sleeping hour with thoughts of when he could see her again. One who tempted him to break his vows and place her before the Guild.

"I'm glad you didn't." He tugged at her pelisse. "You may as well remove this. You'll be staying for a time, no?"

He didn't reckon he'd have her all night long, although that was his most ardent wish. Her father and sister would likely take note if she failed to return home until the morning.

Her lips parted, as if in surprise. "Staying?"

Had she thought he meant for forever? The notion hit him in the chest, and he realized just how desperately he wanted that. To have Arianna here with him every day. To make love to her every night in his bed. To fall asleep with her in his arms, and to wake to the glory of the morning sun and her sweet face.

But that wasn't to be. Not now, not yet. Mayhap not ever. He'd have to settle for the time she could give him, starting in this moment.

"Aye." He grinned at her. "You're staying for a few hours at least, I hope. I've waited two bleeding days to see you again, and it felt like a lifetime."

An understatement, that. It had felt like an eternity.

She worried the fullness of her lower lip, her posture still stiff. "I don't know how long I will have before I risk being missed…"

Logan wanted to kiss her. To flick his tongue over that

lush mouth of hers, to take away the sting of her teeth and banish her every worry. To seduce the tension from her shoulders and make her forget all the reasons why they shouldn't be doing what they were.

He released her instead, settling his fingers on the closures of her garment. "May I?"

She nodded, her countenance still troubled. "Yes, please."

Although they had already progressed far beyond the bounds of propriety, Logan took his time, treating Arianna with the reverence she deserved. He removed her pelisse and draped it carefully over the back of a nearby divan. Her hat and gloves were next, which he also placed with similar concern. These garments, like all the others he'd seen her wear, were fine. However, it occurred to him for the first time that he had seen them before. Arianna was clearly limited in her wardrobe. It was yet one more clue that she was in dire need of funds.

Perhaps her husband had been a wastrel, he reasoned, not liking to think of the cove and yet ever aware he may have had a hand in Arianna's desperation.

His stomach chose that moment to growl as he returned to her side, reminding him that he hadn't taken the time to dine earlier when he ought to have done. He had been with Tierney for much of the day, coordinating the men who would be needed to capture Charles and Clifford Mace. The information Arianna had provided had led their men to the house where he was believed to be in hiding. And then he had returned to a mountain of correspondence.

Arianna's lips curved into a smile, some of the tension appearing to seep from her. "You are hungry?"

Aye, but not for food.

Wisely, Logan kept that errant thought to himself, offering her a wry grin of his own instead. "I forgot to sup. Have you dined yet?"

She shook her head shyly. "I haven't, no. I feigned sickness so my father and sister wouldn't take note of my absence this evening, and there weren't sufficient maids to bring a tray to my room. I didn't dare descend for fear either Father or Juliet would see me and realize I wasn't truly ill."

A new plan began to form.

Logan offered her his arm. "Come with me."

CHAPTER 8

"Another bite?"

Arianna smiled as Logan held the chocolate tart to her lips. It was sinfully decadent, but she'd already consumed two. "I don't dare."

"Why not?" he asked, his gaze hot and hungry on her mouth.

He wanted to kiss her again; she could tell. And she wanted to kiss him as well. They'd dined on a small feast he had prepared for the two of them. The simple fare—ham, cheese, and bread—had been surprisingly delicious. But the chocolate tarts, which he confessed to having purchased earlier in the day, were nothing short of divine.

"Because you have already fed me far too much," she said, although as she issued the denial, her lips moved forward of their own accord, growing nearer to the tempting tart.

She felt comfortable here, with him, in his home. Once more ensconced in the small but cheerful parlor where she had initially awaited him, they were settled on the floor by the hearth, atop a blanket. Arianna had never, in all her life, dined so informally. And she loved the ease of it, the intimacy and utter lack of hauteur. The warmth of the fire, coupled with the wine she had consumed with dinner, had filled her with a lovely glow, a hearty sense that all was well within the world.

For this stolen, forbidden moment, at least.

"You know you want it," he cajoled again.

"Very well," she agreed with a smile at his antics, taking a small bite. The richness of the chocolate coated her tongue, and she had to tamp down a rising moan of happiness at the flavor.

Grinning, he brought the remainder of the tart to his own mouth and consumed it in one bite.

"Floating hell, that's plummy," he said when he had finished chewing and swallowed the treat.

She could not contain her chuckle. How lovely it felt to be here with him, to forget the troubles awaiting her when she inevitably left his side. She hadn't felt this free in years.

"It *is* plummy." She raised her wine glass and took another sip to hide her smile and the effect he had upon her.

She was alternately giddy and terrified.

"Thank you for coming to me tonight," he said, his expression earnest, his hazel gaze burning into hers. "I feared you wouldn't."

She almost hadn't. After her disastrous carriage ride home from the musicale with Juliet, Arianna had been torn between duty to her sister and father and the need to allow herself a modicum of pleasure. But as she had retreated to the haven of her private room, she had lain on her bed, staring into the plasterwork on the ceiling above, knowing that she had to seize this small chance for happiness while it yet remained. Because there was precious little joy in her life. Scarcely any reason for smiling. No one to look after her with such agonizing care. No one who fed her chocolate tarts and held her in his arms as if she were the most exquisite woman he had ever beheld.

"I couldn't resist the opportunity to see you again," she admitted, though it was difficult to allow herself to be vulnerable to him.

When they had made love, she had been swept away in the wildness of the moment, the intensity of their passion. And she had persuaded herself that there would never be another chance for their paths to cross. Yet, Logan had been stubborn and determined.

And here they were.

"I'm damned glad you couldn't." Slowly, Logan licked the chocolate from his fingers.

She watched as his tongue flicked over his skin, stealing every last speck of the sweet. And she could not help but to think about that tongue of his on her skin, tasting her just the same as he did the remnants of his chocolate tart.

"You took a risk, inviting me here," she pointed out, thinking of the secretive nature of their connection, to say nothing of the trust he had placed in her.

For surely the Guild would frown upon an intimate relationship between an informer and one of its men. She could not help but to wonder if pursuing her would cause him to lose his position.

"You're worth it," he said, his voice low and intimate, his gaze caressing.

Worshipful.

No one had ever looked at her the way Logan did.

"How can you know that? You scarcely even know me," she pointed out, for although it felt as if they had known each other forever, in truth, it had been mere days since the first time they had met.

Even if everything had changed within that short, precious time.

He smiled, resting his arm over his bent knee in a rakish pose. "I know you well enough. Besides, every risk has its reward, and none better than the chance to have you here with me again. The chance to be able to hold you in my arms. The chance to kiss you."

There it was, the acknowledgment of the desire, running fierce and hot. Up until now, her dinner with Logan, despite the two of them being alone in his parlor, had been markedly chaste. Instead, they had spent their time chatting as if they were old acquaintances. She'd relished the opportunity to deepen their acquaintance. To get to know the man to whom she had given herself. It seemed they had conducted their affair in the opposite fashion, leading in with passion and now deepening their understanding of each other, growing their bond.

"Would you like to kiss me again?" she asked breathlessly, seizing upon the opportunity to have what she longed for most.

More of him.

"I've thought of nothing else since we parted," he said, his voice smooth and decadent as velvet, rumbling over her.

"Then perhaps you should," she ventured boldly.

Because this night, quite possibly, could be all they had left. All they could ever have. She had already risked so much in coming to him. And she had her father and her sister to consider.

"Come closer," Logan told her, crooking his finger.

She did, leveraging herself on the weight of one hand as she slid her rump nearer. As she did so, her glass of wine fell and spilled, making an indecorous mess of the blanket.

"Oh good heavens," she exclaimed, searching for a napkin which would soak up the liquid before it set in with an irreparable stain. "Forgive me. I'm so clumsy."

His hand stopped hers as she reached for a cloth. "Leave it."

"But your coverlet," she protested. "If I don't sop up the wine, it will be ruined."

"I don't give a damn about the bleeding blanket." He brought her hand to his lips for a reverent kiss. "All I care about is you."

"Oh." She swallowed, uncertain of what else to say. Her mind was failing her, as it always seemed to do in his presence.

Her heart thudded hard, and she forgot to breathe. Forgot about all the reasons why she must not allow her guard to fully fall, why she could never risk developing tender feelings for him. Logan was all there was, his gaze searing hers, his mouth delivering a trail of hot little kisses along her inner wrist.

He inhaled deeply, as if savoring her scent. "You even smell of violets here. I love the scent on your skin. It drives me mad."

The perfume was her favorite and used sparingly, for it had been a luxury from her days as Edgar's wife, and she couldn't afford to purchase more now.

"How mad?" she asked Logan, entranced by the way it seemed as if he could not get enough of her.

His gaze clung to hers. "Mad enough to kiss you."

She smiled, a heavy ache spreading from her belly, lower. "I thought we had already agreed that you should."

"We did, but I was trying to be a bleedin' gentleman."

His coarse admission wrung a laugh from her. How delightful he was, hard and grave yet tender and sweet. She had been drawn to the danger she sensed in him that first night, but he had captured her with the warmth he was so quick to bestow. He had charmed her with ease. Had found his way past her defenses.

One more night with him, she told herself. What could be the harm? And how could she deny herself what she wanted, when it was here before her, waiting for her to seize it?

"What if I don't want you to be a gentleman?" she asked, summoning her bravado.

Logan cursed. "You'll be my undoing, beautiful."

She cupped his jaw, feeling the sharpness of the angle, the prickle of the whiskers he must have shaved earlier that morning, only for them to reemerge tonight. "It is only fair, as you shall be mine as well."

He kissed her then, his lips capturing hers in a connection she felt to her toes. It was as if she had not kissed him in an eternity. How had days passed without this man's mouth on hers? She clutched his shoulders, her body turning toward his, seeking more. His arm slid around her waist, holding her tight to him. She felt safe and protected and desired.

Arianna thought for a wild, reckless moment, that if she could always have this, if she could never leave his side, nothing would please her more.

The kiss deepened, his tongue tracing the seam of her lips. She opened for him, and he tasted of chocolate and sin and pent-up desire that needed to be answered. It seemed to Arianna as if she could not have enough of him. She pressed her lips fiercely to his, trying to claim him in the only way she dared. Showing him just how much she wanted him.

And then her fingers were moving of their own volition, creeping to the neatly tied knot on his cravat. Pulling it open. Finding buttons on his waistcoat and shirt. Her fingertips discovered heated skin at the base of his throat where she had plucked the three buttons free of their moorings. Pure fire licked through her.

"Arianna," he growled against her lips.

She wasn't sure if he was protesting or urging her on, but in the next breath, his hands were moving up and down her spine, then gliding to her nape. Hair pins were pulled expertly away, her chignon falling apart in heavy waves that spilled down her back. Not a protest, then.

He broke the kiss for a moment, studying her in the low light. "Tell me what you want, love."

Did he need to ask?

"More," she told him breathlessly. "More of you. More *everything*. I need you, Logan."

His lips slammed down on hers in a kiss that was possessive and hot. Their tongues tangled as he guided her to her back on the blanket, careful to keep her from the spilled wine. And then his hands were slipping beneath her skirts, his nails dragging over her stockings, trailing up her calves to her knees. His touch dipped into the hollows there, a place she had never particularly imagined would be so receptive to touch. But it was as if every part of her were new beneath his questing fingertips.

He reached her garters, his fingers flirting with the bare skin of her thighs above them. And then higher still, to her folds, parting them. When his thumb rolled over the sensitive bud hidden within, she gasped into his kiss, writhing against him in a quest for more.

More of his touch, more pleasure. More of everything he would give.

He tore his mouth from hers, his body pinning her to the floor with scarcely any weight as he took care to leverage himself on a forearm while he pleasured her with his other hand. His mysterious eyes were smoky in the low light, glittering with the reflection of the crackling flames in the hearth.

"So hot and wet. Better than I remembered."

She could manage nothing more than a gusty sigh as his caresses sent her perilously nearer to the edge of the cliff she had been occupying ever since his lips had skated over her hand. Sooner, perhaps. From the moment he had gently removed her pelisse, sliding it from her shoulders and draping it over his arm in proprietary fashion.

She liked the feeling that she was his and he was hers.

"I didn't intend to seduce you when I asked you to come 'ere," he murmured, his lips almost grazing hers as he spoke, his brow furrowed with the effort of restraining himself. "This ain't the way of it for me. I intended to woo you and win you in the proper vein, but damn it all to hell…"

His words trailed away, and she wondered what else he might have said. What he had intended. But then, it hardly mattered.

"Woo me and win me?" she asked, cupping his face in both hands, drawing his head gently back enough for her to see his full countenance, to study him in detail, to memorize the slashing cheekbones, his proud jaw, the long blade of his nose, his full, sensual lips that knew how to kiss so well, his hair, glinting with fire in the glow cast by the candles and hearth. "What do you mean? You've already done both. Can you not see? Why else should I be here alone with you tonight?"

His fingers replaced his thumb now, swirling over her demanding nub with faster, bolder strokes. "You're all I can think of, from the first moment I wake until my eyes close. And even in sleep, you haunt me."

His words and his touch shattered her. The rush that seized Arianna stole her breath and had her arching her back, shoulder blades digging into the floor beneath the blanket as she surrendered to the wild torrent of sensation he had unleashed. It was glorious, the force of it so tremendous that she could do nothing but hold her breath and grind herself shamelessly into his hand, searching for more pleasure until pricks of blackness dotted the edges of her vision.

When the last wave of bliss ebbed, she was filled with a

heavy, sated sensation, still aching for him, and yet so very alive. Touching herself had never been so satisfying.

But then he surprised her by withdrawing his fingers and kissing her cheek. "I need to know what you want, sweeting. This ain't about me. It's about *you*."

His words made the last of the walls she'd forged around her heart crack and crumble. Her life had never been about her. That this man she'd known for mere days could see her, understand her needs, was astounding. She understood then, the full implication of his words.

She traced the line of his cheekbone, thinking him the most beautiful man she had ever beheld. "I want to be with you, however we can be. Even if it is nothing more than stolen moments and we need to hide what we're doing from the world, you're worth the risk."

His jaw tightened. "You're sure?"

Arianna was filled with doubts and misgivings and guilt about a host of things. But on this, she was unhesitating. "Yes."

He kissed her sweetly, and then there was a flurry of undressing between the both of them. Stockings and stays, chemise and gown, shirt and trousers and boots were all dispensed with ease, little kisses along the way. Her lips found his jaw, the strong cord of his neck. His mouth brushed her temple, the hollow at the base of her throat, the curve of her breast. She had a moment to see the length of him, thick and long, fully erect. But then, he was on her, kissing her again.

They came together as they had been moments earlier, only this time without the barrier of cloth keeping them separated. Any embarrassment Arianna initially felt was soothed away by his worshipful expression as he lowered his powerful body over hers, his hand coming between them to weigh her breast. His lips left hers and his head dipped, and he took her nipple into his mouth, sucking hard.

"Oh," she exclaimed softly, her fingers running through his too-long locks, red and gold and brown glinting in the intimacy of the firelight.

He released her nipple. "You like that, love?"

"Very much so," she confessed.

He grinned, and then moved to her other breast. "Aye, me too."

He suckled the peak, drawing another sweet volley of pleasure from her that seemed to shoot out across her body and land between her thighs. Her hands found his shoulders and then explored the warm plane of his back. His skin was smooth, and she relished the delineation of muscle. He was so very strong, and yet he touched her with delicate care, always putting her needs and wants before his own. Asking her for what she wanted.

He kissed a path down the swell of her breast, to the hollow between both and kissed her there, directly in the center of her chest. The gesture was so touching and yet so erotic. She shifted beneath him, seeking more contact. His rigid cock pressed against her mound, sending a quiver of pure need through her.

"More," she demanded on a gasp. "Please, Logan."

"I'll give you everything you want," he promised, blowing a stream of hot air over one of her turgid nipples. "But first, I need to taste you."

"Taste me?" she repeated, breathless and aching, her body heavy and needy and greedy for his touch.

For anything he would give her.

"Mmm," he agreed into her skin as he kissed a line of fire down her body. Traveling over her navel, past the swell of her belly. Until he had settled his wide shoulders between her parted thighs and his handsome face was unbearably near to her sex. He slid his hands beneath her, cupping her rump in each hand, and pulled her toward him. "Like this."

She was stunned and more than a trifle self-conscious as he hauled her most intimate flesh to his mouth and kissed her. First just one chaste buss over her bud. Then the flick of his tongue up and down her seam. Wet and hot, gentle yet firm. She hadn't known such acts were possible. Nothing could have prepared her for the sensation of Logan's tongue on her, licking her up as if she were a chocolate tart offered for his delectation, his to consume.

"Better than dessert," he murmured against her, as if he had sensed the direction of her thoughts.

But then, perhaps she was so wild with wanting that she had mumbled something aloud. All she knew was that his tongue was undoing her mind as surely as her body. He was licking her up, making deep sounds of satisfaction that told her he was every bit as roused by pleasuring her with his mouth as she was.

She forgot embarrassment, surrendering to his worshipful ministrations. He sucked on her bud the same way he had her nipples, and Arianna gasped and cried out, hips bucking from the floor as sensation overwhelmed her. His fingers brushed over her opening before one slipped inside.

Another moan tore from her as he filled her with his finger, sinking deep, thrusting in and out of her slick channel as he sucked hard on her greedy nub. Heat arced through her like lightning in the sky. His finger inside her felt so good, her inner muscles clamping down on him, holding him there as desire careened to a dizzying height.

The familiar tightening began deep in her belly. One more suck and thrust of his finger deep inside her, and she was going to...*dear heavens*, she was...*oh*. Suddenly, she reached her crescendo, everything inside her splitting apart as she was seized in the unrelenting grip of pure, unadulterated bliss.

He kissed her inner thigh and then rose over her, settling between her legs, the thick head of his cock brushing over her throbbing folds. They were pressed tightly together, the coarse hairs of his chest abrading her nipples, his bare skin warm and firm against hers. She clutched his shoulders, her nails digging into pliant flesh. He was all muscle and lean, masculine strength. And all hers.

He kissed her cheek, then her lips, devouring her mouth with the muskiness of her on his tongue. *More* became a ceaseless litany in her mind. The hollow ache inside her demanded to be filled. Nothing would do but him. She held him tightly, kissing him back with the rising fervor which would not be contained. It was bigger than she was, strong and insistent and demanding.

His mouth still locked upon hers, he dragged himself up and down her slit just as his tongue had. The slippery sounds of their bodies moving together made her even more desperate for completion, her heart pounding harder than ever, her blood like warm honey singing in her veins. When he toyed with her overly sensitive bud, rubbing her with the broad head of his cock, she was dangerously close to spending again.

Logan broke the kiss, his face hovering over hers, his expression slack with need, lips glistening with the evidence of her desire, eyes burning like twin flames. "You want me inside you?"

She writhed beneath him, seeking connection. Seeking everything.

"God, yes," she told him. "Please, I need you so badly."

"Floating hell," he growled, pressing his forehead to hers as he sought entrance below. "I'll try to be gentle."

"I don't want gentle," she whispered. "I just want you."

"You have me," he said, a new intensity in his rich, deep baritone. "I'm yours always."

Always seemed impossible, but then he moved and she forgot to care about the worries of the future and what might happen beyond this night. His cock dipped lower, finding the place where she was pulsing and more than ready for him. He entered her in a slow thrust that stole her breath.

She was aflame.

"My God," he gritted, kissing her cheek, nuzzling her ear. "You feel so good, love."

She threaded her fingers through the silken strands of his hair, then down his nape, over his back, needing to touch him everywhere she could. To absorb the intoxicating heat and strength of him.

"So do you," she murmured back.

Their lips met in another kiss, words no longer needed. Clinging tightly to each other, they forged a rhythm together. Arianna's legs wrapped around his waist and he plundered her mouth as he moved within her. His fingers dipped to the place where they were joined, strumming her swollen bud.

He circled over the sensitive knot in rhythm to his lovemaking, faster, harder, bringing her to the edge. She moaned into his lips as another forceful rush of pleasure overtook her. White-hot bliss surged as he thrust hard into her one more time, her cunny convulsing around him, loving him there, keeping him planted within her. Until his shoulders tensed and he tore his mouth from hers with a hoarse cry.

Logan withdrew from her body, leaving her pulsing with the tiny reverberations of their shared desire. She knew a moment of emptiness, of feeling bereft, but then he covered her lips with his, kissing her sweetly, and the hot spurt of his seed painted her belly as he spent all over her, marking her as his.

CHAPTER 9

Logan awoke in his bed, Arianna snuggled in his arms. She was wrapped up in him, her unbound hair a wild halo on his pillow, and he never wanted to move. After making love in the parlor, they had moved to his chamber, making love once more before they'd both succumbed to a deeply sated sleep. It hadn't been his intention to fall headlong into slumber, and now as he examined Arianna in the glow of the candles still burning, he wondered just what the hour was.

As if sensing his wakefulness, Arianna stirred, her long lashes fluttering open to reveal sleepy gold-brown eyes in the soft early-morning light and glow of the remnants of the fire in the grate.

"What is the time?" she asked.

He drank in the sight of her—those beautiful sleepy eyes, her mussed hair, the faint line of confusion between her brows—and *God*, she was lovely. "I haven't an inkling."

How he wished he could stay here forever with her, just like this, naked and warm in the cocoon of his bedclothes. But then she moved, breaking the spell and dashing his buffle-headed thoughts. She was already scrambling from the bed, leaving Logan alone and oddly bereft. He didn't even take the opportunity to admire her sultry feminine curves, limned by the fire and rising sun. Logan threw back the coverlets and sprang to his feet, uncaring about his own nudity.

"I must go," she said, sounding frantic, looking on the floor in search of something.

Her hastily discarded garments, he realized belatedly when she bent and scooped up her crumpled shift from the pile before pulling it over her head. Thankfully, they'd had the presence of mind to bring them here from the parlor.

"Can you not stay?" he found himself asking.

Forever, he almost added, watching her pull her shift into place, mesmerized by the sway of her full breasts beneath the linen. *Mine*, he thought. *Mine to protect.*

He was a bleeding lunatic, it was true. But he didn't want to let her go. Didn't want to watch as she walked away from him again.

Her inky curls pooled around her shoulders as she hastily retrieved her stockings. "Of course I cannot stay here. It was reckless enough for me to come at all. But lingering as I've done…"

Logan discovered his trousers in a heap by the hearth and stuffed his legs into them. "If you linger longer, what will happen?"

"My father will discover that I've been gone." She perched on the lone chair he kept in his room for when he sat at his writing desk and drew on one of her stockings, securing it with the garter. "Or worse, the servants. I can't afford to cause undue gossip for my sister. She's trying to find a husband before…"

"Before what?" he asked, sensing they were dancing

around the reason for Arianna selling her information about the London Reform Society.

He hadn't pressed her for further information, hoping she would willingly offer the revelations on her own.

"Before it's too late," Arianna said quietly, keeping her gaze averted as she donned her other stocking and garter.

The little bits of knowledge he had about her came together, in the fashion of a bird piecing its nest. And he thought he understood.

"Your father is heavily in debt," he guessed grimly, for he recognized the signs.

Archer Tierney was a moneylender, after all—he had been before joining the Guild, and he'd continued with the business after. Logan had aided him on many occasions, and he understood the desperation some men possessed as they sought funds. It was a desperation that would make a man allow his daughter to betray dangerous men on his behalf.

"I don't wish to speak of it," Arianna said miserably as she came to her feet before picking up her abandoned stays.

He fastened his trousers and stalked to her, taking her hands in his. "Let me."

"I can do it."

"Aye, you can," he agreed, giving her fingers a squeeze as he looked down into her face, willing her to meet his gaze. "But you needn't. I'm here to help you now, and it ain't just with your stays. With your father, too."

She stiffened, her chin going up, her stare colliding with his at last. "You can't help me with him, Logan."

"Of course I can." He released her fingers and made short work of fastening her stays. "As easily as this."

Logan spun her gently about so she faced him again.

Her eyes dropped to the floor, but not before he spied the sadness lurking in their depths. "He's lost almost everything. I don't know if there is a way out. The most I can hope for is to keep his creditors at bay long enough for my sister to finish her Season and find a husband."

He hated the hopelessness in her voice. Hated that she was rushing to leave him, that she had to go at all. Hated that her father and her dead husband had left her in such an untenable position.

"Is that the reason you collected the rewards?" he asked, already knowing the answer. Of course it was. Arianna was selflessly putting herself in peril to help her father and her sister. But that still didn't explain everything. Unless... Understanding dawned. "Your father is the source, isn't he?"

Her reaction told him everything he needed to know—her eyes widening, shoulders stiffening.

"I can't tell you how the information was given to me, or by whom," she said coolly before seizing her petticoats from the floor. "Don't ask me questions I cannot answer."

"Why can't you answer them?" He bent to retrieve her gown, not above keeping it from her until she would listen to reason. "What is it you fear? If it's the Society, I promise I'll keep you safe from them."

Her countenance was torn, and he could not shake the feeling that she wanted to unburden herself, to trust in him completely, not only with her body but with the rest of herself as well. And yet, just when he hoped he had gained ground, she shook her head.

"I must go," she said, worrying her lower lip.

Damn it. He'd been so certain she was on the verge of confiding in him.

He sighed, relenting for now. "Very well. If you won't tell me, I can't force you. But I draw the line at allowing you to wander through London alone at this late hour. I'll return you to your father's town house myself."

"I'll take a hack." She reached for her gown. "Please, Logan, I must make haste."

He scowled at the suggestion he would allow her to flit away into the night, without protection. "You ain't going to find one worth a damn at this time of the morning. I'm taking you, and that's final."

He expected her to argue, but she nodded and allowed him to help her into her gown. When he was fastening her tapes, she spoke again, so softly he had to strain to hear her.

"I wish it were different for me," she said, voice steeped in weariness. "For us. The thought of leaving you gives me this dreadful ache in my chest, as if I can scarcely draw breath."

He knew what she meant, for he felt the same. It was akin to losing a part of himself. Being with her was reckless and unwise. He was, in effect, betraying the Guild, putting himself at unnecessary risk. And yet, he could not stay away from her.

Logan spun her around to face him, kissing her slowly, lingeringly, before raising his head. "It *can* be different for us. Trust in me. When you're ready to let me in, I'll be waiting. You already know where to find me."

"You make me want to have hope," she whispered, her lower lip trembling, the sheen of tears glistening in her expressive eyes.

He caught a teardrop on his thumb as it slipped down her cheek. "Then have it. We'll find a way to extricate you from this tangle and to keep you safe. I vow it."

And he meant those words with every conviction he possessed. Fate—and the Guild—had brought Arianna into his life. And he was bloody well going to keep her there where she belonged.

He fetched her pelisse and draped it over her shoulders before tangling their fingers together. "Come, beautiful. I'll see you safely home."

"Where have you been?"

Her father's voice cut through the eerie quiet of the town house.

Arianna emitted a gasp, her heart pounding hard, and whirled to face him in the shadows flickering around the meager light of the lone taper she had lit to find her way through the darkened halls.

"Father," she managed past a tongue that had suddenly gone dry. "You are at home."

"Yesh, I am," he slurred, making the reason he was still moving about the house in the darkest depths of the night apparent. "I sh-stayed in this evening. I'll ashk you again, where have you been?"

"I..." Her mind went blank as a night without stars. "I was..."

"You were doing something scandalous, were you not?" His voice was colder than she'd heard it before, disapproving despite the notable effect of the spirits he had consumed. "Come with me. We need to have a dishcussion, daughter."

"Can it not wait until the morning?" she asked desperately, not wishing to have a disastrous audience with him when he was in such a state.

And not when she was returning home after having spent hours in Logan's arms, her foolish heart duped into believing, for a moment, that she could truly have a chance at happiness after all.

"No," her father denied. "It can't. I've been meaning to shpeak with you."

He moved toward her in the darkness, his motions awkward and fumbling, as the scent of brandy assailed her.

"I was paying a call upon a friend," she lied, clutching her pelisse in a tight grip. "Forgive me for staying out so late. I hadn't realized the hour."

"A friend?" her father repeated, sounding suspicious. "I knew of no social callsh you were making this evening."

She did not dare to admit that she had been meeting a man, alone. Her father may be in his cups, but he would still understand the significance of such a revelation. What explanation could she offer? She hadn't supposed her father would be at home. He spent most nights at his club, after which point, she feared he strayed to gambling dens, further deepening the hole of his ever-mounting debt.

"It was a musicale," she said, seizing upon the first excuse that rose in her mind.

"Without Juliet?" He staggered to the right and caught himself against a wall. "You're meant to be finding her a hushband."

Dear heavens, just how much had he consumed this evening?

"Juliet attended a ball at the Rivendale Assembly Rooms with Miss Throckmorton and Lady Weldon," Arianna reminded him, and that much, at least, was true. With her sister beneath the auspices of the formidable Lady Weldon for the evening, she had been able to steal away to meet Logan.

"It ishn't proper to be a lady alone at thish—er, *this*—time of night," her father countered, and she could hear the frown in his voice.

Part of her longed to tell him that he hadn't a bit of compunction about her being alone at night when he had sent her to the Guild. And in notorious dens of ill repute like The Velvet Slipper, no less.

Resentment rose, making her chest go tight. Logan's words returned to her in that moment. *You shouldn't have to look after yourself. You should have a man willing to throw himself onto the fire so you can walk across the bleeding flames without getting burned. Not a man who tosses you into it to save himself.*

At the time, she had bristled at the suggestion that she needed someone to protect her, that she could not protect herself. She'd always, even in her marriage to Edgar, prided herself on her sense of independence. But she was beginning to understand the true meaning of independence, and it was not sacrificing herself again and again for those she loved, whilst they failed to offer her the same sacrifices in return.

"You didn't disapprove of my being alone in the evenings on other occasions," she reminded him, her resentment lending her bravado that had been previously absent.

"Obligations are different," he countered, his voice stern despite the signs he had been over-imbibing yet again.

"And why should I have obligations to honor when you apparently have none?" she asked, her frustration making her bolder still. "At least, none that keep you from drowning yourself in drink, gambling wildly with funds you don't have, and then selling off everything of value in this household?"

"How dare you?" he roared, lurching forward suddenly.

So suddenly that it took her by surprise when the back of his hand struck her cheek hard enough to make tears rise in her eyes. With a shocked gasp, she pressed a hand to her throbbing face, her breaths ragged and shallow. He had struck her.

Father had raised his hand against her.

He had *hurt* her.

He'd never done so before. Not physically.

"Look at what you've made me do," he accused, swaying unsteadily on his feet. "Impertinent female, daring to shpeak to me that way. I've done *everything* for you, and you repay me by gadding about in the night, courting scandal."

"The greatest scandal I courted was doing what you asked of me," she countered, rubbing her stinging cheek. "Did you not know the manner of places you sent me? The Velvet

Slipper is little better than a house of ill repute, and yet you had me go there to fetch your five hundred pounds."

"Lower your voice, damn you!" her father barked, going pale. "I've told you to never talk of it."

Yes, he had. Of course, he had. Only, she hadn't realized the magnitude of the danger she had been inviting, all in the name of helping her father to continue to be a wastrel. Mother would no longer recognize the man before Arianna. His face was bloated, his nose red, his hair a thinning, greasy slick over his head, and he had gained a great deal of weight about the middle from indulging in excess drink.

But it was not his physical appearance that her mother would have reviled. Rather, it was his actions, leading them all so close to ruin, placing them in peril, drowning himself in spirits and becoming so caught up in his need to gamble that he could neither stop nor help himself.

"Wherever I was this evening, it is no concern of yours," she told her father, feeling numb.

The man before her did not love her. He was nothing more than a drunken, cold shell of his former self who had lost the capacity to care. And she was tired of doing his bidding. Tired of everything.

"I'm your father. You live beneath my roof. I'll not have you sullying yourself and ruining Juliet's hope for a match with the Earl of Newbury."

She flinched at the realization that her father only cared where she had been because he didn't want her to tarnish her younger sister's reputation by inviting scandal. That he was likely now viewing a marriage between Juliet and Newbury as yet another chance for him to obtain funds. That he harbored no qualms about using both his daughters to help himself and gain what he wanted.

"You needn't fear," she said with a calm she did not feel, proud of herself for keeping her voice from trembling with suppressed anguish. "I would never dream of ruining your chance to sell your youngest daughter to the highest bidder."

With that pronouncement, she rushed past her father, sending hot wax dripping down her pelisse in her haste to escape. She waited until she reached the privacy of her chamber before she allowed the tears to fall.

CHAPTER 10

Stationed at a window across the street from the house where Charles and Clifford Mace were said to be hiding, Logan watched as other members of the Guild, accompanied by men from Whitehall, slid into their respective places. The entire operation had been carefully orchestrated, with a much larger number of men assigned to the task than would be under ordinary circumstances. Each man knew where he was meant to be and what he was meant to do. The Maces were dangerous traitors, men who had proven their willingness to kill. They were also hiding in a tenement where families were dwelling, increasing the peril for all around.

No one wished for any harm to come to innocent men, women, and children. And, flushed from their hiding places, their lives one swing of the hangman's noose from being over, the Maces could be capable of anything.

Logan could only hope and pray this operation would unfold according to plan and without anyone else getting hurt.

"It's almost time," Tierney said, snapping his pocket watch closed.

He was seated at another narrow window in the squalid room that had recently been home to two separate families, a reminder of just how grim life was for some. Logan wasn't shocked by what he'd seen and nor had his superior been, however; they'd both spent much of their lives in the rookeries. Logan didn't know much of Tierney's past beyond his rise to power as a moneylender, but they shared an unspoken understanding, a deep sense of camaraderie, which could only be had by two people who have undergone the same struggles.

The Guild had paid the families handsomely for the use of their rooms for the next few hours. Now, it was a matter of waiting for the moment to strike.

They'd spent the last few days gathering information, with the Guild and Whitehall watching everyone who came and went from the building. The men within matched the descriptions of the Mace brothers. Both with blond hair, tall and thin, blue-eyed with a long blade of a nose. They kept their excursions to a minimum, often only leaving the tenement after nightfall.

"Do you think they'll surrender themselves without a fight?" Logan asked Tierney the question that had been dogging him with vicious persistence ever since he'd been informed of today's mission.

"I wouldn't if I were in their boots," Tierney drawled. "After the plot against the Tower, when they're captured, they'll both swing for certain."

"As they deserve," Logan said, keeping his gaze trained on the movement across the street and below. "All the innocents killed senselessly by their plotting."

"The Maces didn't act alone, but until we can find the rest, they'll do for now."

"Aye, they'll have to," Logan agreed.

Silence descended for another few minutes or what could have been an eternity as they awaited the beginning of their attempts to capture the Maces.

"Care to tell me what a beautiful mort was doing at your rooms the other night?" Tierney asked calmly. "I reckon you weren't merely playing a game of blindman's bluff."

Logan froze, his heart thudding hard in his ears. Tempted as he was to turn, however, he kept his gaze on the scene beyond the dirt-smudged window.

"Chapman told you I had a visitor," he guessed, wondering how much Tierney knew.

The man was devilishly resourceful when it came to finding out every last thing there was to glean about a situation. Logan had been a bleeding fool to suppose he could meet with Arianna and Tierney wouldn't discover it.

"Not Chapman," Tierney answered calmly. "Loyal to a fault, that one. Suffice it to say that you ain't the only one with little birds."

Bleeding hell. He hadn't reckoned it would be one of the scamps. Perhaps Tierney had offered a fatter purse in exchange for the information. Either way, the mere presence of a beautiful woman alone at his rooms wasn't enough cause for suspicion. As he had the thought, however, guilt made his chest go tight and heavy. Because he had betrayed Tierney and the Guild with Arianna. And he would do it again.

And again.

"A cove can't have needs without the Guild spying on him these days?" he asked, careful to keep his own voice as unperturbed as possible.

"A cove can have all the needs in the world, and he can fuck himself raw if he wishes it, with all the whores in Christendom and all the ladies, too," Tierney said cheerfully. "But what he can't do is shag an informant and keep it from the Guild."

Damn it. Tierney knew Arianna and the Major were one, and that she had been at his rooms. Whoever had been watching him must have been doing so for a number of days, and from near enough to discern enough of her features to recognize her and report back to Tierney.

He clenched his jaw. "You told me to seduce her."

"Ah, I see you're not denying it, then."

His grip on the soiled curtains tightened. "Denying it seems a moot point when you already know who she is and why she was at my rooms."

"Leaving late at night looking disheveled does tell a tale," Tierney pointed out coolly, exhaling loudly. "I'm told the Major looked thoroughly tupped, as did you. Or shall I call her by her true name, Lady Arianna Stewart?"

The acrid scent of smoke reached Logan, and he realized Tierney had somehow lit a cheroot and was smoking as they waited at their posts. Smoking and interrogating him at the same time, as if he were perfectly calm and hadn't a bleeding concern in the world. As if they weren't across the way from two dangerous men they'd been instructed to shoot if necessary.

Logan had been prepared to do whatever he must today, to kill a man if need be. But he hadn't been prepared for Tierney's questions. Nor had he been ready to discuss what was between himself and Arianna.

"You've had me followed," Logan said. "For how long?"

"You ought to know I leave nothing to chance." There was the slow, windy sound of another exhale as Tierney paused. "And I trust no one. This is the first time I've had cause to doubt your loyalty, however."

Logan ground his molars together, frustrated. "I'll remind

you yet again that you are the one who suggested I seduce her to see what I could learn."

"Go on, then," Tierney prodded. "Tell me what you've learned."

He had learned that he loved waking up with Arianna in his arms. That the scent of violets would forever make his cock go hard at the thought of her. That she was kindhearted and good, that she was likely being forced to do her father's bidding to help him pay off his debts. That she was loyal to a fault. That her hair was softer than silk, and there was no better sight than her raven curls on his pillow. That he would surrender everything —even his position in the Guild—if it meant she would be his.

Logan swallowed hard against a rising lump of emotion in his throat. What the hell was wrong with him?

"I'm waiting," Tierney added wryly.

He inhaled sharply, then exhaled, knowing he had to offer up some sort of information. Wishing he had a cheroot on hand to smoke. "I've learned that her father is heavily in debt, and that she's likely selling the Society secrets on his behalf to help him recoup funds."

There, that was the truth.

"And?"

"And…" Logan could think of naught that was not private between himself and Arianna.

"Nothing else? You were alone with her for hours. Surely, she must have told you more than that."

Tierney knew damned well that they had not been talking during much of their time together, and what they had said to each other hadn't been with the Guild in mind. He'd already intimated as much, but he wanted Logan to confess it.

He wouldn't do it.

Fortunately, Logan was spared from further confession

by the signal from one of the men below that they were about to move in on the tenement where the Maces were hiding.

"It's time," he said, his senses on heightened alert.

On the opposite side of the street, there was a sudden flurry of movement as the men rushed in. And then, the burst of gunfire rent the air.

∼

THE HOUR WAS LATE, and Arianna knew the last risk she ought to be taking was in seeking out Logan yet again. However, she couldn't seem to stay away. Driven by the words he had uttered when they had last parted, she had slipped from her chamber after fulfilling her sisterly duties earlier in the day and escorting Juliet to another tedious societal function.

When you're ready to let me in, he had said, *I'll be waiting. You already know where to find me.*

Now, she descended from her hired hack and hastened through the shadows to Logan's rooms. Her disastrous clash with her father had left her shaken. He'd slept through breakfast and then disappeared at some point during the day, either to his club or to gamble. She was grateful their paths had not again crossed, for she knew not what she would say to him by the harsh light of day. She felt suddenly, hopelessly adrift.

And there was only one person she wished to turn to for comfort.

She knocked sharply on the door, praying he would be at home. They hadn't arranged a meeting for this evening when she had last left his rooms. She hadn't intended to run to him.

"Who's there?"

To her relief, the voice from within was a familiar, low growl.

"It's Arianna," she said, casting a look about the busy street at her back in the hope she wouldn't be seen or recognized.

She had worn her veil as a precaution. Despite her argument with her father, she had no wish to dash Juliet's chances of making a successful match. If Juliet no longer had to rely upon Father, Arianna would be free to leave. And although she had little more than a pittance as her widow's portion, she would seek employment if necessary. As she had tossed and turned during her fitful sleep the night before, she had determined that she had options available to her. She could become a governess or a paid companion. Although neither situation was ideal, it would certainly prove preferable to remaining at her father's mercy.

The door opened to reveal Logan's tall, muscled form illumined by the lights flickering at his back. He was dressed informally in shirtsleeves and trousers and nothing more, his white shirt sullied with rust-red streaks.

"Come in," he told her, an urgency in his voice that had been absent just moments ago as he looked over her head into the street behind her. "Make haste."

She did as he asked, stepping quickly into his small apartments, the door closing at her back. There was a difference in him this evening that she noticed instantly. A distinct lack of the charm and lightheartedness she had come to expect from him. The dichotomy had appealed to her—a man of darkness and danger, and yet, for Arianna, he had teasing smiles and sultry kisses and so much more. But there was scarcely any hint of the seductive lover she knew.

"Forgive me for coming to you without word," she said hesitantly, searching his countenance. "I can go if you would prefer it."

"No, don't go." He remained unsmiling, threading his fingers through his hair as if he were frustrated with something or someone.

Himself, perhaps?

Or worse, her?

She bit her lip, still feeling uncertain, despite his concise directive. "I fear I've been presumptuous."

In the low light of the entry, it occurred to her that the stains sullying his shirt were a familiar color.

Dried blood.

Worry swirled through her, making her stomach knot with more than just the fear that she had called upon him at an unwelcome time.

He reached for her then, his hands settling on her waist in a possessive hold that was comforting and thrilling all at once as he pulled her into his body. "You're here now, and this is where you'll stay."

She was flush against his chest and it felt so right despite her concern, the rigid planes of his body hard and lovely against her curves.

Her hands flew to his shoulders as she stared up at his beautiful, harsh face. "Something is amiss. Have you been injured?"

He plucked the hat and veil from her head, tossing them unceremoniously to the floor behind her. "Now I can see your face."

He hadn't answered her question, and the intensity in his voice, the way his hazel stare traveled over her, only served to intensify her apprehensions. "Logan, are you hurt? There's blood on your shirt. Will you not tell me what is wrong?"

"The blood ain't mine." He released her suddenly, stepping away.

His clipped words shocked her. "Oh."

"I was about to get into the bath when you knocked." He

ran his fingers through his hair again and glanced down at his shirt front, grimacing. "I'd forgotten. Shouldn't have touched you like this."

If the blood streaking his shirt was not his, that meant it belonged to someone else. Someone else who had either been wounded or worse.

She swallowed hard, her fingers going to the closures on her pelisse, needing to shed it lest any of the blood had transferred. She had known from the beginning, of course, that he was a spy. That he performed perilous deeds and sought dangerous men. But she had never before seen the evidence of violence.

"I didn't kill 'im, if that's what you're thinking," Logan said grimly. "Someone else did."

The blood on his shirt belonged to a dead man.

Shock coursed over her, leaving Arianna cold. "Who?" she managed to ask, then swallowed a rush of bile.

Had it been Charles or Clifford Mace? Had the information she'd sold to the Guild led to their deaths? Suddenly, the full implications of what she had been carrying out on her father's behalf hit her, with the force of a blow to the midsection. The air rushed from her lungs, her chest constricting. There was a ringing sound in her ears, the edges of her vision darkening.

She swayed, her pelisse falling from her fingers and sliding to the floor.

"Arianna?" Logan caught her, hauling her against him again. "Look at me, love. Breathe. In and out. Slowly."

She clutched his upper arms, obeying him, keeping her gaze trained upon his and concentrating on breathing. Gradually, the darkness faded, the ringing dissipating.

"Was it..." she began to speak and then faltered as another rush of emotion threatened to choke her. She licked her dry lips and then managed to continue. "Was it my fault?"

Her vision blurred, and this time it was tears, pooling to roll hotly down her cheeks. He released his hold on her waist and cupped her face tenderly.

"Don't weep, beautiful," Logan murmured, lowering his head and dotting her face with kisses.

Dimly, she realized he was catching her tears.

"I'm r-responsible," she managed, grief and shock and guilt clambering up her throat, making it tight and difficult to breathe.

"You 'ad naught to do with it," Logan said firmly, kissing her jaw, the tip of her nose. "It wasn't Charles Mace who was killed. It was his brother, Clifford. And what 'appened today was Mace and his brother's fault for plotting treason together and inciting a mob that led to the deaths of innocents. It ain't your fault."

But despite his comforting reassurance, her guilt was not assuaged. Her fingertips dug into his muscled arms. "But a man is dead because of me."

"Clifford Mace was a dead man because of his own actions," Logan said soothingly, kissing more of her tears away. "He'd be swinging from the noose soon enough if he weren't already gone to Rothisbone. You can't blame yourself. You aren't responsible for what he's done."

The rational part of her mind knew that what Logan was telling her was true. But even if Clifford Mace had been guilty of committing treason, she had never imagined that the information her father had given her to sell to the Guild would lead to a man's death. She had supposed the conspirators would be captured and sent to prison to await their trials.

"I never wanted any of this to happen," she said, her breath hitching on a sob. "If I hadn't sold that information to you—"

"Then we never would've met," Logan interrupted,

bussing her cheek again. "And if you hadn't told the Guild where Mace was hiding, there would be one more dangerous man in the world tonight, roaming free and plotting something even worse."

"Is Charles Mace in prison, then?" she asked, realizing Logan had yet to reveal the fate of the other brother.

Logan's expression hardened. "No. The bastard escaped after taking a shot at me. But we'll find him soon enough."

She gasped. "He shot at you?"

"Aye, but he missed, and then he scuttled away like the rat he is."

Thank heavens Mace's aim had been faulty. If something had happened to Logan... No, she could not contemplate such a horror.

A new sense of fear crept into her at the notion of Charles Mace somewhere in London. What if he learned who had been responsible for informing the Guild of his whereabouts? What if he came looking for Logan in retaliation?

"Does he know who told the Guild where to find him?" she asked.

"Your secret is safe with the Guild," Logan reassured her.

But was it safe with Father?

Once, Arianna would have been certain of the answer to that question—it would have been a resounding and heartfelt, emphatic *yes*. But that was before Father had become so swept up in his debts and spent each day thoroughly in his cups. That was when he had been a different man.

"Arianna?" Logan prodded gently. "What's the matter, love? You've gone pale again."

She had to tell Logan the truth. Now, before it was too late.

"It's my father," she said. "You were right. The information about the Society did not come from me. It came from him. He's somehow involved himself with them quite deeply. I have no notion of just how much."

"He's betrayed them, then." Logan's gaze searched hers. "I assume it was because he's pockets to let and needed the rewards being offered."

She nodded. "Yes. I would have told you sooner, but I…"

"You didn't trust me."

She bit her lip, hating that he was right. She had put her faith in her father, foolishly and wrongly, and it had been broken.

"I didn't know what was right," she conceded. "My father wasn't always as he is now. He was different before my mother died. But when she left us, he changed. He began drinking to excess. I didn't realize just how deeply he'd sunk until after my husband's death and I returned home. I had no notion he'd been gambling, amassing debts. Over the last few months, he's been selling off everything of value in the house. My mother's jewels, furniture. I've given him my widow's portion. And still, he continues to gamble…"

"The bastard made you sell the secrets for him," Logan finished, his tone forbidding.

"He didn't force me," Arianna explained. "He told me our circumstances were quite desperate. My younger sister Juliet needs to marry. I've been trying to do whatever I must to make certain she can have her Season before we're utterly ruined. Collecting the rewards seemed a viable option, until now."

"Floating 'ell," Logan bit out. "He placed you in danger to pay for his own vices."

Logan was right. Father had placed her in danger. And if he continued to gamble as she suspected he was and over-imbibe each day as she knew he was, then this circle of misery would only continue, without end.

A shuddering breath left her as she struggled to calm her wildly vacillating emotions. "What am I to do?"

"We'll figure it out together," he promised her softly. "I'll keep you safe, beautiful. Trust me."

She nodded, knowing instinctively in the deepest depths of her heart that he would try. Unlike everyone else in her life, he had never let her down.

Yet.

CHAPTER 11

After a seemingly endless day fraught with upheaval, violence, and emotion, Logan was precisely where he wanted to be: in his bed, with his woman in his arms. They'd bathed together in his cramped tub, taking turns tending to each other in an intimate act he'd never performed with another woman. But how important it had been, to feel that connection. He'd washed her hair and she had scrubbed his back. He had soaped her breasts, and she had tenderly threaded her fingers over his scalp, rinsing the suds.

Now, he was content to hold her, her head resting on his chest, their hearts thumping in a reassuring rhythm that was somehow in unison. He stroked up and down her back, the coverlets keeping him from the luxury of her sweetly scented skin. But the night possessed a chill, and he had no wish for her to be cold. Beyond his bed, the flames on a candelabra flickered against the darkness of the night, the fire in the grate burned down low.

"Logan?" she murmured softly into the stillness.

"Hmm?" he asked, playing with the damp tendrils of her midnight curls now.

"Are you awake?"

"Aye, love." He didn't think he could sleep this night. Not after the scenes he had witnessed earlier in the day, and not until he came to a firm decision on what he was going to do next.

"Tell me something that only you know," she said, echoing the words he'd said to her on that first night. "Something you've never told another."

He smiled, still toying with her hair. "I bought the Winters soap we used in the bath tonight because I hoped it would smell like your scent."

And yes, touched in the head as he was, he'd intended to lather himself in the concoction. One way he could be nearer to her even when they were apart. He wouldn't lie, although the scent of the soap had been floral and pleasant, it wasn't as divine as her violet perfume. Having her here with him while he bathed had been its own reward, however.

He felt her lips move against his bare chest and knew she was smiling, too. "You did?"

"I did," he admitted. "After that first night."

Which proved just how bleeding much of an effect she had on him.

Arianna was quiet for a moment, using the tip of her finger to draw a circle around one of his nipples. It was a place on his body that had never seemed particularly sensitive before. But everywhere she touched him came roaring to life, and the light stroke sent heat directly to his groin.

"It is a lovely soap," she murmured, "but it doesn't smell quite the same, does it?"

"No," he agreed, nuzzling her crown with his cheek in a tender show of affection he'd never given to another. There was something about Arianna that made him want to cherish her, to worship her. To take care of her. To hold her and never let go. "Nothing could smell as bleeding good as you do."

"I'll have to use my scent more sparingly," she said. "It's far too dear. I could never afford another bottle now."

"I'll buy you one," he found himself offering. "Hell, I'll buy you a damned dozen of them so you never run out."

She chuckled, but there was a hint of sadness in her voice. "It's not done for a gentleman to give gifts to a woman who isn't his wife."

There it was, the reminder that she was a lady. When they were together, it was so damned easy for the rest of the world and everyone in it to fall away. For him to forget that she was the daughter of a viscount. Because even if that viscount was a tosspot wastrel who cowardly used his own daughter, he was still a lord. A lord outranked a rookeries-born thief-turned-spy like Logan. And as a lady, Arianna was well beyond his reach.

"I'll give them to you anyway," he said, his voice going hoarse with emotion. "To the devil with anyone who says I can't."

"I shouldn't be surprised that is your response." She stroked his chest as she spoke, sending another pleasant surge of awareness through him.

But he didn't want to make love just now. He wanted to savor the moment and their bond.

"My turn," he said, trying to distract himself from any inconvenient lust. "I've answered your question, and now you owe me a secret as well."

She'd already confided the most important one to him this evening—that her father was behind the missives and the sale of the information about the London Reform Society. He'd suspected as much, of course. But hearing it from her lips, her willing admission, pleased him. Because it meant, for the first time, that he'd earned her complete trust. She was willing to give him more than just her body, and he was grateful for the distinction.

"A secret that I alone know... Hmm, I haven't many secrets, I don't think."

Her hand continued its lazy trail of caresses, and he loved her touch, loved the warmth of her curves pressed against him, loved her naked and in his bed.

"Surely you've more than just the one," he said, grasping a handful of curls before allowing them to fall to her back.

"Well, I do detest balls," she surprised him by answering. "I don't suppose I've ever told anyone that before, but I've always found them to be an utter misery. They're crowded and hot and filled with people who are eagerly awaiting your misstep, tittering behind their fans and hoping you'll trip over your hem or dribble lemonade down your bodice."

He'd never been invited to a ball. It wasn't the sort of place he'd long to be either. Had never given a damn about what was proper and what wasn't, about the glittering world of wealthy nobs.

"Why do you attend them, then?" he asked, curious, but suspecting he already knew the answer.

It was the same motivation that had propelled her through her life thus far, from what he could discern.

"Obligation," she said, confirming his instincts. "Duty. One attends a ball to find a husband. Or to help one's sister find one."

So much of the gentry's world revolved around marriages. And for Arianna, her entire life had been one vast sea of responsibility, it would seem.

"You married out of duty, too?" he asked.

"Yes, because it was expected of me. It is a daughter's burden, of course, to marry and please her parents. I wish I had not now, for my marriage wasn't a happy one."

It was the first she had spoken of her past since that first night. He knew enough from making love with Arianna that her former husband had not been a considerate lover. It was hardly surprising to learn that her marriage hadn't been pleasant. But he hated that she'd been forced to endure it at all. Hated any hint of past pain she'd suffered at the other man's hands. At the hands of her family. All people who should have loved and protected her.

All people who had failed her.

"You deserved far better than settling in the name of duty," he told her fervently, stroking her hair.

"I wasn't miserable," she said quietly. "My husband wasn't in love with me. In fact, he scarcely noticed I existed. I suspect we both married out of the same sense of familial obligation. He left me at a coaching inn on the way to Brighton for our honeymoon, having entirely forgotten I was accompanying him."

"Christ, what an idiot," he muttered, wondering how anyone could have failed to be drawn to not just her ravishing beauty, but her innate goodness and urge to care for those around her. "He was clearly dicked in the bleeding nob."

Arianna's caress trailed to his shoulder. "Thank you."

"For what?" he asked, his cock stiffening despite his every intention to remain impervious to her touch.

Simply being with her had been enough. But his body's reaction to her, now that the furor of their earlier emotions had subsided, was taking precedence.

"For defending me," she said softly. "No one ever has before."

Anger on her behalf had him clenching his jaw. "They damned well ought to have done."

And he intended to rectify that by being the one who defended her now. For as long as he could.

For forever, whispered that same voice inside him. The one that had become increasingly more insistent, the longer Lady Arianna Stewart remained in his life. It occurred to Logan in that moment, with her lying so trustingly against him, her warmth and softness pressing into him, that he wanted her to always be in his life. That he never wanted to let her go.

But what could he offer a lady? She was a viscount's daughter and he was a spy. As he'd told her, being in the Guild wasn't the life for a man with a wife. There was far too much danger. No, these stolen moments were all they could hope to have. He would have to find some way of making certain she wasn't forever at her father's mercy.

"Logan?"

Her low, sultry voice cut through his thoughts. He glanced down to find her watching him, head tipped back.

An errant curl fell across her cheek, and he swept it away, relishing the silken softness of her skin. "Yes, beautiful?"

He could not help but to linger there, by the mouth that drove him mad, those lush red lips that haunted his every waking and sleeping hour. With his thumb, he swept over her lower lip in a slow, tender swipe.

"Kiss me," she said.

And he was lost, all his good intentions cast to the instant flames of his desire. He lowered his head, claiming her lips as his, and she tasted every bit as sweet as he remembered. He groaned into her mouth, surrendering to his need, his fingers tangling in her hair as he cupped her head, angling her so he could deepen the kiss.

Her fingers coasted from his shoulder to his neck, leaving a trail of fire in their wake as she found his jaw and stroked. She touched him with such tenderness, taking her time, as if every touch, every second mattered more than the last. And he did the same, allowing his other hand to dip under the weight of the coverlets, over the delicate protrusion of her shoulder blade, to the indent of her spine. Her skin was even softer here, and warm from the counterpane.

When she'd first appeared at his door this evening, he'd been in a different state. Seduction had been the furthest notion from his mind. He still had yet to answer Tierney's questions about his relationship with her; the mission with the Mace brothers had eclipsed most of the day. But his troubles faded away as he gently rolled her to her back and settled between her parted thighs.

How natural it felt, her beneath him. How right.

He knew then that he could not deny either of them, regardless of what was to come. They had now, this moment, this night. They had this passion burning brighter than the sun, and every bit as likely to burn them.

He eased the weight of his body into her softness, taking his time to savor her lush beauty. Kissing his way across her belly, then higher, over the curve of one perfectly rounded breast. Logan leveraged himself on one forearm, using his other hand to trace the flare of her hips. He lowered his head, sucked a hard, pink nipple into his mouth, and was rewarded by her breathy moan, her body undulating.

His senses were acutely aware of everything. Of her curves pliant and warm, the soft sounds of her sighs as he flicked his tongue over the beaded tip of her breast. Of the heat beckoning from between her legs, where he knew he would find her slick and ready. He was aware too of the floral scent of the Winters soap mingling with the musky perfume of her desire. Of the flickering candlelight bathing them in a warm glow. Of the taste of her kiss still on his lips, the tenderness of her hands on his body, caressing his chest and shoulders, her fingers sifting through his hair.

The sound of his name in her throaty voice. "Logan."

"That's right, beautiful. I've got you."

Ah, God. How was he to last? It was too much, being with her, and too good. Too perfect. His cock was unbearably rigid, pressing against her inner thigh. But he was determined not to rush their coupling. Their time together was finite. And he wanted to savor every moment they had now.

He moved to her other breast, sucking, licking, kissing. His free hand slid from her hip, traveling along her side, over the delicate tracery of her ribcage, to cup her full softness. She fit perfectly in his palm, her hard nipple, still wet from his mouth, eager and responsive as he swirled his thumb over the tip.

"Oh," she said on another sigh.

He flicked his tongue over the taut bud, loving the way she writhed. "You're so beautiful." He kissed the swell of her breast. "And silken." Another kiss. "And mine." He trailed his lips higher, kissing along the slight protrusion of her collarbone. "All mine."

"Yes," she hissed, her hands leaving his hair to move down his back, her nails lightly raking over his skin.

Suddenly, he had to have the words from her. Needed to hear her acknowledgment.

He kissed her throat, still playing with her breast, lightly pinching and pulling at her greedy nipple. "Say it. Tell me who you belong to."

"You," she gasped, hips moving, seeking. "I'm yours, Logan."

"Damned right you are," he growled, in the grip of something indefinable, something that was larger than he was. It wasn't mere lust, and some distant part of his mind acknowledged that. But whatever it was, he wasn't going to examine it now.

He took her mouth then, the kiss hungry and deep. She clutched him, making delectable little sounds in her throat that made his cock go even harder. He feasted on her lips as he slid his hand back down her silken skin to the juncture of her thighs. She was slick and hot as he parted her folds, finding the hidden nub of her pleasure and teasing it.

"Mmm," she hummed into his kiss, hips bucking as she sought more.

And he gave it to her in slow whorls over her pearl until he increased the pace, recalling just where she liked to be touched and how. He sensed the need building inside her, felt it in the way she tensed, in the urgency in her lips, her breaths growing ever more ragged. Just when he had her where he wanted her, he lifted his head, breaking their kiss to stare down into her honey-brown eyes that glistened in the low light, burning into his very soul, or so it seemed.

He slicked his fingers down her folds to her entrance and sank a finger deep into the hot grip of her cunny. She clenched on him, her eyes widening as he began to fuck in and out of her slick channel.

She made another inarticulate noise of pleasure, lips, swollen and dark from his kisses, parting as she gasped. His cock, still pressed into the haven of her inner thigh, was leaking. He wanted to sink inside her more than anything. But first, he wanted her to take what she needed.

"Come for me, beautiful," he urged, a second finger joining the first as he found the place inside her that made her wild, his thumb pressing hard on her bud at the same time.

As if on command, her cunny tightened in a series of spasms as her pleasure shuddered through her. There was no better sensation than her clenching around him, warm and wet and perfect. He rose on his forearm to drink in the sight of her in the shadows, body bowing up to meet his, head tipped back, mouth parted on a husky moan. She was more than beautiful, all feminine curves, creamy, pink, and lush.

"Good girl," he praised, working his fingers in and out of her as she rode out the waves of her orgasm.

Finally, he couldn't withstand the force of his own need for her any longer, and he withdrew, gripping his cock and coating himself in her wetness, slicking it up and down his rigid length.

"You want me inside you, love?" he asked, for when she told him what she wanted, taking control over her own pleasure, there was no more potent aphrodisiac in all the world.

"I want you inside me now," she said breathlessly, shifting to accommodate him, wrapping a leg around his waist so the head of his cock was perfectly nestled against her opening.

She didn't have to tell him twice.

Logan tipped his hips. One thrust, and he was inside her welcoming heat, her cunny gripping him in a velvet hold that threatened to undo him entirely. Another thrust, and he was all the way inside her, fire licking up his spine. He stayed as he was for a moment, relishing the sensation of being fully seated, so deep. So good. God, so very, very good. And then, the wet warmth of her pulsing around him forced him into action.

His hips pumped into a rhythm that had them both groaning and gasping, straining together as they sought a mutual release. Her nails dug into his shoulders and she met him thrust for thrust. He moved faster, driving into her harder, the heavy emotions of the day combining with his frenzied desire. And she was every bit as frantic, clinging to him, legs locked firmly around him. They were one, feeding each other kisses, bodies sinuously gliding together as desire overtook them.

She made a feverish sound of need, twisting her hips so that each thrust brought him up against her pearl. He gripped her hip and fucked her harder, all the pent-up desire and frustration and worries uniting as he gave them both what they wanted.

She came on a wild cry, clamping down on his cock and quaking beneath him as the force of her pinnacle roared through her.

Ah, fuck. It was too much. He couldn't last.

He tore his mouth from hers and withdrew from her sweet cunny just in time to spend all over her belly and thighs.

CHAPTER 12

Arianna sat beside Logan as the carriage rocked over pitted roads, taking them from his rooms, back to her father's Mayfair town house. The hour was once again late, and the possibility her absence had been noticed by Father yet again was real. Her stomach tangled in a knot that tightened with each clop of the horses' hooves as the heavy weight of guilt over Clifford Mace's death returned.

"You're quiet," Logan observed, his arm around her shoulders tightening, drawing her more firmly against his side.

"Forgive me," she said, voice hushed as she looked up into his handsome countenance. "I was woolgathering."

He kissed her temple, nuzzling her hair, the gesture so tender it made her want to weep. After they had made love, he had offered to set her up in a house of her own for long enough that she could escape from beneath her father's roof. She had declined, of course, for accepting such a tremendous gift from him would be tantamount to becoming his mistress. Her pride balked at the notion, it was true. But so did her conscience, for she knew she yet had an obligation to Juliet until she was married. If Arianna accepted a living arrangement provided for by a man and it was ever discovered, the scandal would prove too great to overcome.

It touched her heart that Logan wanted to aid her, but in the end, she knew that it was she alone who could extricate herself from her untenable circumstance. When Juliet was married, Arianna would find herself a situation, for she had no desire to submit herself to another unhappy union where she was completely at a man's mercy. Governess, companion, it mattered not. What did matter was that she would be far beyond the reach of Father's control, and she would never again sell another secret to the Guild, not on his behalf or anyone else's.

When Logan raised his head, his gaze was searching in the glow of the carriage lamp. "I wish you would reconsider your refusal of my offer to help you."

She smiled wistfully, hating that they had to part. If only they could spend all night in his bed, wrapped up in each other. If only life was different.

"You know I cannot accept a roof over my head from you any more than I could accept a dozen bottles of violet scent," she told him softly. "It isn't proper."

His jaw clenched. "Is it proper to put yourself at risk to settle your father's debts?"

"I was foolish for agreeing to do so," she acknowledged. "I know that now. I didn't fully understand the magnitude of the repercussions until today."

"Promise me you'll not attempt to sell any more secrets about the Society on his behalf," Logan said. "If your father has knowledge of where Charles Mace has run to, he must come to the Guild himself."

She fervently hoped Father was not so thoroughly entrenched with the Society that he would know where Mace had escaped to, but she couldn't be certain. It was certainly one more source of worry for her, fearing just how deeply he had become involved.

"I promise you I'll not sell any more secrets," she said easily, for that was one vow she could keep.

She had seen with her own eyes the evidence of what the last secret had cost a man—his very life. And she would never again be responsible for such a terrible price.

"Good." Logan gave her shoulders another tender squeeze. "But I don't like you returning to your father's town house."

"It is my home," she said simply. "We have discussed it already. I must remain there until my sister marries. I fear what will become of her otherwise."

"And where will you go after?" he pressed.

It was a question he had asked her earlier as they had helped each other to dress, but she had distracted him with a kiss instead of answering.

"Wherever I must," she said now.

He frowned down at her. "And what the bleeding hell does that mean?"

"You needn't worry about it."

"The hell I won't," he said urgently. "You're my concern now, whether you like it or not."

But she wasn't, not truly. Their relationship was shrouded in secrets and shadows. They had the darkness of the night but could never have the day. They couldn't be seen together in public. To the world, they were strangers.

Arianna rested her head on his shoulder, allowing herself the small solace of his nearness, the warmth of him radiating into her. "I like being yours. Far too much."

He kissed her crown, his fingers idly stroking her shoulder. "When can I see you again?"

Part of her knew what her answer should be. *Never.* It would be the best for him, the best for her. At some point soon, their paths would invariably go in separate directions. And yet, how could she deny herself?

"Soon," she said, though she knew she ought not to promise more.

Every late-night excursion she took to see him was a risk. And there was always Juliet to consider.

"That ain't a day," he said, his voice low and silken.

"I shouldn't keep meeting you this way," she protested, forcing herself to think again of her sister.

"Then let me find rooms for you."

She sighed heavily. "You know I can't allow it."

"Your sister, aye," he grumbled. "I understand the need to protect your siblings."

Arianna recalled what Logan had told her before about his family. *They think I'm dead, and they're better off believing it*, he'd said. He hadn't spoken of them again, and she found herself wondering more about them now, about his past. About everything to do with him.

"How many siblings do you have?" she asked softly.

Emotion sparkled in the depths of his mysterious eyes. "Seven."

His voice had gone hoarse as he gave her the simple reply. There was a great deal of sadness in him, she thought, where his siblings were concerned.

Arianna rested her hand on his thigh, needing to touch him, to offer some manner of comfort, however small.

"Were you close to them?" she asked, recalling his words to her about his family on that first night. *Not any longer*, he'd said when she'd questioned him then. But she knew him better now. She'd been with Logan enough to know he had a good heart. That he cared. That he protected those around him.

"I love them." It was his turn to sigh, a great, gusting breath that told her just how much of an inner struggle he waged. "I'd give my life for any of them, but life in the gaming hell wasn't for me. I needed to do something that was my own, something I could be proud of. And when I found the Guild, I knew what that something was. Only, it meant I 'ad to sacrifice my family to keep them safe."

It was the most he had revealed about himself thus far, and the loss of *h* in his words told her just how affected he was. But there was a part of his story that was something of a shock to her as well.

"Your family owns a gaming hell?" she asked, wondering if her father had ever frequented the establishment.

Not that it would matter; Logan was not responsible for his family's business. And it was plain Logan himself was no longer a part of it.

"Aye," he said, stroking his jaw with his free hand, his expression intense. "'Tis called The Sinner's Palace."

"Do you not miss them?" she asked, thinking that he surely must, for although she grew vexed with Juliet's selfishness, she still loved her sister dearly.

The notion of never seeing her again was impossible to contemplate.

"Every bleeding day." He sighed again. "But I've no choice. I knew what joining the Guild meant. I can't afford to bring danger to them or to The Sinner's Palace. I've taken an assumed surname to protect them and kept my distance and silence. Because I know that if they had an inkling I was alive, they'd fight me like the devil to bring me back."

She remembered what he'd said, too, about the Guild not being the profession for a man with a family. It pained her to think of him forever alone, carrying on with life without anyone to care for him. He had so much to offer. But then her heart squeezed in painful jealousy at the thought of him with someone else.

A foolish reaction, that. She and Logan had no future

together. They came from different worlds. They were temporary lovers. Nothing more. He was a brief, cherished spot of light in the dark disappointment of her life.

"You're determined to keep them from finding you, then?" she asked to distract herself from the unwanted longing within her. Longing she had no business entertaining.

He nodded. "It's for the best."

"You're a good man, Logan…" Her words trailed away as it occurred to her that he'd told her he had taken an assumed surname, but she didn't know what either it or his true surname was.

"Martin is the name I've been using," he said quietly, studying her intently in that way he had, which made her think he could see all her secrets. "But my true name—"

"Hush." She stayed his confession with a finger pressed to his lips. "You needn't tell me. I should never have pried. As a member of the Guild, your secrecy is paramount to your safety."

He kissed the digit, then captured her wrist in a gentle grasp and pulled it away. "I want to tell you. I trust you, Arianna. I wouldn't 'ave you in my bed if I didn't. My true name is Sutton. Logan Sutton."

His complete faith in her—a man who spent each day of his life embroiled in danger, who guarded his mysteries with his life—humbled Arianna.

"Logan Sutton," she repeated, liking the name on her lips, the knowledge of who he was beyond the charming mercenary who had seduced her with wicked kisses and knowing grins and those enigmatic eyes.

One day, there would be a Mrs. Logan Sutton, and he would make that woman very happy, she was sure of it. Logan would never forget his wife at a coaching inn.

But that woman won't be me, she thought with an unaccountable wave of sadness.

The carriage rocked to a halt in the next moment, before either of them could say more.

Arianna forced herself to look away from him, pulling aside the Venetian blinds to see the familiar looming shadows of the mews behind her father's town house that she had left hours earlier. "We've arrived. I must go."

The knowledge that she must leave this carriage, leave his presence, filled her with a physical ache. But she hadn't a choice. Dawn would arrive soon, and the few servants who remained would be stirring, to say nothing of the servants and occupants of the neighboring homes. Juliet was still unwed, Arianna's situation was still hopeless, and Logan likely had far more important matters to attend to than her.

He caught her arm when she moved toward the carriage door. "Don't. Not until you tell me when I can see you again."

It hit her then, with a certainty that left her breathless. She had fallen in love with him. She *loved* Logan Sutton, dashing East End spy with a secret vein of honor, man who could never be hers.

Oh dear God.

The knowledge felt like the weight of a thousand stones upon her chest. If she continued meeting with him for secret trysts, there was far more at risk than her reputation and Juliet's Season. There was also her fragile, stupid heart.

"Perhaps we shouldn't see each other again," she forced herself to say through the sadness threatening to choke her.

"We shouldn't see each other again?" he repeated, his eyes like twin, burning coals, searing into her with their potent flame. "Why not? I want you. You want me. What more is there to worry over?"

"Juliet must wed," she said softly, "and I must have a care

to avoid gossip. If I am to seek a proper situation after she marries, I cannot be tainted by scandal."

He stilled, his jaw going taut. "Tainted by scandal, or tainted by it becoming known you've 'ad a lowborn scoundrel like me in your bed?"

She hadn't meant to pay him insult with the word *taint*, but she could see clearly now that she had. Her heart ached anew to think she'd hurt him with her hasty explanation, made only to guard herself from future pain when the inevitable day came that they had to part ways forever.

"That has naught to do with it and you know it." Impulsively, she leaned forward, cupping his face in her gloved hands and setting her mouth on his for a kiss farewell.

He tasted earthy and salty, like sadness and the love they had made earlier, and she had to close her eyes tight to keep the welling tears at bay.

With a cry, she tore her lips from his. "I'll always remember you. Farewell, Logan."

"Arianna, damn it, don't go yet," he pleaded.

She shook her head. "I must."

And then, before she burst into tears before him and her resolve weakened beyond her ability to walk away, she threw open the door to the carriage and hurtled herself into the bleak darkness of the night.

L͟o͟g͟a͟n͟ ͟w͟a͟s͟ ͟h͟a͟v͟i͟n͟g͟ a terrible bleeding day.

He'd scarcely slept after returning home to a cold, empty bed that smelled of Arianna and the love they'd made together. And although he'd known she was right when she'd said they shouldn't see each other again, that it would be best for the both of them, he'd spent the hours since watching her disappear into the night dreaming up ways their paths might cross again. He knew where her chamber was. He could climb that fiendish tree again…

But no, he shouldn't be thinking about any of that just now. Shouldn't be thinking about her or longing for her at bloody all. Because he was currently seated across from a grim-looking Archer Tierney who had once more delivered an unexpected summons.

And who was watching him now with an unreadable expression on his harsh face.

Tierney leaned forward on his desk, leveraging himself on his elbows in a pose that was indolent. It was deceptive, that pose, and Logan knew it.

"You've brought more than your fair share of trouble to the door of the Guild, Sutton," Tierney stated, his tone cutting. "First it was the petticoats, and now it's your damned family."

The reference to his family immediately had Logan stiffening in his chair, gripping the arms so hard his knuckles ached. "What's this about my family?"

"They've been looking for you," Tierney said. "One of your two dozen brothers."

Looking for him? How the devil did they know he was alive? He wondered even as relief washed over him, the worry tangling his gut in knots relenting ever so slightly.

"I've only four of them," he informed Tierney, suddenly in a rush to know more. "Nothing is amiss with any of them? Or my sisters? What of them? Are they well?"

"I haven't killed your brother yet, if that's what you're wondering," Tierney drawled, his tone unconcerned.

The relief was dashed.

"Jesus, Tierney," he bit out. "Stop speaking in riddles and tell me what's 'appened."

"Your brother paid me a call not so long ago," Tierney explained. "Hart Sutton, to be precise. He claimed there was word at the Beggar's Purse that you and I were seen together. Demanded I tell him what I know of you and where you've gone."

He had met with Tierney at the Beggar's Purse, before he'd joined the Guild. But the tavern was perpetually filled with drunkards and whores. Neither he nor Tierney had supposed anyone lucid enough to see them had been about. Nor that they would remember it so long after the fact.

"Who the bleeding hell would have seen us there?" Logan asked, feeling as if he'd received a blow.

"Don't know who it was. Your brother wasn't keen on providing his sources," Tierney replied. "I told him I'd give him the information he was looking for if he paid me. And then I gave him a name that has nothing to do with the Guild."

Logan knew Hart, and he knew the rest of his brothers and sisters, too. Stubborn, the Sutton clan. They never surrendered, and they always looked out for their own.

He raked a hand through his hair, shocked by the revelation. "What name?"

"The Earl of Haldringham," Tierney replied. "An old tosspot and a bloody terrible gambler. There's nothing for your brother there, but by the time he sniffs around and realizes it, we'll be gone."

While Logan was still in shock over learning his siblings had been searching for him, Tierney's last words hit him equally hard. Surely Tierney wasn't suggesting they would be leaving London.

His heart quickened as he thought of Arianna and all the unfinished business they had. "Gone?"

Tierney gave a short nod. "We've been working out of this building for far too long as it is. The longer we linger, the greater our chances of discovery, if not by your brother, then someone else."

"Leaving London?" he pressed. *And Arianna*, he thought to himself.

"Here now, Sutton," Tierney said, pinning him with a glare. "I'm the one asking the bloody questions here. You've set your brother on me, and you've been bedding an informant and lying about it."

Aye, even if he hadn't directly set Hart on Tierney with questions, he could acknowledge he was likely partially responsible. It was possible that he had been seen the night he had saved Jasper's wife. And he most certainly *was* bedding Arianna. Or, at least, he had been. She'd seemed adamant about them no longer seeing each other last night.

He gripped the arms of his chair so hard he feared they'd snap. "I'm sorry about my brother."

Tierney raised a brow. "But not about continuing to fuck Lady Arianna Stewart?"

Logan ground his molars with so much force his jaw ached, just to keep himself under control. To keep from launching himself across the desk, grabbing Tierney by the cravat, and planting him a facer.

"Watch what you bleeding say where she's concerned," he warned Tierney.

He'd tear any man limb from limb who dared to pay her insult. Arianna was his, damn it.

Not any longer, he thought grimly. She'd made that more than apparent last night.

"Are you threatening me, Sutton?" Tierney asked. "Because that wouldn't be wise."

Logan ignored the implicit menace in his superior's words. "Are you having 'er followed?"

Tierney flashed him a feral grin. "I have everyone followed. Trust no one. Suspect everyone. That way, you'll never end up with a dagger in your bloody back."

Logan wondered what had happened to Tierney to make

the man so jaded and untrusting. "Are you going to Whitehall with what you've learned?"

He had to know, for if there would be repercussions for Arianna, he'd do everything in his power to protect her, however he could.

"Not yet," Tierney said, stroking his jaw. "But I'll be watching. One more misstep from you isn't going to be pretty, old chap. For now, you'd do best to keep your meddling family far away from the Guild and to keep your cock in your damn trousers."

Logan nodded grimly. "Yes, sir."

"Good." Tierney paused, drumming his fingers idly on the desk. "Now, then. There's the matter of Charles Mace. We need to do everything we can to capture him. With his brother dead, the bastard will be even more desperate, perhaps even out for revenge. There's no telling what he'll do if we don't find him."

"By all accounts, Mace and his brother were as thick as thieves," he agreed. "What do you want me to do?"

"I want you to get every bit of information you can from Lady Arianna and her father," Tierney said. "I presume Lord Inglesby is the source of her knowledge. He's long been known to sympathize with the London Reform Society, and he's in dun territory."

Logan wondered just how long Tierney had known the full truth. It was apparent he'd been aware before Logan himself. Had he been too blinded by lust for Arianna to see what was now so blatantly obvious? It was a sobering realization. He'd always reckoned himself impervious to any distraction.

Until her.

"I'll not go to her in false pretenses," he warned Tierney.

Tierney shrugged. "I never told you to do so. But I am telling you to keep your distance. No more bedding her. If

Lady Arianna is acting with her father, then she could be guilty of treason as well."

Logan's mouth went dry. "Everything she's done has been at her father's command. She's trying to protect her sister. She's innocent of wrongdoing."

Tierney's green stare was harsh and unrelenting. "So you say. But you're thinking with your prick, and we all know pricks haven't any brains."

"She's innocent," he repeated firmly, for he believed in her.

He *knew* her. Arianna was not a liar, and nor was she a manipulator. Had he harbored any doubts, her devastation at the death of a villain like Clifford Mace had made that abundantly clear.

"Get me the information, keep your wits about you, and for the love of Christ, do something about your family," Tierney ordered, rising from his chair in the signal that Logan was being dismissed.

Logan surged to his feet, eager to leave the office before he did or said something foolish. Something that would mean his certain expulsion from the Guild.

"I'll send word to you when I have what you require," he said, tamping down his protective ire where Arianna was concerned.

"See that you do," came Tierney's stern reply. "Your future in the Guild depends upon it."

Logan took his leave from the office, stalking into the familiar hall, wondering what the hell he was going to do next. Arianna had told him it was for the best that they no longer see each other. Tierney had demanded answers from her. And his thinly veiled threats about going to the Guild and not believing in Arianna's innocence had the heavy weight of worry pressing on Logan's chest.

He couldn't allow anything to happen to her.

If anyone was going to prison for colluding with the London Reform Society, it was going to be her selfish wastrel of a father. Not her. *Never* her. Not while Logan yet had breath in his lungs.

"There you are," called a voice at his back. "We've got a problem that's yours at the door, and it ain't going away."

Logan spun around to find Lucky following him, the guard's countenance grim. "A problem that's mine?"

His mind instantly leapt to Arianna. Was she here? How the devil had she found the Guild headquarters? And what was she doing gadding about in this part of London, alone?

"Come," Lucky said, jerking his head in the direction of the front door. "It's the Sutton wot won't go away."

Sutton. Not Arianna, then. Hart?

Floating bleeding hell.

Wordlessly, Logan followed Lucky to the front door, which had also been barred. Someone was knocking incessantly on the other side. Logan stood carefully out of sight as the guard pulled open the portal.

"Mr. Tierney ain't seeing callers," Lucky announced, his tone sharp and final.

"Get the bleeding hell out of my way if you want to keep your teeth," returned a familiar voice Logan knew all too well.

It *was* Hart.

Tierney's warning to do something about his family and make certain they stayed away from the Guild echoed in his mind. Everything within Logan tensed. The urge to throw the door to the side and see his brother was strong. He missed his family. Desperately. But it wasn't safe for them to be within his circle, to know about his work with the Guild. The risk was too great. The danger more pressing than ever, and he was already on the wrong side of Tierney as it was. He couldn't afford another false step.

"Missing half my cogs already," Lucky told Hart, sounding unconcerned by the threat.

"I'll knock out the rest of them," promised Hart with a menace Logan well knew he could support.

His brothers were all damned good with their fists.

"I've been given orders," Lucky countered, grim. "Tierney ain't about anyways. Only Mr. Martin is."

Hart was his brother, his problem. Logan was the one who would have to warn him off. If Logan had half a prayer of protecting Arianna, he had to abide by Tierney's edicts. Which meant making certain his family stayed far, far away from the Guild.

"Who the devil is Mr. Martin?" Hart demanded.

Logan stepped forward, joining Lucky at the door. And there was one of his beloved brothers, with the Sutton dark hair and hazel eyes. A rush of emotion welled up within him, but he firmly tamped it down, telling himself it was for the best. That he had to keep his family at a distance for their own welfare. That he had to protect them, to protect Arianna.

"I am," he said coldly, holding Hart's stare without faltering.

It killed him to do it. To act as if his brother were nothing more than a stranger. He hadn't been prepared for this meeting. Not now, not like this.

"Loge," Hart said, disbelief in his voice as he stepped forward.

But Lucky moved with haste. The guard extracted a pistol and pointed its barrel directly at Hart.

"Stop where you are," Lucky growled.

Fear coiled in Logan's belly like a serpent. He couldn't allow any harm to come to his brother. He had to put an end to this.

"I'm not who you think I am," he told Hart, inwardly willing him to accept his words and go.

But Hart was too damned dogged for that.

"The hell you're not," his brother ground out, looking as if he had no intention of leaving.

He forced his countenance to remain emotionless. "I'm not."

"I came here to speak to Tierney about—"

"Haldringham," Logan finished for him.

Hart looked stunned. "You know."

Logan nodded. "Aye."

"Let me speak to you instead," his brother entreated.

Christ above, he wished they could. But everything was such a bleeding muddle right now. And he had to take care, so much care. With Hart, with Tierney, with Arianna. With everyone.

"No," he told Hart firmly, though the denial felt bitter and acrid on his tongue.

And still, Hart refused to relent. "Yes. Damn it, you're my brother."

There was only one way to make certain the ties were severed. He had to do it. Had to say the words that would make him hate himself later.

"Your brother is dead," he said calmly. "You'd do best to forget him. Do not return." He gave Lucky a nod. "Close the damned door."

On cue, the guard slammed the portal in Hart's face.

CHAPTER 13

"You are to wish me happy, sister dearest," Juliet announced, looking pink-cheeked from the crisp air and pretty as she entered the drawing room, newly returned from a drive in the Earl of Newbury's curricle. "His lordship has asked for my hand."

Relief washed over Arianna as she put the embroidery she'd been halfheartedly working on—mostly poking her fingers with the needle—aside and rose to her feet. The Earl of Newbury would make Juliet a suitable husband. He did not possess the easy, dashing charm of Willingham, but neither was he in need of a wife with a sizable dowry. And with Juliet wed, Arianna would be free to carry on with her life.

Without Logan in it.

The thought made her throat constrict. But for what must have been the hundredth time since she had run from his carriage that night, she told herself that ending their affair had been for the best. He was a spy with no place in his life for a wife, and she was a lady who needed her respectability.

For now, said a wicked voice within her. With Juliet safely married, Arianna would truly be free to pursue Logan as a lover again if she wished...

She struck the unwelcome thought from her mind, knowing she mustn't dwell upon him. That she must look to the future instead of dwelling in the past. And a lady with no choice but to earn her way in the world had to take great care with her reputation.

"My felicitations," she congratulated her sister as she reached her, forcing a smile of joy that was not entirely felt, for the turmoil in her own heart. "I am happy for you."

She'd spent the last week poring over advertisements in *The Times*, seeking out potential situations for herself. The news that Juliet had chosen a husband was both welcome and timely. For that morning, positioned between countless requests for board and lodging, and just before the genteel apartment to be let and the sale of a pair of handsome bay geldings, had been a listing wanting an experienced governess of respectable connections, with a knowledge of the French language, for a respectable family in Yorkshire.

Arianna was not experienced, it was true. However, she did have a great deal to recommend herself. Her French was excellent, and she was adept at both music and drawing. She also knew more than a smattering of Italian. She had already written her letter of introduction. Completing the missive had not been without the accompanying sting of sadness. Once, she had hoped for a family of her own. Now, she would be relegated to tending to the children of others.

"Thank you," Juliet said. "I would not have accepted, for you know I was holding out hope Lord Willingham would come up to scratch. However, given what you told me about Father's finances, I deemed it prudent."

Her sister's words held an eerie similitude to the way Arianna had felt upon accepting Edgar's proposal some years before. Logan's words returned to her. *You deserved far better than settling in the name of duty*, he'd said. And did not Juliet deserve that too?

She clutched her sister's arms, studying her for signs of regret. "Is this truly what you want, Juliet, to marry Lord Newbury?"

There was a hint of wistfulness in her sister's smile. "It is not the grand love I had hoped for, but his lordship is most kind to me. He has promised that I shall have what I wish in all things as his countess."

Heavens, Juliet would likely run roughshod over the soft-hearted earl. But then, knowing Juliet as she did, that was probably just the sort of husband she was looking for. He wasn't handsome enough to make her swoon, but he was wealthy and had just given her carte blanche.

"As long as you are happy, my dear," she told her sister, catching her in an impulsive embrace.

"I will be happy to be gone from here," Juliet murmured, returning her hug. "I couldn't bear to lose everything and be reduced to penury."

She couldn't entirely fault Juliet for wanting financial security. Arianna had seen for herself just how vital it was to be certain one had enough upon which to live. Otherwise, a lady was reduced to the benevolence of family members or earning her bread for a living.

And Father's benevolence had proved far from munificent.

"Have you shared the news with Father?" she asked. "He will be pleased."

Thankfully, their father had not been about when she had returned from her last late-night tryst with Logan. He'd not been present much at the town house for the last week, but then, she had also been doing her utmost to avoid him.

"Not yet," her sister said. "I wanted to tell you first."

Arianna released Juliet and took a step back, keeping the

smile pinned to her lips. "I suppose we shall have a wedding to organize."

"I'll be planning it with Lady Newbury," Juliet said. "His lordship said it would be quite meaningful for his mother to do so, particularly since she has so recently lost the previous earl."

"Oh." Arianna could not keep the disappointment and surprise from her voice. "Of course, you must. Lady Newbury will be your new mother. You'd be wise to keep her contented and forge an excellent relationship."

Heaven knew Arianna had never enjoyed a relationship at all with Edgar's mother. The duchess had been cold and joyless and disapproving. After Edgar's death, the extent of her relationship with Her Grace had been a distinctly grudging greeting if their paths crossed at societal gatherings.

Still, Arianna was somewhat dismayed at the notion that her sister had no intention of including her in the preparations for her nuptials. But then, this was Juliet. Why should she have expected any differently?

"I knew you would understand," Juliet said, bussing her cheek. "You are always so good to me, sister. After I am married to Newbury, I shall see if his lordship is amenable to having you live with us."

She would *see* if his lordship was amenable.

As if Arianna were a distant, impoverished relative who would likely be turned away instead of the sister who had sacrificed the last few months, putting her very life at risk, to make certain she could be happily settled. Of course, Juliet didn't know the depths of the recklessness with which Father had been involved. Perhaps she ought to tell her...

No, she decided swiftly. The fewer people who knew of their involvement with the London Reform Society, the better. Particularly after Clifford Mace's death and Logan's words of warning. The peril was far too great.

"Thank you, dear," Arianna forced out instead, striving with every modicum of pride she possessed to keep her smile in place. "That is kind of you."

"Newbury said my kindness is one of the qualities that attracted him to me," Juliet said shyly, raising a hand to her carefully arranged golden curls. "Along with my hair, of course. He says I'm the picture of English beauty."

Arianna, meanwhile, never would be. Her hair was black as a raven's wing, her eyes mud-brown, her lips too large for the perfect rosebud pout so revered by polite society. She tried to tell herself Juliet was being obtuse and not deliberately attempting an insult, but that rather rang hollow.

Making excuses for her family had fast become a habit. As had putting them before herself. Only, she hadn't seen it before. But she saw it now. Saw it as clearly as her sister's blue eyes that so perfectly matched the sapphire earrings dangling from her lobes, part of mother's parure that Arianna had saved from Father's frenzied pawning.

"I wish you and Newbury a lifetime of happiness," she said, needing to escape the room. The house. Perhaps London itself. "If you'll excuse me, dear, I am going to go for a walk."

"A walk?" Juliet's nose crinkled. "But it's no longer the fashionable hour."

This time, Arianna's smile was genuine. "I don't care."

With that, she left her sister and her abandoned embroidery behind in the drawing room. She required air. Movement. *Freedom.*

Arianna collected her pelisse, hat, and gloves, and then ventured to the busy street, walking the pavements. Her heart was heavy, burdened by the sacrifices she had made for her sister and father. But most importantly, by the realization that she would not see Logan again. That she wouldn't know his passionate kisses or tender caresses. That she would never lie in his bed, wrapped up in him, and play their little game of telling each other secrets no one else knew.

A week had passed since she had last seen him, but it felt more like a lifetime.

How had she been so foolish as to fall in love with a man she could never have? If she had better guarded her heart, kept him at a proper distance, this never would have happened. And she would not know this gaping hole inside herself, the loss of him which far transcended the grief she'd felt for Edgar.

As she turned a corner, Arianna became aware of a carriage that appeared to be following her at a discreet pace. A subtle glance over her shoulder, the brim of her bonnet an unwanted obstruction, confirmed the hovering presence of the conveyance. Swallowing hard, she forced herself to walk faster, thinking she was likely mistaken. Why would anyone be following her? But just as the question arose, the carriage pulled beside her, the door flying open.

A scream of terror rose in Arianna's throat.

~

"Bleeding hell," Logan muttered as he leapt from the still-moving carriage.

He hadn't intended to frighten Arianna, but she was screaming to wake the dead, and there was only one way to stop it. He hauled her into his arms, flush against his chest, and clamped a hand over her mouth.

"Hush, beautiful. It's me," he said into her ear.

She quieted instantly, the fight draining from her body. "Logan?"

"Aye, 'tis me. Get into the carriage," he instructed her, well aware that they had captured the interest of far too many curious onlookers for his liking.

"I can't get into the carriage with you," she protested. "Someone will see."

"The faster you do it, the fewer people to take note," he reasoned, releasing her and lacing his fingers through hers, tugging her in the direction of the waiting vehicle. "Come."

She looked as if she were about to argue, catching the tempting fullness of her lower lip between her teeth, her honey-brown eyes darting around to ascertain just how much of an audience they had. But now that he had her, he wasn't about to let her go. Logan pulled her toward the carriage.

"You'll only make it worse if you keep putting up a fight, love," he said reasonably. "Come into the carriage."

With a sigh, she obeyed, allowing him to hand her up into the waiting privacy before joining her and slamming the door closed to ward off any further gossipmongers eager for tales to tell. She settled primly on the bench, fidgeting with her pelisse, and he seated himself at her side as the carriage rolled back into motion. The coachman, a trusted Guild man, knew what to do, where to go.

"You've abducted me," Arianna accused without heat, still plucking away at her black pelisse.

His lips twitched as he took her in. Her cheeks had been kissed with pink from the chill in the air, and tendrils of midnight hair had come free of her coiffure to curl mischievously about her heart-shaped face. Had it been a mere week since he'd seen her last? It felt more as if it had been a bleeding eternity.

"You accompanied me of your own free will," he countered easily.

"Did I have a choice?" she queried tartly.

Her question reminded him of the various ways her

freedom of choice had been stripped from her, first in her marriage and later in her widowhood as she'd been forced to obey her father. He bleeding *hated* that. He'd meant what he said when he'd told her she deserved better. Arianna deserved only the best, and to the devil with everyone else around her.

He held her gaze. "With me you always have a choice. If you wish to leave, I'll stop the carriage. Say the word."

Stay here with me, he pleaded inwardly. *I've missed you. I want you. I need you.*

But he kept all those inconvenient feelings to himself. The reason he'd sought her out was to carry out Tierney's orders, not to persuade her to continue their liaison, regardless of how desperately he wanted that. Tierney had made it clear that he expected a thorough investigation of Arianna and her father.

The Guild had spent the last week hunting for Charles Mace to no avail and moving their headquarters to a new location thanks to Hart's stubborn insistence in finding him. Logan knew he owed Tierney all the answers he could get. Still, he couldn't lie to himself. The chance to see her again had been a potent lure.

Arianna was silent for a moment, before shaking her head. "Don't stop the carriage. I presume you're carrying me away with you for a reason."

If only he were truly carrying her away with him. Carrying her off to a place where it was no one but the two of them, and they could make love for days and the rest of the world could go to bleeding hell.

"I needed to speak with you and your father," he said instead of giving voice to all those wayward longings. "I intended to pay a call on the both of you, but I spied you walking. Where were you going, and why were you alone?"

He strongly disliked the notion of her walking about as

she wished when Charles Mace was out there somewhere. Whilst they had no reason to suspect Mace knew of the role she'd played in the information which had been passed to the Guild, Logan didn't like leaving anything to chance. Especially not when it came to Arianna's safety.

"I don't know where I was going," she admitted on a sigh. "Anywhere, I suppose, as long as it removed me from my father's house for a time."

He frowned, not liking the sound of that. "Is he asking you to sell more information?"

"No," she said, her brow knitted with worry. "Not yet."

Her response set his jaw on edge. "You promised me you wouldn't involve yourself in this damned business any longer."

"And I shan't. But I cannot promise he won't ask." Her countenance was as sad as her voice. "Not any more than I can promise I won't be absconded with by dashing rogues."

He winced at her pointed observation. "I better be the only bleeding rogue who's absconding with you."

Now and forever, Logan wanted to add, but wisely kept silent on the last. He couldn't offer her anything beyond pleasure, and she deserved far better. She deserved a man who could make her a proper husband. Deserved to find happiness with a cove who worshipped the very ground upon which she trod. Who would do anything to make her happy. A man who would die before forgetting her at a goddamned coaching inn.

"You are the only rogue I *want* to abscond with me," she said quietly.

And curse her, there went his resolve.

"Floating hell," he cursed grimly. "You shouldn't say that unless you mean it."

He was thinking of her parting words that night, of how she'd told him she couldn't afford to be tainted by scandal.

Trying to do everything in his power to honor her wish. Aye, hauling her into his carriage on a busy Mayfair street hadn't exactly been wise, but he hadn't had much choice. Touching her now was a distinctly different matter. If he did, he wouldn't want to stop.

She was worrying her lower lip again, watching him with those same shadows in her eyes that haunted him. "I do mean it. I shouldn't, but I do."

He swallowed hard, a rush of longing sweeping over him that was so intense, he had to ball his hands into fists at his sides to keep from reaching for her. "You're making this bleeding difficult for me, beautiful."

"You're the one who brought me into this carriage," she pointed out.

There was silence then, their stares holding, nothing but the familiar sound of the carriage and the road beyond interrupting the quiet.

"I'm fulfilling my duty," he bit out, feeling inexplicably hollow.

Duty was all he had, but it had never felt so bloody lonely before. Arianna made everything else pale in comparison. Even during the last week they had been apart, she'd never strayed from his thoughts. The yearning for her hadn't diminished. It had only increased.

She nodded. "Of course. You've come on Guild business."

"You told me farewell," he reminded her, hating the sadness in her voice.

Loathing himself for being responsible for even a modicum of it.

"I was trying to do what is right for my sister and for my own future."

"What is your future?" he found himself asking.

It wasn't why he'd come. Wasn't the dialogue he was

meant to be having with Arianna. But now that they were together, he couldn't deny himself.

"I am hoping for a situation as a governess," she said simply. "I've found a family in Yorkshire that is in need."

The thought of her moldering in Yorkshire, caring for some nameless family's children, nettled. It wasn't right. She didn't deserve to be hidden away, subject to the whims of others. But it wasn't as if he had a hold on her. Even if he were to leave the Guild tomorrow, he didn't have the funds to start a new life with her, and nor did he have another means of earning his living. He could return to the family he'd left behind, perhaps find work in The Sinner's Palace. And yet, after the way he had disappeared, he could hardly ask them to forgive him. No, he had nothing to offer Arianna.

Why, then, did the thought of her leaving London to become a governess leave him feeling as if he'd been torn in two?

"Is that truly what you want?" he asked her.

She shook her head. "What I want is immaterial. It is what I have to do, if I want to be out from beneath my father's roof."

His mind was whirling. Thinking of ways to postpone her departure. Thinking of reasons why she should stay.

"What of your sister? I thought you needed to remain until she weds."

"Juliet has announced her intention to marry." Arianna's smile was meager.

Forced, he thought.

"You can't go to Yorkshire," he blurted, his restraint snapping.

Logan succumbed to the urge to reach for her, pulling her close. And she nestled into his arms as if it were the most natural place for her to be. He inhaled deeply, catching a hint of the sweet floral note of violets.

"It is where the situation I've found is. If they choose me, then I must go." Her face burrowed into the knot of his cravat, her arms sliding around his midsection and holding tightly.

"God, I've missed you," he confessed, wishing she wasn't wearing a blasted bonnet so that he could bury his face in her hair. As it was, the muslin and lace of her millinery thwarted him.

"I've missed you, too," she admitted, her voice small and muffled.

How had he managed to endure the last week without her? Moreover, how would he endure a lifetime of it? The future loomed, bleaker than he'd ever imagined. An abyss from which there would be no escape.

He couldn't allow her to go. It wasn't right. This was where she belonged, here with him.

"You're not going to Yorkshire," he said firmly.

"I must, Logan. I haven't a choice."

"You *do* have a choice, damn it." The words fled him, uncontrollable, and he knew then, that just like the perfect rightness of the way she felt in his arms, that *they* were also right and true.

There was another choice. He could give her one. There was nothing stopping him but common sense.

"I don't." She tipped her head back, her lovely face no longer obscured by the brim of her bonnet, golden-brown gaze searing him from the inside out. "There's no other way. I'll not remain in my father's household, and nor can I rely on my sister after she is married."

The answer, impossible as it seemed, was there before him. The only answer. He couldn't lose her. "You could marry me."

CHAPTER 14

*A*rianna had misheard Logan.

She must have.

It was the rumble of the carriage wheels, the jangle of tack beyond, the hoarse cry of a coachman here or there, which had garbled the words he had just spoken to her. Which had mangled them irreparably and made her weary mind find hope where she should not.

She blinked, thinking she was also imagining the expression on his countenance, earnest and awaiting. Tender, too. In the maddening sway of the carriage, settled as she was in the comfort of his embrace, their bodies disconcertingly near, the last week of desperate loneliness fell away. But then she blinked again, and his beautiful lips were still quirked in a half smile of reassurance. And his hazel eyes were still burning into hers with expectation.

"What did you say?" she asked, sounding far more breathless than she would have preferred. Far more buoyant, too.

"You told me that you didn't have a choice aside from going to Yorkshire and becoming a governess," he explained patiently. "I said you do 'ave a choice. You could be my wife."

The slip into rougher patterns of speech was telling. Logan meant what he was saying. But she told her frantic heart to calm itself, for she would not allow him to marry her in pity.

"You're a member of the Guild," she reminded him. "You said yourself it was no profession for a man with a family."

"I could leave it."

He spoke with such ease, as if the suggestion were entirely without repercussions. As if he could simply walk away from the Guild.

"For me? Because you pity the straits in which I have found myself?" She shook her head again. "No. I won't allow you to give up your work to save me. You'd only come to resent me for the choice. I have one unhappy marriage behind me, and I'll not subject myself to another."

"It ain't pity that I feel for you, love," he said, raising a brow as his beautifully sculpted lips kicked into a rakish grin.

It was desire, of course. The reminder of all the passion they had shared made heat settle in her belly and had an answering ache pulsing to life between her thighs.

She licked lips that had gone dry, thinking of the myriad reasons why they could not marry, why such a union would never work. "A marriage must be founded on something more than mutual lust and the guilt you feel over my circumstances."

"What I feel for you runs far deeper than mere lust."

And what she felt for him was love. He'd not spoken the word, aside from using it as a term of endearment. Her marriage to Edgar had been far from a love match, but neither did she think she could bear a union in which she loved her husband and he did not return that tender emotion. Surely, such a marriage would be every bit as doomed as her first had been.

"I won't allow you to sacrifice yourself for me," she denied softly. "I thank you for the offer, but I must respectfully decline."

Even if doing so tore her heart into a thousand tiny, jagged shards. Because she wanted to marry him. *Good heavens*, how she did. She hadn't realized just how much until this moment. Hadn't believed it a possibility. But she loved him far too much to let him surrender everything he'd worked for, everything he was, for her sake.

"Marrying you is the furthest I could get from sacrifice," he said, threatening her resolve.

"Logan," she murmured, her heart aching. "Please…"

"Please what? Are you saying you'd rather go to Yorkshire and become a governess than marry me?" He paused, lifting a hand to cup her cheek in the gentlest of gestures. "I'm not a nob, and I'm not the son of a nob. I'm not worthy of a lady of your breeding. I understand that. But I would never ask you to place yourself in danger for me. And neither would I leave you at a bleeding coaching inn."

He was contrasting himself against the other two men of her life: Edgar and her father. Both had disappointed her. Neither had left her feeling protected or loved.

But Logan did. Even if he hadn't said the words, he cared for her. She knew that much. Could it be enough?

"I don't care that you aren't a lord," she told him. "That matters naught to me. It's the fact that you would give up everything for me… I don't want you to do that. I could never forgive myself if I asked it of you."

"You haven't asked it of me. I've offered of my own free will. You mean more to me than the Guild."

But she could not accede with such ease. There was something about the suddenness of his proposal which did not sit well with her.

"You told me you came to speak with my father and myself," she countered, trying to steel herself against the tender sweep of his thumb along her cheekbone, the longing in his eyes. "You had no intention of asking me to marry you when I first entered the carriage."

"You're right," he admitted softly. "I sought you out with a different purpose. But as has been the case from the moment our paths first crossed at Willowby's, I didn't know what I needed until I saw you."

She knew what he meant, for she had felt the same way. Such a stirring awareness, compounded by attraction, searing need, and a deep, abiding sense that she had finally found someone with whom she could find herself at ease. She'd never been comfortable in her skin as Edgar's wife. It had been a role she had played, and not well, if the miserable year of her marriage was any indication.

No, she'd known from the first, in an instinctive, intrinsic way, that Logan was different. Everything had been right and comfortable when it otherwise should not have been. Being intimate with him had been a natural progression of that deep-seated familiarity. The way she felt for him was bigger than she was. He was hers, and she was his.

"You feel the same way," he pressed as he worked to make sense of her emotions and thoughts. "Tell me you don't."

She couldn't.

It would be a lie.

Still, she had to try. "You cannot truly want to marry me. You want to protect me, but I'm not your burden to bear."

"Never call yourself a burden." His voice was stern, teeming with emotion. "Nothing about you is a burden. Not one bleeding thing."

He was still stroking her cheek, and she felt the resolve she'd been clinging to with such tenacity shifting. "But do you want to marry me, Logan? How can you, when we scarcely know each other?"

"How can I not?" He kissed the tip of her nose, the

gesture reverent. "All I know is that I can't lose you, beautiful. I need you in my life, at my side, in my bed. I need you forever. I was too bleeding pigheaded not to say it before, not to realize it. I never should've let you go that night."

Longing surged, so persistent it was almost painful, accompanied by a deep and abiding yearning she couldn't deny. She wanted to say yes. Wanted to marry him. How could she not? She loved him. It was new and strange and wild, this feeling inside her.

Still, she had to be certain. For his sake as well as for hers. Her last marriage had not been a pleasant experience, and she did not want to entrap Logan into a situation that would one day potentially make him miserable.

She caught his wrist in a gentle grasp, staying his movement as she searched his eyes for the answers she sought. "But giving up the Guild just to marry me? How can you? What will you do?"

"Let that be my worry, Arianna." He leaned into her, his breath a warm benediction falling over her lips. But when she expected him to kiss her, his mouth instead flitted over her cheek, along her jaw, dotting little pecks that had her sighing, all the way to her ear. "Say you'll marry me, and we'll make a plan for the rest. Don't go to Yorkshire. Don't leave me. Stay. Be my wife."

How precious, those words, coming from him.

Her breath seemed to freeze in her chest. Did she dare to accept? He did not seem like a man who had been importuned by the moment or her plight. He spoke in certainty and measured tones. His gaze had not faltered. And his lips feathered over her throat now, just above the collar of her pelisse, finding her pulse.

Her head tipped back, a shudder of surrender going through her. "I...don't know what to say."

"Say yes," he urged against her neck, stringing another trail of kisses back to her jaw.

She hesitated another few heartbeats longer. Long enough for his lips to at last coast over hers in the barest tease of something more.

"Yes," she whispered against his mouth, hoping neither of them would regret it.

~

IF HIS FLORID cheeks and the stench of spirits in the air were any indication, Arianna's father was deep in his cups. And if the state of the drawing room was any indication, Lord Inglesby had been pilfering his furniture, pictures, and everything else of value in his town house with the frantic hope he could settle his debts.

Little wonder Arianna's father had been desperate enough to betray the men he'd likely been colluding with. Logan wasn't accustomed to the plummy life of a viscount, but he could plainly see the places where paintings had been removed from their hangers on walls and furniture had once stood in dark patches on the otherwise faded Axminster.

They had taken Logan's carriage back to Inglesby's town house after Arianna had agreed to his madcap plan of marrying him. He had delivered her near enough to her Father's home that she was able to return alone without anyone being the wiser. He had waited a quarter hour to allow her to settle herself before paying his call.

And now, in addition to interrogating the man about anything else he knew concerning the Society and Charles Mace, Logan also intended to ask for Inglesby's blessing upon their union.

Union. Strange word for a marriage. It sounded so bloodless, so simple.

Floating, bleeding hell.

He was going to be a husband. *Arianna's* husband. The shock of it still left his head feeling a bit as if it were spinning in the clouds. He hadn't understood, until he'd had her in his arms, what he'd needed to do. Not until she'd told him she would be going to Yorkshire, and the notion of her leaving him, of being beyond his reach, of never seeing her again, had gripped him with a pall like death.

Marrying Arianna was right, and he knew it. He would deal with Tierney however he must.

But first, Lord Inglesby.

They were seated on the remaining furniture, which had seen better years. Arranged in a tidy triangle. Staring at each other. Arianna had performed stilted introductions upon her father's arrival, using Logan's assumed surname, for they could not be certain whether or not her father could be trusted. Given her father's current state, he was glad of the decision. The man was drunk as David's sow.

"Thank you for agreeing to meet with Mr. Martin, Father," Arianna said, at home in her role of hostess, even if there was an edge of concern in her voice and her gaze strayed between her father and Logan in troubled fashion, as if she wondered which of them would require more of her reassurances. "Shall I call for some tea, or perhaps another restorative?"

"None for me, thank you, my lady," he told her with as much gallantry and formality as he could muster for the woman he intended to make his wife. "Though you are kind to offer."

He would not allow a hint of impropriety to shadow either his offer for Arianna's hand or his mission, which would possibly be his last for the Guild.

"I can't imagine this will be a particularly long call," Inglesby said with a notable slur as he pinned Logan with a disapproving stare before turning to his daughter. "Nothing is required, my dear. You may go and see to your sister whilst I speak with Mr. Martin."

It was apparent from the viscount's expression that he had intended the last as a firm dismissal.

"Forgive me, my lord," he inserted smoothly before Arianna could protest, "but I must request Lady Arianna's presence."

The viscount, who bore precious little resemblance to Arianna save black hair which was thin and graying, and a much larger and more masculine form of her delicate nose, made a low sound of disagreement.

"And why should you believe yourself welcome to request anything in my home, Mr. Martin?" Inglesby demanded gruffly. "You go too far."

"I am here at the command of Whitehall, Lord Inglesby," he explained quietly. "That is why."

Some of the ruddiness fled the viscount's countenance. "Whitehall? Why should they send such a shabby blackguard in their name?"

Arianna's soft gasp at her father's rude demand cut through the silence. He hadn't expected the viscount to welcome him, and that had been before he'd decided he was going to marry the man's daughter. He knew who he was, where he was from. He was Logan Sutton, born to the rookeries, the roughness of his youth still marring his speech, dress, and education. But his coarseness had also been excellent reason for Whitehall to keep him in their employ.

"Mr. Martin is neither shabby nor a blackguard," she was saying, storming to his defense.

She was loyal, his woman. To a fault. The evidence of that was seated before him.

Logan held up a hand as if to say it was hardly of any

import whether or not her father paid him insult. For it wasn't.

"It is a fair question," he mused, stroking his jaw idly. "I'll own that I'm not dressed for a ball, my lord. But the work I do ain't done in the ballroom. I'm with the Guild."

He waited for that news to settle into Inglesby's brandy-soaked upper story.

The rest of the color drained from Arianna's father's face. "The Guild?"

Logan nodded, smiling faintly, for he couldn't help himself; seeing the man who had so selfishly placed her in peril squirm was its own source of satisfaction. "Aye, the Guild. I trust you're familiar with our work. We report directly to Whitehall, as I'm sure you know."

Because you sent your own daughter to us, to do your dirty deeds, you bleeding scoundrel, Logan thought grimly, but decided to be politic and kept that bit to himself.

"Why have you come?" Inglesby bit out.

"I have questions for you, my lord," Logan said smoothly, casting a glance toward Arianna to determine how she was faring during this uncomfortable interview.

Her honey-brown gaze met his, and he read concern in their glittering depths. Her hands were laced primly in her lap, her face otherwise betraying not a hint of her thoughts.

"What questions can you posh-possibly have for me?" her father demanded on another slur, dragging Logan's attention back to him.

"Concerning your involvement with the London Reform Society," he explained. "Specifically, with members who are now accused of committing treasonous acts."

"I know nothing of the Society or its members," her father blustered.

He held Inglesby's gaze, which was blue and cold. "You're lying, my lord."

"How dare you?" Inglesby spat, rising from his chair and staggering to the side, collecting himself before losing his balance entirely. "Get out of my home, you cur."

Logan rose as well, not keen to allow another man to tower over him, even if he was an aging drunkard who likely hadn't the capacity to harm a mouse. "I dare because it is true. You may have sent your daughter on your behalf, but do not mistake my coarse speech and plain dress for stupidity. I know you are the source."

The viscount staggered again, clutching the back of his abandoned chair for purchase as he swung toward Arianna, who had also risen from her seat. "You've betrayed me!"

Arianna flinched, her countenance softened with regret, her hands now catching in the drapery of her gown, her elegant fingers twisting the muslin. "I haven't betrayed you, Father."

"Do you have any inkling of the danger you've placed us in?" her father demanded.

Logan moved to stand at Arianna's side, for he was her protector. Against her father, against the Guild, against the bleeding world if need be. She would never be alone again, nor at the mercy of men who didn't deserve her.

"Do you mean the danger you willingly placed your own daughter in, for the sake of funding your vices?" Logan cut in unable to keep the anger from his voice as it rang through the depleted drawing room with the crack of a whip. "I know what you've done, my lord, as does the Guild. Lady Arianna is an innocent in this tragedy of your making."

He would not allow Lord Inglesby to lay the blame at her door. Her only fault was in loving her father too much. The man quite plainly was not worthy of her tender feelings, nor her loyalty.

"I understand now," Arianna's father said, listing to the right before catching himself on the beleaguered furniture.

"You've whored yourself for this baseborn rogue, and you betrayed your own father."

Arianna's soft gasp of hurt sliced through Logan with the power of a knife's blade. Keeping from launching himself at Inglesby and demanding the bastard issue her an apology required all the control he possessed. A Herculean amount of it.

"Now it is you who oversteps, my lord," he said coldly. "You'll not pay her insult. Your daughter has done everything in her power to help and protect you, and you've done naught but throw her to the bleeding wolves. I'll give you a final chance to atone for your sins, and if you ain't willing to cooperate, I've no choice but to return to the Guild with it. Tell me what you know about the London Reform Society and Charles Mace. Have you received communication from him, or anyone connected to him, in the last week?"

Inglesby's narrow-eyed stare was concentrating upon Arianna, quite as if Logan were not even present in the room. "How could you? My own flesh and blood?"

The viscount lunged toward Arianna, arm raised as if to strike, moving with far more alacrity than Logan would have thought possible. But Logan was quicker. He stepped between father and daughter, Arianna safely at his back, his gut clenching at the realization that Inglesby had intended to hit her. Had he done so before? *Fucking hell.* Logan would never allow him to hurt her again.

"You'll not harm Lady Arianna," he bit out. "Not now, nor ever again. She is under my protection now."

Inglesby recoiled. "Under your protection? What do you mean?"

This wasn't the manner in which he had hoped their dialogue would proceed. But there was no hope for it. The viscount was either too deep in his cups for rational thought, or too much of a selfish scoundrel. Logan was inclined to believe it was a mixture of both.

"We are to be married, Father," Arianna answered, stepping from behind the protective shield he'd created with his body, her chin held high, voice firm.

The viscount's horror was written all over his face. "You cannot mean it."

"Lady Arianna has paid me the vast honor of agreeing to be my wife," Logan confirmed, newly filled with a deep and abiding sense of rightness at the words. "You may wish us happy."

"No." Inglesby shook his head. "I forbid it. I'll not have my daughter sullied by such a mish…misalliance."

"It ain't for you to forbid," Logan told him. "It's 'appening whether you like it or not."

There went his attempt at keeping the rookeries from his speech. But then, perhaps the timing was perfect, the reminder of his past a much-needed dig at Inglesby's pride. Because Logan *was* going to make Arianna his wife, and there wasn't a thing her bastard of a father could do to stop him.

"What have you done?" Arianna's father demanded of her.

Logan watched her, admiring her beauty and strength, amazed by her self-possession, not just in this moment of supreme upset, but in all those which had come before it. She was mesmerizing. Breathtaking.

"I have done what you asked of me," Arianna answered her father clearly, her voice laced with an air of finality. "And now the time has come to do something for myself. Please, Father, I beg of you that if you know anything about where Charles Mace is hiding himself, tell Logan now."

"You expect me to trust this lying whelp from the rookeries?" her father sneered, swaying once more on his feet. "Never."

Logan wondered, and not for the first time, just how long

Ingelsby had been giving the bottle a black eye. Had he started in the morning, to be so thoroughly soused?

"This is your last chance," he told the man with a calm he did not feel.

Inside, he was seething. Furious that Arianna had been subjected to this man's callous mistreatment, his manipulation and abuse.

Never again, he vowed inwardly. *She is mine now. Mine to protect. Mine to defend.*

Mine to love.

Love? A fine time for such a realization to occur. He kept his gaze trained upon Ingelsby, awaiting a response, telling himself he would fret over the implications of this new knowledge later.

"I know nothing," the viscount said, "other than that I want the two of you to be gone from my sight and gone from this house at once."

Logan nodded. "Fair enough, my lord. You had the opportunity to share what you know. If it's discovered that you've played a part in helping Charles Mace, I'll not be responsible for what becomes of you."

It was as gentle a warning as he could muster for the man, and only offered for Arianna's sake. Because she loved her father, regardless of whether he was worthy of it.

"Get out," Ingelsby snarled. "Both of you!"

Logan laced his fingers through Arianna's. "Come, love."

He hadn't expected for her father to demand that she leave his house immediately, but then, he wasn't willing to leave her here, either. Especially after what he had just seen. She was coming with him, even if he had to toss her over his damned shoulder and cart her away.

To his relief, Arianna didn't put up a fight. Instead, she clung tightly to him, and together, they took their leave. In the hall beyond the drawing room she turned to him, however, her expression stricken.

"What am I to do?" she asked, tears glittering in her eyes.

He was proud of the strength she had shown before her father, and he ached for the pain she must be feeling within. "We shall go to your chamber and fetch anything of import," he said calmly. "You'll come home with me."

"But we aren't yet married," she protested.

"We will be as soon as I can manage it," he promised. "Let's make haste."

He had no wish to prolong the ugly scene which had unfolded with her father.

Together, they mounted the staircase and ascended in silence. There was so much he wanted to say to her, but words would have to wait. For now, the most important task was to remove her from her father's household as quickly as possible. He would have to go to Tierney with this latest failure and with news of his impending nuptials both. But that, too, was a worry for another moment.

The hall upstairs, much like its counterpart below, was notably bereft of pictures and ornamentation. It would seem Lord Inglesby had been mining the floors to pay his debts in equal measure. And if his state in the drawing room was any indication, the man would only sink further into dun territory, until there was no escape. Thank God Logan had found Arianna when he had, before she had become involved in something worse. Before it was too late.

They reached a closed door and she turned to him. "This is my chamber."

Before she could go within, another door opened and a blond mort rushed into the hall, her resemblance to Arianna undeniable, despite the difference in hair and eye colors. The sister, he reckoned.

"Arianna, who is this?" the lady demanded, casting a suspicious eye in Logan's direction.

It was, he thought with amusement, the way he reckoned she might look upon a chimney-sweeper or street urchin who had dared to make himself known to her.

"This is Mr. Martin," Arianna introduced awkwardly, "the man I am going to marry. Mr. Martin, this is my sister, Miss Juliet Hargreave."

Her sister gasped. "Marry? But...you've never spoken of this man."

Logan sketched an ironic bow. "It is a pleasure to make your acquaintance, Miss Hargreave."

"But...but..." Arianna's sister was stammering now, apparently so astonished at the prospect of her sister wedding such a lowly beggar as himself, that she could not complete a coherent sentence. "Why is he here with you now, just outside your chamber? I am shocked! I know you are a widow, but this is positively scandalous by anyone's standards. If word were to reach Lord Newbury and his mother of this, I should think it would lead him to cry off and refuse to marry me. And if he refuses to marry me, I shall be utterly without hope."

Ah, thinking of herself. It was a family trait, Logan thought. In everyone but Arianna, who had been left to be the selfless sacrificial lamb.

"I know it must come as a shock to you," Arianna told her sister quietly, still gripping Logan's hand as if she feared he might disappear and leave her to fend for herself with these self-centered vagabonds she called family. "The news is sudden. However, you needn't fear for yourself. I am certain Lord Newbury will remain as pleased as ever to take you as his wife. He is quite smitten with you, is he not?"

Miss Juliet's shoulders straightened. "Of course he is. How could he not be?"

"Indeed," Logan muttered to himself, thinking it a miracle that Arianna had soldiered on for as long as she had.

As far as he was concerned, Lord Inglesby and his youngest daughter deserved each other quite handsomely.

"Father and I have had a misunderstanding," Arianna explained, simplifying the ugly scene which had unfolded below for her sister's benefit. "He deemed it best if I leave. I'm gathering what I'm able, and I'll send word to you of where you can find me."

"You cannot mean to say you are...*running off* with this man?" her sister asked, her lip curling with distaste. "I shall be ruined if you do."

"I fear you're already ruined, and it hasn't a thing to do with your sister's marriage to me," Logan informed her dryly, nettled by her continued concern for herself alone.

"How dare you say so, sir?" Miss Juliet demanded, turning the force of her displeasure upon him.

Arianna withdrew her fingers from his and crossed the hall to her sister, taking her in an embrace that her sister halfheartedly returned. "I'm certain this is a shock to you, dear. It's not my intention to cause any scandal or to harm you in any fashion. I wish nothing but a lifetime of happiness for you and Lord Newbury."

With that, she released her sister and turned to Logan, the sadness in her eyes making him want to toss Miss Hargreave out the nearest window on her behalf. But she loved her sister, he reminded himself. Just as she loved her undeserving, selfish arse of a father. Her heart was far more forgiving than his, as was her ability to see the best in others. He'd have walked away from this bleeding town house long ago, without looking back. But then, even if he'd been born a lowly Sutton, he was still a man, and as such, he would have had choices available to him that Arianna hadn't.

That changed for her today.

"Come, let us gather what we can," he told her quietly, before offering another abbreviated bow to her sister. "Miss Hargreave."

He offered Arianna his hand, and she took it, their fingers lacing together tightly.

CHAPTER 15

As the carriage swayed over London roads, taking them from her father's town house, Arianna's meager possessions haphazardly packed into the conveyance along with them, she slanted a glance in the direction of the man who would be her husband.

He was watching her, his gaze intent.

"Your father would 'ave struck you today," he said, his voice raw.

There was no use denying it. Once, she would have believed Father incapable of raising his hand against her. But that had been before losing Mother, when he had been a different man entirely.

"Yes," she agreed simply. "I believe he would have done."

"It's 'appened before."

His grim words were not a question; they rang with certainty.

She swallowed hard. "Only once."

His jaw hardened, but she knew the fury in his expression was not meant for her. "One time too bleeding many. It's a man's duty to protect those weaker than 'imself."

She'd not heard Logan's accent slip so consistently since she'd known him. That he was so unsettled, and on her behalf, was humbling.

"He is not himself," she said quietly, knowing the excuse did not ameliorate her father's actions.

"Never again," Logan told her, his tone vehement, his eyes burning into hers. "Not while I'm on this side of the bleeding dirt."

She nodded, tears stinging her eyes yet again. She blinked hard. Arianna had never been the sort to resort to emotion. Her stoic nature had carried her through all her years thus far since her mother's death. Mother had been their family's anchor, keeping their boat from drifting away in a vast ocean. Her death had cut them free, and they'd been hapless ever since.

Despite Arianna's attempts at maintaining her poise, the urge to weep had been strong since that awful confrontation with Father. But she had held off, thinking instead of what she must do. Now, with the pitying expression upon Logan's handsome face, she felt all the tentative fortitude within her begin to crack like an old, weakened foundation.

"Pray, don't look at me that way," she said, voice thick with emotion.

He smiled tenderly, her sweet charmer returning to chase the gruff protector away as he gave her fingers, which had been inextricably linked with his for much of the day, a comforting squeeze. "In what way, beautiful?"

"As if you pity me."

He brought her hand to his lips, placing a kiss upon its top. "I told you before, pity ain't what I feel for you." He turned it over, pressing a kiss to her palm, making her wish she were not wearing gloves. "I'm proud of you, in awe of your resilience, humbled by the goodness and selflessness in your heart. You're a far better woman than I am man, and that's for certain."

She didn't feel particularly good just now. She felt wicked and bad. She'd left her father feeling betrayed and her sister hurt and shocked.

"I am hardly good and selfless," she said. "If I were, I would not have done what I did."

He found her bare flesh beneath the glove, at a tender spot on her wrist, and kissed there, too. "You have spent years being a dutiful daughter and sister. The time has come for you to do what pleases you instead of them."

He was being so tender, so sweet. It was almost impossible to believe he was a hardened spy, the same man who had been streaked with another's blood. The harshness of that night had fled his countenance, and it was easy to pretend, as she watched him deliver a nip to her bare flesh, that he was nothing more than a charming beau come to court her instead. If only their lives would have been blessed with such ease, and she could have met him in a ballroom instead of a den of vice. It would have been better for Father, she thought. Better for Juliet, too.

Gently, Logan tugged her glove from her hand, placing it on his thigh. And then his head lowered, and he pressed a kiss to the place where her thumb met her palm.

But would it have been better for me? she wondered as he kissed the vee between her middle and forefinger next. For if she had met Logan Sutton in a ballroom, he would not have been the man she'd fallen in love with, protective and fierce, mysterious and dangerous, seductive and smooth yet also wild and rough, all at once.

"I've failed them," she whispered.

Her confession—the fear that plagued her, the gnawing disappointment in herself—had him glancing up from his ministrations, his auburn brows high, his sensual lips drawn into a thin line. "Your father failed *you*, and your sister is only concerned for herself. It's a bleeding miracle you sacrificed yourself for them so long. They ought to have been kissing your hems instead of chasing you from your home and accusing you of courting scandal."

"I am courting scandal," she pointed out, for they were unmarried, no preparations having been made, and she had nowhere to go.

"We'll marry as soon as we're able." He kissed the tip of her pinky and then surprised her by drawing it into the velvet warmth of his mouth and sucking.

Heat flooded between her thighs, the ever-present need for him clamoring within. "But where shall I go until then?"

He nipped the outer curve of her palm, giving her a grin that melted something in her core. "You'll be in my bed, where you belong."

If he was trying to distract her by wooing her, he was certainly succeeding. There was no other place she longed to be more than back in his bed, their bodies naked and pressed together. How incredible it was to believe such previously unattainable happiness could be hers to seize. Except, marrying her would likely cause him trouble, and she must not forget it.

"But the Guild," she reminded him as much as herself. "What shall you tell them?"

"Let that be my worry." He laced their fingers together again, palm to palm. And then he cupped her nape in his other hand, his touch sure and loving, the caress sending a thrill down her spine. "I'll protect you above all else; you needn't fear. You're mine now, Arianna."

His hazel eyes burned into hers, and she *felt* like his. "And you're mine."

How astounding it felt, to claim this handsome, fierce man as her own.

"Always," he said softly, his head lowering, the warmth of his breath feathering over her lips in the prelude to a kiss. "I've always been yours."

It felt that way as his mouth brushed over hers. It felt as if she had known him forever, as if they had been predestined. She returned his kiss, her fingers curling in his coat. As their lips slanted together, the sadness fell away, making room for the heady blossom of desire. Nothing else mattered, not the future, not the past, not the pain of her father's defection, not Juliet's accusations. There was only the two of them, Arianna and Logan.

His tongue sought entry, and she opened for him, the kiss deepening, the taste of him filling her with fire. She was suddenly desperate for him in a new way. It wasn't just the ache between her thighs, the instinctive need to have him there, inside her, filling her and bringing her to shuddering release. Rather, it was something more. It was love, too.

She had sacrificed herself for her family's sake, and now Logan was sacrificing himself for her. Arianna recognized his selflessness, and she was both humbled and driven by it. She wanted to tell him, but words seemed paltry and ineffectual, incapable of conveying the depth of emotion, the strength of her love and gratitude, too.

She tipped her head back, breaking the kiss, their gazes colliding, his hooded and partially hidden by thick red-brown lashes. How beautiful he was.

"Logan," she said softly, his name and nothing more, a wealth of meaning in her voice and eyes.

He understood what she was asking, for he released her slowly, before plucking her hand from his shoulder. Drawing her fingers to his mouth, he caught the tip of her glove in his teeth and tugged, pulling it free. Yes, that was what she wanted, and he knew it better than she did.

"Lift your skirts," he told her, voice low, steeped in the promise of sin and seduction.

She didn't hesitate, catching the muslin, bringing handfuls to her waist, revealing her stockinged legs and the sturdy nankeen boots she'd donned earlier for walking. He caught her waist in his hands and hauled her into his lap with easy, fluid motions until she was on her knees. The low ceiling of the carriage knocked her bonnet askew, and she reached for the ties, swiftly undoing the ribbons and sending the hat sailing to the floor.

Her hands found purchase on his broad chest, and for a moment, she allowed herself the luxury of absorbing his heat and enjoying the play of muscle beneath her fingers. He shifted her, bringing her into direct contact with the rigid length beneath the placket of his trousers. Arianna could not stifle the moan that rose, nor quell her instinctive reaction as she rocked into him, driving herself against his hard cock.

Their eyes remained connected all the while, the unabashed longing in his making her stomach flutter. No man had ever gazed at her with such undisguised hunger. It was intoxicating, the way he made her feel, the power his desire gave her.

He doffed his own hat, his head falling back against the squabs, a rake in repose, sunlight glinting off the reddish-brown strands of his too-long hair. "Go on, beautiful. Take what you want."

Her need was insistent, but she struggled for control, wanting to savor him in a way she hadn't before. One of her hands fled his chest to cup his cheek, the scratchy abrasion of his whiskers a delight to her senses. She stroked his jaw, then traced the carefully sculpted curves of his upper lip.

He held still all the while, allowing her to explore him as she wished, not uttering a word. She followed the seam bisecting his perfect lips next, then traced the outer edge of the full lower. How wondrous to think he was finally, truly, *hers*.

She stroked his cheek, admiring the harsh angles of the bones beneath his taut skin, the complex dichotomy of a man —equal parts hardness and softness, so it seemed. There was his broad frame, his muscles, the stubborn turn of his jaw, the large hands that sifted through her raised skirts. And yet, his skin and voice were so smooth, his hair and lips silken, his tongue wet velvet as it glided over her.

He found her knees beneath the pooled fabric of her petticoats, gown, and pelisse, then. He swirled in slow, deliberate circles, caressing her with nothing more than the pads of his thumbs as he watched her, that mysterious hazel gaze scorching hers. It was teasing and light, that touch, and yet, it made the throbbing deep inside her quicken.

What a potent freedom, to have his touch whenever she wished it. When she was his wife, they would no longer have to hide in darkness. What a thrilling rush it was now, to see him in the daylight, to have his big body beneath hers as they rode through London, amidst a sea of people, no one the wiser of what was happening within the carriage.

She longed to kiss him quite desperately, and he had told her to take what she wanted. With slow deliberation, she stroked his throat above the collar of his coat and the linen of his simple cravat, absorbing the ripple as he swallowed, feeling the thick cords there, not stopping until she cupped his nape. And then, she lowered her lips to his, accepting his invitation. The kiss was light at first; a whisper of her mouth over his.

He swiftly deepened it, his hands sweeping past her knees, going higher. Beyond the garters holding her stockings in place, skimming over her upper thighs. Ah, *merciful heavens*, the effect those wicked hands had upon her as they moved. They turned her to flame, made her into a wanton.

Upward, they traveled, large and strong and comforting and enticing. Callused hands rasping over sensitive skin until he caught her hip in one hand and the other slipped between her thighs where she ached for him most. *At last.* He rewarded her with a teasing glance up and down her folds as they kissed each other breathless. And then he gave her more. It was electric, the effect of those knowing fingers parting her, slicking her wetness over her eager flesh. He knew just what she wanted, where to tease.

Arianna's tongue tangled with Logan's as his fingers at last brushed over the swollen bud of her sex. It was so right, his lips beneath hers, his touch, fluttering over her bud in tender swipes that made her forget everything but him. Worries and sadness faded.

She rolled her hips into his questing hand, seeking more. The sensation intensified as their kiss deepened, his fingers circling her nub faster and harder as little sparks of pleasure began to shoot through her. She tunneled her fingers through his thick, auburn hair, grasping handfuls as he pleasured and kissed her as if he were every bit as hungry for her as she was for him.

Perhaps it was the upheaval inside her, the need to become mindless, or the time they had spent apart. Whatever the reason, she peaked quickly, crying out into his kiss as the first wave of bliss washed over her. He made a low sound in his throat, as if he was pleased, and then his finger traced her seam, gliding through her wetness to find her entrance. He pressed, and her body accepted him with ease, the digit penetrating her deep.

It was exquisite agony, and she rode his finger, grinding herself down on him as her inner walls still reverberated with the effect of her release. She gasped into the kiss, then moaned when a second finger joined the first, and the wet sounds of him gliding in and out of her body in a fast, frenzied rhythm filled the air.

"Floating hell," he murmured against her lips as his thumb stroked her sensitized pearl while his fingers worked her, "you're so wet and ready."

She gave a needy sigh of agreement, all she could manage as her desire was protracted to dizzying heights. Arianna was mindless as she kissed him, showing him with actions how much she cared. Telling him all the things she could not say with words.

His fingers abruptly withdrew, leaving her panting, an emptiness deep within. She wanted more. Wanted him to make her forget the pain of what had happened earlier, forget the uncertainty awaiting them. Her hips moved, chasing the pleasure only he could bestow.

"Just a moment, love," he crooned against her lips as he gentled the wildness of their kiss. "I'll make it better soon."

And she knew he would, because that was what Logan Sutton did. He made everything better. Her world had been joyless and grim before he had entered it.

He caught her lower lip in his teeth and tugged as he worked to free himself from his trousers. She gasped when the head of him, thick and full, pressed against her entrance.

"Rise up on your knees, love," he urged, brushing his cock up and down her folds.

She scrambled to do as he had asked, lifting her lower body to accommodate him fully. Her cunny pulsed as he slicked his cock through her wetness.

"How does that feel?" he asked, his voice a low rasp that only served to make the ache between her legs grow stronger.

"Good," she managed. "You feel so good against me. But I want you inside me."

"Then take me," he urged. "I'm all yours."

His words spurred her on. She had done this before. She was no novice.

Arianna lowered herself slowly, impaling herself on his thick length. As before, it took her body a moment to grow accustomed to the immense size of him. She inhaled sharply at the brilliant pleasure verging on pain as he stretched her and filled her. She lowered herself the rest of the way, and it was good, so very good, the tip of his cock brushing against an exquisite place.

With his hands on her waist to guide her, she began to move as she had before, finding the rhythm that made them gasp and groan into each other's mouths. She rolled her hips to take him deep, then rose on her knees to allow his cock to slide through her channel. Her eyes fluttered closed as she surrendered to the abyss of pleasure.

"Yes, love," he rasped into their kiss. "Fuck me. Fuck yourself on my cock. Just like that."

His coarse words made her wetter, sending a rush of moisture from her and making her clench on him. It was wicked, being fully clothed and yet having him inside her, those sinful, sculpted lips of his saying filthy things.

His fingers tightened on her waist as she rode him in earnest, taking the pleasure he had told her to seize for her own. Driving all thoughts of past, future, and anything but the present from her mind.

"Look at me," he commanded.

And she obeyed, opening her eyes to lose herself in the heated magnetism of his hazel stare. His handsome face was slack with passion, his eyes glittering, the obsidian discs of his pupils dilated wide.

"My God, you drive me to the edge of madness."

"Yes," she hissed, never stilling in her movements as she rocked on his rigid length, taking all of him and then nearly allowing him to slide free again and again. "You feel so good inside me. So deep."

He was moving with her now, aiding her by thrusting his hips upward, filling her at an angle that had her gasping, liquid pleasure making her very bones feel as if they may melt.

"Spend for me," he said.

It was there, another pinnacle. Within reach. She was going to...she was almost...

Oh.

She rode him harder. Faster. And suddenly, something inside her broke. Her orgasm began low in her belly, a desperate seizing that had her tightening on him as pleasure arced through her. She cried out, her body convulsing as the sweet glow of delirious bliss washed over her.

He rocked into her from below, his lips still chasing hers, feeding her frantic, hungry kisses she could not get enough of, his grip on her waist tightening. "I'm going to come," he murmured into her mouth.

On each other occasion they'd made love, he had not spent inside her. But she didn't want to break this connection. Didn't want their joining to end so abruptly.

"Stay with me," she begged breathlessly, cupping his face. "Don't leave."

She knew what she was asking, understood the risk.

"Fuck," he swore, his voice strained. "You're sure?"

"Come inside me," she said, brushing her lips over his as she continued to ride him in time to the swaying of the carriage.

He gave her what she wanted, throwing his head back against the squabs, the tendons in his neck strained and pronounced above his cravat as he reached his own peak. The hot rush of his seed inside her sent another ripple through Arianna and she rocked on him, her inner walls contracting around his cock as she milked every last drop from him.

Heart pounding, breath ragged, she collapsed against his chest. He was still within her, his own heart beating in a rhythm to match hers beneath her ear. His arms came around her, holding her tight. He pressed a kiss to her temple, and for those few, stolen beats of their hearts in unison, Arianna allowed herself to believe that all would be well.

CHAPTER 16

This interview wasn't going to proceed any better than the one with Arianna's father had. Of that, Logan was bleeding certain. But, having left her at his rooms under the watchful guard of Chapman so that she might see herself settled, he knew he had to do some settling of his own as he slipped on foot through the alleys near the new Guild headquarters.

Namely, he had to relay his failure to Tierney and to inform him of his impending nuptials with Arianna, along with his desire to leave the Guild for good. He would be lucky if Tierney didn't slit his throat.

Or worse, turn him in to Whitehall on suspicion of colluding with traitors to the Crown. But Logan owed it to the Guild and to the woman he loved to have this meeting. He was well aware that Tierney could misconstrue his reasoning in marrying Arianna and leaving the Guild. The timing was damned suspicious, and even he could admit it, knowing his innocence and Arianna's. The decision, sudden.

But how to explain the complexities of it? Logan's booted feet traveled over dirty cobblestones as he approached the printer's shop where Tierney had repositioned the Guild, producing pamphlets in an effort to flush some of the London Reform Society members in hiding from their holes. He'd thought the Guild was his purpose in life. It had given him the meaning, the sense of pride, which had been missing from the role he'd played in his family and at The Sinner's Palace.

But then, he'd met *her*.

And in Arianna, he'd found so much more. He'd found *everything*.

With a heavy sigh, he moved past a narrow alleyway separating the nearby shops. He was so tangled in his thoughts that he failed to hear the flurry of movement behind him until it was too late. Before he could turn to defend himself, there was a hard grip on his arm and the unmistakable barrel of a pistol pressing into his back. Logan froze.

Floating fucking hell!

Was he being robbed by a cutpurse? He wasn't armed save a dagger, secreted within a hidden pocket in his coat. How foolish he'd been to leave his pistol behind, yet another mistake he could ascribe to being too consumed in thoughts of Arianna and facing Tierney. He'd been careless. Reckless.

Stupid.

And now, he would pay the price.

Another hand gripped his other arm.

He reached slowly with his right hand, scarcely moving, thinking he had to get to the blade. To defend himself.

The sound of a conveyance rolling forward, approaching them from behind, filled him with dread. Whoever it was who had his pistol jammed into Logan's back, the bastard intended to force him to go elsewhere. His blood went cold at the thought.

"Get into the carriage, Logan," commanded a familiar voice at his back suddenly. "There ain't any other choice."

He'd recognize that voice in his sleep, for it belonged to his eldest brother, Jasper.

How the devil had he found him here? He jerked his head around, realizing the other iron-hard grip on his arm belonged to another of his brothers, Rafe.

"What the hell are you doing?" he snarled at them, for being kidnapped by his brothers was the last bleeding problem he needed just now. "You're dicked in the bloody nob if you think I'm going anywhere with you."

Jasper and Rafe ignored him, wordlessly forcing Logan toward the carriage. Someone issued a loud whistle, and the carriage door swung open to reveal the hulking Hugh, who leapt down, looming with the beastly strength that rendered him such an asset as a guard at The Sinner's Palace.

"Christ, not Hugh," he muttered as the giant of a man seized him in his unrelenting grip as well.

He attempted to leverage an elbow into Hugh's ribs, but it was no bleeding use. He struggled, to hell with the pistol—he knew Jasper wouldn't shoot him. The weapon had been a prop, meant for shocking him. But no matter how hard he struggled, his boots were sliding on the uneven stones as he was pushed and pulled into the gaping door of the carriage. Logan fought, kicking, tripping, headbutting Hugh in the nose.

But though his attempts resulted in a satisfying crack as his skull connected with Hugh's beak, Logan still found himself unceremoniously hauled into the waiting vehicle. The four of them fell in a heap as the door slammed closed, a whip cracked, and the carriage jolted down the road.

∾

Gervase Somerville, Viscount Inglesby, was a desperate man.

In the grim shadows of his study, nothing but a lone, flickering taper to light the darkness, he composed a missive in shaky scrawl. It was the last letter he had wished to write, having hoped he was done with this wretched business at last, escaping with his life intact. But there was no hope for it now. He hadn't a choice. Arianna was going to lead them all beyond the cliffs of ruin and straight into the pits of fiery hell.

Curse his hand, trembling from the need of more spirits. Barrel fever, some called it. A sickness. And mayhap it was. No different than an ague, and most definitely a plague. But losing his wife, Elizabeth, had been a terrible blow. Since her death, he'd needed a way to numb the pain. No one understood the hollow emptiness inside, the void which could never again be filled. Not Arianna. Not Juliet. Not anyone.

He had begun with wine, but that hadn't proved sufficient. Stronger spirits had proven a boon. Brandy, gin, anything he could find. A bit in the morning when he woke. Then more to get him through the day, as often as necessary, and another dram to sleep. Until it had become two drams, then three, then ten, and still, he required more to keep the memories at bay.

He hadn't had a drop of brandy since the drawing room, when Arianna and Mr. Martin had announced their intention to marry. The horror of it coursed through him now as he struggled to review the cipher key for his message: a man from the Guild, wedding Gervase's own daughter. If word reached the Society members before he could inform them himself, his involvement with the Guild would be more than apparent to all. He was already suspected, for he was one of a council of less than five who had been aware of the hiding place where Charles and Clifford Mace had retreated following their attempt on the Tower.

He needed that brandy now. Felt the lack as an ache in his

bones. His palms were sweating, his guts churning with nausea. Soon, he would have a drink and soothe his ragged nerves. He would drink to forget.

Drink so that he would not be forced to think about his daughter whoring herself to a lowborn Guildsman. So that he would not have to worry about what would become of him if he failed to settle his debts. So that he would not be haunted by the betrayals he had committed.

Once, he'd believed in the Society's cause.

He'd been younger and idealistic. He hadn't been broken by life. But there was no place for causes now. He had debts. Needs. Daughters dependent upon him.

Only one daughter beneath his roof soon.

Bless sweet, biddable Juliet. He'd always thought Arianna was the most responsible daughter. She'd done her duty in her first marriage, and again in returning to his household as a widow and aiding him by securing the rewards being offered by Whitehall. She'd never questioned him, never exhibited such insolence and brazen daring, until he'd sent her to meet with the Guild.

It was all because of that damned whoreson Mr. Martin. And if anyone was going to pay the price, it was going to be that devil instead of Gervase. How dare the scoundrel take advantage of Arianna? And to sit there, as a guest in Gervase's own drawing room, and speak with such unguarded boldness, nary a care for his station…why, it had been an outrage upon a betrayal of the worst order.

Arianna had been a dutiful daughter. She'd been the distance he needed between himself and the Guild so that he could safely collect the blunt being offered by Whitehall. Without her…

Without her, he was doomed to resort to attempts to recoup his losses at the tables.

And because of her, they were all in desperate danger.

Dimly, he realized he'd been staring at the cipher key for so long, mired in his troubled thoughts, that the ink on his quill had dried. His hand shook as he dipped his nib into the well with such violence, he sent it spilling across his desk.

Cursing, Gervase shot to his feet, frantically fumbling for a handkerchief from within his coat. He found it at last, pulling the crumpled square of linen free and using it to blot up the spreading midnight stain.

Blast Arianna for putting them in such a precarious position.

And blast Logan Martin for the role he'd played.

Perhaps a drink to settle himself was necessary after all.

Leaving the soaked handkerchief, he walked unsteadily to the sideboard, palms damp with sweat now. Yes, a drink was all he required.

After that, he would finish the missive's code and send it on its way, praying it would find Charles Mace before it was too late.

Logan glared at his brothers Jasper and Rafe.

He'd spent far too much time lingering within the familiar confines of The Sinner's Palace's office, staring down the barrel of his eldest brother's pistol and deflecting questions he couldn't bleeding answer.

"You may as well stop pretending you're going to plump me with that gun," he told Jasper.

Whilst there was a chasm separating them now, born of his defection from the family, he didn't harbor any doubts that he was safe. Suttons protected their own. And he was still a Sutton, even if he went by the name Martin now.

Jasper raised a dark brow, his countenance hard and unyielding. "Who says I'm pretending?"

"After the way you disappeared and left us thinking you'd gone to Rothisbones for all this time, you'd bloody well deserve it," Rafe added.

With a head of blond curls that fell in ringlets that had always driven the morts to distraction, Rafe was one of the rakes in the family, along with Jasper. But although they'd never had troubles charming the ladies out of their petticoats, they had no qualms about exacting punishment from anyone deserving. He'd seen Rafe and Jasper draw blood on many occasions.

"Shoot me and be done with it then," he invited, testing them both.

He'd yet to spy any of his sisters. He hoped to God they weren't involved in this recklessness. And as for his other brothers, Wolf and Hart, they were also mysteriously absent.

"We don't want to cause you any 'arm and you know it," Jasper relented. "We want a patter with you, that's all. You've been gone for more than a year, nary a word of why you'd gone or where. You owe us an explanation, curse you."

Logan loved his siblings. Being with them now, even if they were at odds, reminded him just how much. How deep their love ran, how strong their bonds. Their sire had been a worthless tosspot who'd never given a goddamn about any of them. But together, they had survived, looking after each other, working to build something from nothing. Being beneath The Sinner's Palace roof once again was an eerie homecoming, memories haunting its halls. Happy memories.

God, he missed his family.

They were marrying, finding love.

And so was he. So much had changed in his absence. He wondered what else he had missed, and then he told himself it didn't matter. He couldn't allow them close to him. Not until he was out of the Guild for good. He wouldn't bring danger to their door.

"Well," Jasper prompted. "Nothing to say, brother?"

"Tell us what Tierney's about," Rafe added, his tone gentling a bit. "We fear he ain't up to any good, that you've involved yourself in something dangerous."

They weren't wrong about that. But it wasn't his place to make revelations that would lead them into more peril than they'd already invited by repeatedly tangling with Tierney. First Hart, now Jasper and Rafe. Logan knew he had to put an end to their attempts. Had to make it clear to them, beyond a doubt, that he had no intention of remaining here and confessing.

"I don't need your concerns," he told his brothers. "Feast your peepers on me. Ain't a thing wrong with me. Where's all the danger you speak of?"

He knew where the danger lurked, or at least some of it. Other dangers still remained hidden. Bad enough that Arianna had become entangled in them because of her arsehole father. He couldn't alter what had already come to pass, but he wouldn't also involve his siblings.

"There's danger enough to keep you and Tierney moving," Jasper observed shrewdly. "We came looking for you at Tierney's moneylending business, and you were gone. Slipped through the men I had watching the place somehow. Now you've set up shop at a printer's. What the devil is afoot?"

The news that Jasper had employed men to watch their former headquarters shouldn't come as a shock; they'd known they were being watched. But they hadn't known who was behind it. His siblings were more stubborn and determined than he'd reckoned. He had to convince them to sever ties. To stop looking for him. To stop asking bleeding questions. At least until he had safely extricated himself from the Guild and married Arianna. Too much was at stake, and he wasn't at liberty to explain.

"It's none of your concern," he told his brothers. "I left for a reason. I don't want any part of this place or this family. I don't belong 'ere, and I never did. If it wasn't obvious before, it ought to be now. Leave me the bleeding hell alone."

He was being harsh. Cruel.

But he had to be. What other choice had he? None.

Jasper and Rafe looked as if he'd struck them.

And Christ, but that expression on their faces—the anguish, the betrayal—would never leave him, not in all his days. He knew it. When he'd taken an oath of allegiance to the Guild, he hadn't understood just what it would cost him. He could only hope that one day, his siblings would forgive him and welcome him back into their lives.

"You want no part of us?" Jasper asked hoarsely.

They'd been going in circles for what seemed an eternity. He had to get out of The Sinner's Palace. Needed to get back to Arianna.

"None," he said coldly. "The Suttons are dead to me."

CHAPTER 17

"Saved my life, Mr. Martin did," Mr. Chapman was telling Arianna as they shared tea and a small repast of cheese and bread. A simple meal, and one she had fixed on her own, grateful for a task to occupy her hands and mind.

Because she was worried.

Logan had been gone for hours now.

She replaced her teacup in its chipped saucer, Logan's trusted aide's words only serving to make the knot in her belly tighten further. "When did he have cause to save your life?"

The older man shook his head. "Can't tell you, my lady. But suffice it to say I'd be a dustman by now if it weren't for 'im."

"A dustman?" she inquired, unfamiliar with the term.

"Dead," Mr. Chapman elaborated succinctly. "Blade of a knife stuck between my ribs."

Misgiving tightened around her, sinuous and strong as a vine. She didn't like to think of the danger Logan had faced before she'd known him, nor the danger he might possibly face yet. Danger which could be keeping him away from her.

You must think of something else, she reminded herself sternly for what must have been the hundredth time since Logan's absence had stretched into the evening hours and the night had grown dark.

She'd busied herself by becoming familiar with his small, spartan rooms first. And then by tidying everything in need: a small line of books he had on a table at his bedside, chasing the dust from surfaces, and even straightening his bedclothes which had been drawn haphazardly, as if he'd left his bed in a hurry that morning.

Finally, when there was seemingly nothing else for her to accomplish, she'd sought refuge in the company of Mr. Chapman. He was a quiet man of serious nature, but it was apparent he admired Logan greatly.

"You'll not find a better man," he had confided in her as she'd prepared the water for their tea.

"I know," she had returned, a wealth of meaning in those two words.

She took a sip from her tea now, hoping it would soothe her unsettled stomach.

"Reckon I shouldn't 'ave said that," Mr. Chapman said into the silence, regret coloring his voice. "Mr. Martin wouldn't wish me to speak so plainly to 'is woman."

Logan's woman.

How she liked the way that acknowledgment made her feel, cutting through the worry, reminding her that he had promised he would return to her. That he would protect her now. That she was his, forever. Strange, perhaps, but she felt more at home in these humble rooms than she ever had in either her husband's home or her father's.

She gave Mr. Chapman a reassuring smile. "You needn't

worry about speaking plainly with me. 'Tis honesty that I prefer."

"I'm not accustomed to ladies," her companion said, breaking off a hunk of bread and taking an impolite bite that spoke far more to hunger than table manners. "Begging your pardon for my wayward tongue. I never did learn to hold it when I ought. And I reckon I'm too old to learn the way of it now."

"You paid me no insult," she said quietly, casting a glance toward the darkened window, wondering where Logan was, when he would return. "I am thankful to you for keeping me company."

"You're worried," Mr. Chapman guessed.

She sighed, turning her gaze back to him. Years and the elements had weathered his countenance, carving grooves into his forehead. Like Logan, his speech was rough. Perhaps more so, even. She would wager they hailed from similar parts of East London. Was that the nature of their bond, that they came from the same place? Or was it the Guild? Or something more, yet? She wondered if Mr. Chapman was someone Logan had known before; he'd mentioned that his family thought him dead, but he'd said nothing of anyone else.

"He has been gone for hours," she admitted, rubbing her arms through the sleeves of her gown, for they had grown cold despite the cheerful fire crackling in the nearby hearth. "I fear for him."

"Ah, my dear. You're in love with him, are you not?"

Mr. Chapman's shrewd observation shocked her. She hadn't supposed she was revealing the true nature of her feelings with such ease. But then, she'd never been in love before. She didn't know what it looked like or felt like. She only knew that from the moment Logan had come into her life, she'd felt a deep and abiding connection to him that only grew stronger with each passing day.

"Your secret's safe with me," Mr. Chapman added when she failed to respond, his wizened face softening. "You'll tell the lad when you're ready. But you needn't fret. It's plain as the nose on my face that he's in love with you, too."

Her foolish heart leapt at the notion.

She took another careful sip of her tea. "What makes you think so?"

"The way the lad looks at you," he explained.

She knew what Mr. Chapman meant, for she had seen the tenderness in Logan's gaze as often as she had seen the heated fires of desire. But was tenderness love? And if not, might it not *grow* into love, much like a seed taking root in the soil, requiring rain and the warmth of the sun before it sprouted?

She could be his rain. She could be his sun. Whatever he needed.

"No one has ever looked at me the way he does," she confessed to Mr. Chapman.

The older man nodded. "You'll make an excellent wife for the lad."

They'd not spoken of when they would marry yet; Logan had rushed to the Guild with the news before they could plan further.

Mr. Chapman chuckled, evidently spying her surprise as much as he did her feelings for Logan. He tore another hunk of bread off with his meaty paw. "Aye, I know the way of it. I was young once too, and arsy-varsy in love."

"What happened?" Arianna asked, for he'd not mentioned a wife.

"She married another cove," Mr. Chapman said ruefully. "Mary's father disapproved. Wanted her to marry a baker instead, and so she did."

Sadness washed over her at the revelation. "Oh, Mr. Chapman. You must have been brokenhearted."

He waved a hand. "It's in the past where it belongs. But I learned my lesson, my lady. When you love someone enough, don't surrender. You don't want to look back one day and wonder what would've been if you'd only fought a bit 'arder."

Don't surrender. It was excellent advice. She'd certainly been guilty of surrendering in the past, and far more than she cared to admit. If she were honest with herself, she had almost lost Logan because of it.

The door rattled, interrupting the companionable stillness that had fallen, and suddenly, Logan stepped over the threshold, looking weary, his countenance unsmiling.

But here, *thank heavens*.

He was safe.

She was on her feet and flying to him with no awareness of having moved, so instinctive was her reaction. He caught her in his arms, burying his face in her upswept hair and inhaling deeply, as if to fill his lungs with her scent.

"You're back," she said, fighting the sting of tears that had never been far since that damning meeting with her father.

"Aye," he said simply, his strength and warmth surrounding her, his breath falling hotly over her ear now.

She was dimly aware of the scrape of Mr. Chapman's chair as he rose from the small table where they'd been sharing their meal.

"I'll be leaving the two of you alone," he said quietly.

She partially withdrew from Logan's embrace, meeting the older man's gaze. "Thank you for sharing tea and some wisdom with me, Mr. Chapman."

He offered a bow. "'Twas a pleasure, my lady."

"And thank you for looking after her," Logan added, keeping an arm banded around Arianna's waist as if he feared she would disappear if he released her.

Another nod, and Chapman took his leave of them, retiring to his own rooms. When he was gone, she turned back to Logan, searching his expression for a hint of how his meeting with the Guild had gone.

"Have you news?" she asked.

He cupped her cheek, his stare intense and mysterious, gray more than any other hue in this low light. "Aye."

His thumb, callused and cool, stroked her cheek. He seemed preoccupied, as if a heavy weight were atop his shoulders.

"Did it not go well, then?" she guessed, biting her lip to steel herself against a hollow rush of anxiety.

"We'll be married as planned." His other hand flattened on the small of her back, drawing her neatly against him. "If you still wish it?"

"Of course it's what I wish." Her palms settled on his chest, finding his greatcoat damp and cool, the body it shielded firm and well-muscled beneath. "But what of the Guild? Will there be repercussions for you?"

The knowledge that there very well could be had contributed to the ever-tightening coil of worry within her. It was enough that Logan was sacrificing himself to save her from her father's problems. But to think he could be punished, or worse...

"There are always repercussions for every choice in life, are there not?" he asked softly, stroking her jaw now, his expression still unreadable. "The true question is whether or not they're worth it."

She swallowed hard, wondering how it was possible for him to seduce her while her stomach remained in knots and she'd yet to have a proper answer from him. His hand caressed down her throat, the touch so gentle, the barest whisper against her skin, and yet, how quickly he set her aflame.

Arianna's fingers dug into his coat, clutching it tightly. "Are they?"

"For you, beautiful?" His hot stare devoured her face, lingering on her lips. "Always."

She tugged at his coat, wishing it gone, wishing all the layers separating them banished. "You must tell me what they are. I won't have you suffering for my sake."

His thumb flirted with the hollow at the base of her throat, toying with the strands of pearls she'd had the presence of mind to fasten about her neck earlier before fleeing her father's town house. "You wear this often."

Still, he had not answered her question. The maddening brush of his thumb over her tender flesh made her pulse pound harder and longing unfurl like a blossom. Her nipples were already tightened into aching points beneath her stays, all from nothing more than his sleek caresses and the feeling of his big body against hers.

"The necklace belonged to my mother."

"You didn't allow your father to pawn it," he noted grimly.

"No," she said, hardly surprised Logan had spied all the missing furniture, pictures, and other pieces at her father's town house. "I suppose I would have done, if it had come to that. But I would have sooner sold off everything else of value I possessed. This is all I have to remember her by."

And it wasn't the necklace that was important, but what it signified. That lasting connection. When she clasped the pearls about her throat, she thought of Mother and happier times. Of singing together at the pianoforte, of her mother's endless patience and kindness, of her laughter and grace. Of all the years she had been blessed enough to know her.

"I'm glad you saved it," he said softly, trailing his touch over the strands until he cupped her nape, his long fingers sinking into her hair as the hand on her back glided up and down in a steady, mesmerizing caress. "And I'm damned sorry about everything earlier, with your father."

"He has destroyed himself in his grief." She had known it for some time; her every action had been to mitigate his fall. To keep the three of them somehow afloat in a storm-tossed sea of ruin. "But you still haven't spoken of how your interview with the Guild proceeded. Will you not tell me?"

He sighed, the sound heavy, and lowered his head, pressing his forehead to hers for a moment. "Not particularly well, love. For now, I'm to continue on until Mace is captured. But I've made it plain we're wedding as soon as we're able. There's nothing the Guild or anyone else can do to stop us."

She didn't like the edge to his voice. Arianna suspected there was a great deal of information he was withholding from her. Whether it was out of duty or a wish to protect her, or perhaps even both, she couldn't say.

"Will you be punished?" she pressed, needing to know.

He kissed her cheek. "You needn't worry."

Once again, it was not a response.

She reached for his face, forcing him to lift his head before he would further seduce her. "But I do worry. I worry for you, Logan. I'll not have any harm come to you because of me."

She had hoped he would be free of the Guild after today, no longer mired in the dangerous work of capturing enemies of the Crown. But it would seem they were not to be so fortunate. And if, in marrying her, he would only create more problems for himself, then what he must do was as dreaded as it was obvious.

He couldn't marry her.

But as quickly as the realization hit her, she thought of Mr. Chapman's words. *Don't surrender.* They could wait if they had to, at least until Mace was captured.

"You worry too much," Logan told her, but there was no bite in his words.

"You shouldn't wed," she said on a rush. "Not like this, not if it is going to make you the cause of doubt or worse. After Mace is caught, we can marry."

"No." Logan shook his head, his jaw hardening. "I'll not wait to make you my wife. Everyone else can go to the devil. You'll be better protected from this entire affair if we're married."

Her breath caught as she searched his expression. "Does the Guild consider me suspect?"

His silence spoke volumes.

She pushed away from him, spinning to pace toward the fireplace and the abandoned table with its half-eaten repast and cooling tea. The Guild believed her guilty of colluding with the London Reform Society. Why had it never occurred to her before now that she might arise suspicions with the secrets she had sold on her father's behalf? Had it been willful foolishness? Had it been merely because she was secured in the knowledge of her own innocence?

"Arianna." Logan's touch on her elbow had her turning to face him, eyes now swimming with unshed tears.

"I am guilty only of trusting my father and attempting to help him," she said, heart pounding. "You believe me, don't you?"

"Damn it, love." He reached for her, twining their hands together, pulling her into him. "How could you doubt it? Of course I believe you."

"But they don't." She tried to withdraw from his grasp, but he held firm. "You cannot marry me, Logan. Not like this. Not if the doubt cast upon me will affect you as well."

"Yes, I can, and I will." He brought her hand over his chest, pressing it above his heart, which thrummed steadily beneath his greatcoat. "Do you feel this?"

She swallowed hard, blinking at the stubborn tears. "Your heart."

"It's yours," he said softly, reaching for her, cupping her face as tenderly as if she were fashioned of the finest crystal. "It beats for you."

Her own heart thudded harder, her breath arresting in her lungs. "What are you saying?"

"I'm saying that you have my heart, beautiful." He kissed the corner of her lips, then across her jaw, not stopping until he'd reached her ear. "I love you."

The last was a hushed, heated whisper, his lips grazing her as he spoke. Her other hand, not anchored firmly upon his heart, fluttered like a butterfly which was hesitant to land. She didn't know where to touch him. Her knees went inexplicably weak, and had not his arm slid around her waist again, she likely would have spilled to the floor.

At last, her hand found purchase on his broad shoulder. "You love me?"

"Aye." He caught her earlobe in his teeth in a nip that sent pure, molten heat between her legs. "I love you. So you see, I must marry you. There ain't any other choice."

"But you—"

"Hush," he whispered, tracing the whorl of her ear with his tongue. "No more protests. We'll get a common license on the morrow. In a week, you'll be Mrs. Logan Sutton."

Sutton. His true name. She liked the way it sounded. Liked the way it made her feel, deep inside, that sense of rightness, as if all the jagged pieces of her had smoothed, fitting together at last.

"I don't want to cause any more trouble for you than I already have," she protested anyway, fingers curling into his coat.

His hand over hers no longer bore the coolness of the

night, but instead had warmed from the contact of their skins. His heat burned into her, the weight comforting, reassuring, *beloved*.

"The only trouble you'll cause me is denying me." His lips traveled lower, moving over her throat, finding the sensitive cord of her neck and nibbling until she shivered and pressed herself shamelessly into his tall form.

He was making it impossible for her to think. And perhaps that was his intent, to so thoroughly woo her that her only thoughts were of his next touch or kiss. If so, he was succeeding admirably. She surrendered to her own desires, giving in to the urge to kiss his whisker-stubbled cheek, then his ear. Love for him burst open inside her, mingling with the need, and suddenly, she was mindless.

~

LOGAN SUCKED on the creamy flesh of Arianna's throat, just above the strands of pearls that were so precious to her. With her in his arms, all the worry and frustrations of the last few hours melted away, replaced by the resounding need to be inside her. The sweet scent of violets invaded his senses, and her soft, pliant body fit so perfectly against him. Nothing and no one was going to keep him from making her his wife. Not even her, if need be. He'd protect her from herself and her own foolish altruism.

She was determined to sacrifice herself for his sake, and he wasn't going to allow it. Arianna had placed everyone in her life before herself, but that ended now. He would be the one to place her first. It hadn't gone well with Tierney, not at all, and he knew he was treading the thinnest, most precarious of ice. One false step, and he'd fall through the surface to drown.

But none of that mattered.

Nothing mattered more than her. Keeping her safe. Making her his wife. And he intended to do just that. Even if it meant seducing her to keep her from thinking of all the reasons why they shouldn't marry.

Who was he fooling? Seducing her was hardly selfless. Ever since he'd left the unhappy meeting with Tierney, who'd been in a foul mood after having detained his brothers Wolf and Hart—Logan had been able to think of nothing other than returning to her. Nothing more than this, having her within reach. Not having to make love beneath the cover of darkness, only to part before dawn.

Arianna in his bed. In his arms.

When her lips glanced over his cheek in a sweet, tender kiss, the breath fled him, the rush of need for her so fervent and strong that his cockstand was instant. He made no secret of it, smoothing his palm from the small of her back to her rump. He gently squeezed, grinding her against his erection.

Her head fell back on a gasp, and he raked his teeth along her throat, some primitive part of him hoping he'd leave a mark for all to see she was his.

"Logan," she said, his name a throaty plea that made him harder still.

He was wearing too many bleeding layers. Why were they not naked and entwined in his bed? Why were they standing here before the fire and the remnants of the meal she'd taken with Chapman? Why was his head not between her thighs, his tongue on her cunny?

"I want to take you to bed," he murmured, working his way back to her ear.

"But...have you eaten?" she asked, moaning when he licked the hollow behind it.

"I want to eat you," he told her wickedly.

"*Oh.*"

A world of meaning in that lone sigh. She didn't protest. He wouldn't have allowed it anyway. He was ravenous indeed, but it bleeding well wasn't for bread and cheese. It was for her.

"Yes, oh," he said darkly, nuzzling her throat before lifting his head to gaze down at the sight of her, lips parted, eyes glazed now with passion instead of the sadness that had cut him to the marrow when he had first returned. "Now."

Logan released her and tore at his greatcoat, dropping it heedlessly to the floor. He toed off his boots next, holding her gaze. His bedroom was ten paces away, but it may as well have been on the moon. He wanted her with a sudden need that threatened to tear him in two.

"Logan," she said, a hint of censure in her breathless voice. "You cannot disrobe here."

He raised a brow. "Aye, I can."

He thought she would counter him, that she would be scandalized. But although it was a trifle uncivilized to strip one's self bare in the midst of a main room, no one would see save the two of them. Chapman would know better than to return now, barring a fire or a murder. And Logan wanted her so much that he was reasonably sure neither flame nor death would keep him from bedding Arianna this night.

He shrugged out of his coat and then reached for the knot of his simply tied neck cloth. He'd intended to look the part of a trustworthy cove today, not quite elegant but not the back-alley spy who stole through the nights, either. Now, he found himself wearing far too many trappings of civility. His bleeding waistcoat would be better served pitched into the fire.

Arianna didn't shy away, however. Nor did she look away with missish indignation. Instead, her honey-brown gaze remained intent and bold, burning into his. Here was the same commanding, elegant woman who had so entranced him at Willowby's, only different. Because now, she was his.

Logan's fingers—turned dumb by her regard—tangled in the knot, unable to loosen it. And then, there was the calm brush of her small, dainty hands shooing his clumsy, great paws away.

"Let me," she said.

She could have said *follow me to hell*, and he would have obeyed just the same. His hands fell to his sides, unnecessary encumbrances, and her clever fingers made short, wifely work of undoing the cravat. She slid it from his neck, the linen a rasp over skin made sensitive by her nearness. Every part of him burned for her.

When she'd finished with her task, she remained, her fingers next moving over the buttons of his waistcoat, plucking them free one by one. He longed to reach for her, but another part of him wanted to hold still, to allow her free rein over him. So much of her life had been decided by others or for others. He wanted their lovemaking to always be mutual. To give as much as he took. For her to seize the pleasure and respect she'd forever deserved and yet had never been given.

"I thought it wasn't done to disrobe here," he couldn't resist teasing.

She paused in her ministrations, and he could have kicked himself in the arse. "You are correct. It most certainly isn't."

And then, she belied her words by stripping the waistcoat from his shoulders. It, too, dropped to the floor with a dull sound, falling atop the rapidly growing pile of discarded garments. Her fingers moved to the line of three buttons at the neck of his shirt, pulling each one from its mooring. He called his hands to life again and obliged her by grasping his shirt and hefting it over his head in one swift motion.

He stood before her bare-chested, clad in only his trousers. But she remained politely swathed in far too much cloth. Petticoats, stays, and a gown kept them apart. She caressed his chest and he forgot about the barriers. *Hell*, he even forgot his own bleeding name for a moment.

Remaining still for her required all the control he possessed. So delicate, that touch, tracing over his clavicle to his shoulders, following the muscles of his upper arms, then upward again. She was undoing him, this woman, these sweet, tentative strokes of hers all but bringing him to his knees.

As before, the seducer had become the seduced. The power she had over him was infinite. He knew then that he would do anything for her, anything to keep her at his side. He would betray his vows to the Guild. Choose her over his allegiance to aught else.

"You call me beautiful," she said softly, "but you're the one who is beautiful. I never knew a man could be so tempting."

He was damned glad she hadn't, but he kept that thought to himself. Selfishly glad for himself that her husband had been a blockhead and a fool who hadn't realized the utter gem he'd had in this woman. She was fierce, loyal, loving, sensual, and bold.

Lovely, too.

He cleared his throat against the stinging tide of emotion. "'Tis you who is temptation incarnate, love."

Particularly when her wandering hands traveled down his chest, to his abdomen. His breath caught. And then, lower still, one of her hands catching the waistband of his trousers, her fingers hooking over it, her other skating down his falls.

She palmed his cock, and he couldn't quell the hiss of longing that emerged. "I want you inside me."

No sweeter words were to be heard in the English language than these, uttered in her silken, dulcet voice. He caught her hand in his and pulled her into his bedroom, grateful for the candles left burning within so that he might yet see her. He guided her to the bed and stopped, using their linked hands to spin her in a semicircle so that her back faced him.

"My turn," he said, finding the tapes keeping her gown in place with ease.

Although the need to bed her was roaring through him, he was absurdly pleased to take his time, admiring her as she had done to him. He kissed her nape, gratified by her shiver, then divested her petticoats with ease. Logan took a moment to admire the graceful line of her neck, the gentle curve where it met her softly sloped shoulders, the bountiful curve of her waist beneath the short stays she wore.

Sentiment hit him with a rush, lust and deep emotion colliding. Logan drew her against him, knowing she could feel the hard ridge of his cock rising to rude attention, burrowing into her rump. He caught her waist, allowing his palms to glide over her midriff until his hands splayed over the softness of her belly below her busk, and he buried his face in the sweet-scented crown of her hair.

"God, how I love you," he said again, unable to keep the words from her, even if she hadn't returned them.

She'd been neglected in her marriage, mistreated by her father. He couldn't expect her to entrust her heart to him with such ease. Anyone in her place would be wary.

But then, the most miraculous of things happened. One of her hands crept atop his, and her head rolled onto his shoulder, her other arm reaching behind him to clasp his nape.

"I love you too, Logan," she said, and she brought his mouth to hers.

The kiss and the declaration took his breath. Both were more than he expected. More than he deserved. But he was greedy and selfish when it came to this woman, so he drank up her kiss, and those wondrous words sank into his heart, and he intended to keep them there until the day he kicked the damned bucket.

He licked into her mouth, unable to resist, and their tongues tangled and played. She tasted of tea and sugar and everything he desired. Her hunger matched his, her breathy sounds of need proving his undoing. He ended the kiss before it could carry on for too long, reminded of the rest of her garments which needed shedding.

"I need you naked," he told her. "Now."

"Yes," she said, her voice throaty with longing.

Fucking hell, her open, unabashed desire for him made him bleeding *wild* for her.

No more slow seduction now. He forced himself to take one step in retreat. Hands trembling with combined need and longing, he undid the ties on her stays, then unlaced her. Together, they pulled the undergarment from her body, and then she turned back to him, clad in nothing but chemise and stockings.

They slammed together, their minds united in their mutual need, her hands working at his trousers and his hauling her chemise over her head. When he was naked, he took great delight in falling to his knees before her and removing her garters and stockings, kissing each newly bared swath of flesh until they were both overcome, and they fell into the bed together, a tangled twist of limbs and sinuously writhing bodies.

He sucked her nipples and then moved down her body, using his shoulders to wedge her thighs apart and keep her open for him. She was flushed with desire, pretty and pink, the sweet musk of her cunny making his mouth water. He kissed her folds, and her fingers slipped into his hair, her body undulating in welcome beneath his mouth. He knew what she liked, and he gave it to her. Long, steady licks alternating with hard sucks of her swollen pearl. He lashed her with his tongue, claiming her with his mouth as he would soon with his aching cock.

He knew she was close, the way she tugged at his hair and the gasping sounds above goading him on. When he plunged two fingers into her hot, slick channel, she twisted and stiffened, crying out her release as her cunny clamped on him. He stayed with her, gentling his licks and sucks until he felt he'd wrung every drop of pleasure from her body.

But when he rose, she stopped him, clutching his biceps. "Wait. My turn."

Christ, she was using his own words against him. He'd made a monster. A beautiful, greedy, passionate monster. One who was urging him to his back. He obliged her, thinking she would ride him.

Until she rained kisses over his chest, then lower, following the trail of hair that led directly to his straining cock.

"You don't have to...*fuck*."

His words of protest died a swift death when Arianna kissed the head of his cock. She cast a shy glance up at him. "Does this not please you?"

"Aye, it pleases me," he bit out. "It pleases me greatly."

"I want to give you pleasure as you've given me," she said, delivering another small, chaste kiss to his shaft. "Tell me what to do."

He'd never instructed a woman on how to suck his cock before, and the notion of guiding Arianna made him harder than iron.

Logan rolled his hips, scarcely able to keep his restraint intact. "Take me in your mouth."

She did, the dark-red lips that haunted his dreams eagerly wrapping around his cock. He groaned, telling himself he had to last. But it was so good, the velvet warmth of her mouth, the moist heat.

"Suck," he told her.

And she did that, too. He almost howled like a mongrel at the suction, tentative at first, and then stronger as she grew accustomed to the act. She moaned, taking him deeper, and he feared his head would explode. He wondered if having his cock in her mouth made her cunny wetter still, and then cursed himself for the rogue thought, for it made his ballocks tighten with the need to spend.

Only, he didn't want to spend down her throat, enticing though the notion was. He wanted to spend inside her. To fuck her hard and deep and fill her with his seed as he'd done in the carriage.

She had warmed to her task, using her tongue on the sensitive underside of his cock, then taking him back into the wicked recesses of her sinful mouth. But if she didn't stop, he was going to come.

"Enough," he ground out, reaching for her arms and pulling her atop him.

She settled astride him, her cunny mere inches from his rampaging cockstand, her lips swollen and glistening, but there was a frown marring her expression. "Did you not like it?"

"I bleeding loved it, beautiful," he rasped, finding her hips. "Too much. But tonight, I want to come inside your sweet cunny, not inside your mouth."

"Oh," she said, and even in the low candlelight, he spied a pink flush tingeing her aristocratic cheekbones.

She may be a widow, but Arianna was still very much an innocent. He looked forward to corrupting her. *Thoroughly.*

It hit him then with the force of a blow, the realization

that he had a lifetime to love this woman. A lifetime to earn her kisses and sighs. A lifetime to be her champion, to hold her close, to be her defender and her greatest admirer. How incredibly humbling.

"Is something amiss?" she asked, still astride him, the glory of her sex poised tantalizingly near to his leaking cock. "You look so serious."

"Everything is right," he told her. Too right, but he didn't say that aloud, for he had no wish to give in to the fear on the edge of his mind. The fear that this was too perfect, too wondrous. Instead, he tightened his grip on her hips. "Now ride me, love."

He didn't have to tell her twice. She sank down on his cock, taking him deep in one swift motion. The fit was snug, the hot, wet grip of her cunny so damned good. This was where he belonged, inside her.

"You feel so perfect," she said, her hands settling on his chest as she began fucking him in earnest.

He was mesmerized by the sway of her full, creamy breasts, her hard nipples begging for his mouth as she moved. His hungry gaze traveled lower, to where their bodies were joined and he watched the glide of his glistening cock in and out of her pretty cunny. He caressed her hips, then palmed her breasts, leaning up to catch the tip of one in his mouth and give it a good, hard suck.

Arianna moaned and clenched on him.

She liked that, his wicked little wanton wife. Not wife yet, he corrected himself, but soon. It was as good as done. And that word, the possession implicit, *wife*, made him wild.

He released her nipple with a lusty sound. "Mine," he growled against the curve of her breast as he matched her thrusts with unrestrained rolls of his own hips. Fucking her as hard as he could, sinking as deep inside her welcoming wetness as possible.

"Yes," she whispered, a hushed sound, almost like a prayer. "I'm yours."

Too much, those words. Yet still not enough. He suckled her other nipple and then rolled them as one, his cock still filling her, as he leveraged himself on his forearms to keep from crushing her with his weight.

"My turn," he said again, repeating the game they were playing, giving each other pleasure, taking control and then relinquishing it, only to seize it once more.

She cupped his face in her hands, the gesture so loving that something shifted inside his chest, making his throat constrict. For a moment, he forgot the need to move and held still beneath those gentle touches, her tracing the lines of his face as if he were the work of some master's brush rather than a lowly born rookeries rat.

"Kiss me," she commanded.

And he obeyed, sealing his lips over hers, feeding her the taste of her on his tongue—musky and delicious and sweeter than honey. Her hands roamed, leaving his face, finding his shoulders, her nails scoring his flesh as she arched into him, their tongues sliding sinuously together. And then, he couldn't do anything but surrender to the will to fuck her. In and out, he thrust, filling then withdrawing, her cunny clinging to him, his cock coated in her dew.

Again and again and again.

Until she was tightening on him, and he found the rhythm they both craved, slamming into her harder and harder. She came with a lusty moan into his mouth, the pulses of her walls around him nothing short of exquisite. Holding her tight, kissing her as if it were his last, Logan lost himself, coming so hard that little black sparks shot across his vision and a roaring sounded in his ears. He emptied himself inside her, filling her with his seed as he had in the carriage until there wasn't a drop left.

His breathing ragged, heart hammering, Logan broke the kiss at last, intending to roll off her.

But when he would have withdrawn, Arianna clutched him. "No, don't go. Stay."

He kissed her temple. "As my lady wishes."

CHAPTER 18

"You told them where to find us."

The accusation made Inglesby's gut curdle with dread.

The hour was late, the light in his carriage low, and he was on his way home after a reckless night at the tables, during which he had lost five hundred pounds and consumed half his weight in wine. He hadn't expected to find Charles Mace waiting for him within his own conveyance, pistol at the ready, with a warning to hold his tongue and keep from raising the alarm to his coachman if he wanted to remain alive.

Particularly not when the missive he had sent more than a week before—or perhaps it had been a fortnight now—had gone unanswered.

He suddenly wished he'd not had that last bit of port. Perhaps if he hadn't, his vision wouldn't be so blasted blurry, and his brain wouldn't be so sluggish and thick, and he would have been capable of defending himself.

"I didn't," he lied.

But even he knew the sound of his voice was hollow. He'd

never been particularly adept at deception. Less so when he was soused as he was now.

Wretched night.

Why had he reckoned he could use the five-hundred-pound reward to win? It was cursed money. He'd known he should quit after he lost the first hundred, and yet he had carried on, hopelessness rendering him reckless. The port hadn't helped...

"You're lying," Mace growled. "Tell me the bloody truth, Inglesby."

Gervase had feared, from the moment he'd begun to accept payments from Charles Mace in exchange for information he could glean to aid the London Reform Society cause, that he would one day be forced to answer for it. Mace and his brother were dangerous ruffians, who intended to overthrow the government rather than achieve gradual reform. Perilous, treasonous dealings with dangerous men. But Gervase had badly needed the blunt, and he had also been in a unique position of being a friend to the Society and a lord both. He'd done what he had to do.

Later, when his money woes had become insurmountable, and Whitehall began issuing rewards following the failed attack on the Tower of London, a new plan had emerged. He had believed himself clever, using Arianna, eliminating his direct involvement. When the Society had delivered a new payment and another request for information, it had occurred to Gervase that he might mollify his coffers by accepting coin from both Whitehall *and* the Society.

And he'd done precisely that, contacting the Society with a warning that Whitehall had been told about the location and time of their next meeting. It had been brilliant. Until it hadn't, and the Guild had questioned him when his information had failed to produce even one conspirator.

With the lure of the five hundred pounds looming, he had decided to have done with his involvement in such dealings altogether. With the Mace brothers imprisoned or dead, he would no longer need to fear reprisal.

However, only one Mace brother had perished, and the other—the one threatening his very life just now—had escaped. Clearly, the efforts he'd made to assuage the damage had been for naught.

"I'm telling you the truth," he forced out, trying to take care to enunciate his words.

"You're drunk," Mace said coldly, the pistol still pointed directly at Gervase's heart.

It seemed unwise to admit his inebriated state. Any weakness would be seized by such an opponent.

Gervase sat up straighter. "I'm not."

Mace's lip curled. "A drunken liar, that is whom we have to thank for all our efforts, now laid to waste. My brother is dead because of you, Inglesby, and now you're going to pay the price. You led the Guild to us so that he could be butchered like an animal."

Mace's words swirled in his slumberous mind. *You're going to pay the price.*

In blood, surely. For there was no other means he could supply. Tonight had ruined him just as certainly as any bullet would. Perhaps he would be better off dead. But no. He couldn't go to his rewards in such fashion, felled by a vagabond's pistol.

"I told you in my letter, I had no part of it." Desperation curled up Gervase's spine, rendering him cold.

"Your letter was filled with riddles," Mace said. "You claimed your daughter was marrying a man from the Guild."

"Martin," Gervase agreed readily.

He wasn't sober, but he felt clearheaded now. And one thing was certain—this man intended to kill him to exact vengeance for the death of his brother. Gervase had prayed before, prayed over the dying body of his wife, asking the Lord to take him instead. But much had changed since that long-ago day. Grief had cracked him open, and there was nothing left inside but a hollow void he'd attempted to fill in every way he could.

None of them had done one whit to change a bloody thing.

Instead, they had brought him here, facing down the barrel of a madman's pistol. For that was what Charles Mace was, and Gervase knew it now. A lunatic capable of committing any sin and justifying it in the name of his cause. But then, perhaps in that, he and Mace weren't so dissimilar.

The thought was jarring and unwanted.

"What has that to do with what happened to my brother?" Mace demanded, his voice ringing sharp in the carriage.

Foolish to hope the elderly coachman he'd managed to retain with the promise of payment would overhear and stop the carriage. If he did, to what end? Gervase thought about lunging for the pistol, but he knew he'd be no match for the younger, stronger man opposite him.

He thought then of Arianna's defection. Of how she had betrayed his trust, confiding his involvement to the Guild. But this was all the fault of that no-account Martin. If that whoreson had not seduced her, she would have remained loyal.

"Martin is the man responsible for your brother's death," Gervase said. "He's married my daughter. Spare me, and I'll tell you everything you need to know."

"Still no signs of Charles Mace," Logan reported to Tierney, who had arrived at Logan's rooms that afternoon in a surprise meeting he'd requested.

He reckoned it was down to suspicion, for ordinarily, Logan met with him at Guild headquarters. Although Tierney had grudgingly given Logan his approval to marry Arianna, he'd made it more than apparent that Logan was no longer as trusted as he'd once been. He supposed he couldn't blame him. In Tierney's boots, he would have likely been every bit as protective of the Guild. But his allegiance was to his wife now.

Tierney cursed roundly. "The bastard's out there somewhere. I can feel it in my bones."

As could Logan. Ever since announcing his decision to marry Arianna, he'd been working with relentless diligence to see Mace captured so that he would be free to leave the Guild and start a new life with her. And yet, each day, regardless of how many hours he spent scouring London, he returned to Guild headquarters with the same disappointing news. It was as if the man had disappeared.

Which made no bleeding sense. Handbills had been circulated all over London bearing Charles Mace's face. Even the public was clamoring for his arrest.

"My little birds are watching the home of every family member or acquaintance Mace has," he added. "They've all reported back to me with naught."

"With everyone looking for him, it stands to reason he would have to seek shelter with someone he trusts." Tierney passed a hand over his jaw, frowning. "And yet, that's the most obvious place for us to look, is it not? Perhaps we've been looking in the wrong places."

Logan was willing to admit it was certainly possible. Every bleeding place they'd searched for Mace had been wrong thus far.

A sudden commotion at the door distracted him then, and he turned to see Arianna and Chapman crossing the threshold. She was wearing her pelisse, bonnet, and gloves, and although she was buttoned up in the height of modesty, and despite the hovering presence of his superior just over his shoulder, desire slammed into Logan at the sight of her.

They had been married in a small ceremony attended by strangers who acted as their witnesses. She'd been his wife for the span of one week, and it had been the best week of his life, aside from his dismal failure at finding Mace.

She dipped into a formal curtsy, no doubt at the sight of Tierney. "Good afternoon, gentlemen. Forgive me for the interruption."

God above, he loved it when she sounded so stilted and aristocratic, her manners perfectly polite. Especially when they were in bed. But now was not the time for inconvenient and incurable cockstands.

Chapman offered an abbreviated bow and hastened back out the door, leaving Logan, Tierney, and Arianna alone in an awkward silence.

Her gaze darted from Logan to Tierney, and he could practically hear the questions churning in her sharp mind. It was the first occasion upon which she and Tierney had directly crossed paths.

"You needn't apologize, madam," Tierney said coolly, making no effort to hide his distrust. "I was just about to depart."

"Will you not introduce us first?" Arianna asked, another reminder that she was more accustomed to Mayfair drawing rooms than bachelor rooms in a tumbledown part of London.

He cleared his throat. "Mr. Tierney, may I present my wife? Darling, this is Mr. Tierney, a friend of mine."

She cast a hesitant smile in Tierney's direction, and

Logan noted that the cool air outside had painted her cheeks a comely shade of pink. "It is a pleasure to make your acquaintance, sir. I've met so few of my husband's friends."

Tierney's countenance remained hard and impassive, however, as he clasped his hands behind his back and struck an indolent pose that was at odds with the barely leashed power of his large frame. "Little wonder that you have, given the sudden nature of your nuptials."

Logan ground his molars to fight the urge to box Tierney's ears. "Perhaps you ought to be on your way now, Mr. Tierney. I'm sure you have more pressing matters to attend."

Tierney quirked a brow. "I do indeed. As I'm sure you do."

The thinly veiled innuendo in his drawl was not lost on Logan, but he was powerless to answer for it. When he was no longer a member of the Guild, perhaps he and Tierney would have a patter.

One that involved their fists.

"I bid you good day, sir," Arianna said cheerfully, the shrewdness in her eyes telling Logan that she understood the underlying tension laced in their polite conversation.

He waited for Tierney to take his leave, holding his breath that his superior wouldn't make any further callous conversation until the door had finally closed.

"Who was that man to you?" Arianna asked, curiosity shining in her luminous gaze.

"No one you need concern yourself with," he answered cryptically, for she knew that as long as he was a member of the Guild, there were questions he could not answer.

And then, he hauled his wife into his arms as he had longed to from the moment of her return.

"I missed you," he said, lowering his head to nuzzle the sleek silken skin of her throat.

"I missed you as well." She rubbed her cheek against his in the fashion of a happy feline and then withdrew to remove her gloves and bonnet. "It feels like a lifetime since we said farewell this morning."

It did to him as well. He spent every minute that he wasn't in her presence wishing himself back in it.

"Where were you and Chapman?" he asked.

"Paying my sister a call."

Her nonchalant response as she slid the pelisse from her shoulders had him instantly on edge. "At your father's town house? Damn it, Arianna, you promised me you would go nowhere near there."

"I promised you I would not place myself in harm," she corrected gently. "Not that I would never again see my father or Juliet."

His alarm grew. "Are you saying that you saw your father?"

If she had, and if that scoundrel had raised his hand to her, Logan would cut off his hand himself, peer of the realm or no.

"I did." Arianna sighed. "Pray don't be angry with me. It wasn't my intention to see him, but Juliet had sent the invitation to me at his request. He had something to tell me about the Society. Something which I think may be useful to you."

That caught his attention, but he was still far more concerned after her welfare. "Tell me he did not strike you or otherwise cause you upset? For if he did, he will answer to me."

"He did not," she hastened to reassure him, hanging her pelisse on a nearby hook. "He was most apologetic about how everything transpired when last we met. I do wish you would have seen him, Logan. He wasn't even as thoroughly in his cups as he usually is."

It was hardly a recommendation, and Logan wasn't nearly as eager to forgive the bastard. However, he was relieved to hear that Ingelsby hadn't caused Arianna further harm. What he had already done to her was crime enough.

"He should have fallen to his bleeding knees at your slippers and begged forgiveness," he growled. "You can't think to forgive him with such ease, love. He struck you, and then he forced you to put your very life at risk all so he could continue to drink himself to oblivion and dispense with any funds you were able to obtain on his behalf."

"I haven't forgiven him yet," she said solemnly. "But Logan, he told me that he knows where Charles Mace has been hiding. He said he wished to offer the information to the Guild as penance for all that has happened."

"Jesus, love. Why didn't you say so sooner?" He could have told Tierney before he'd left. Now, he would have to go chasing after him. Grimly, he said, "Tell me everything you know."

∾

"Are you certain it is necessary for me to hide myself away here?" Arianna asked Logan, trying and failing to keep from wringing her hands together in anxiousness.

"You're doing it again, love," Logan pointed out calmly, as if he wasn't about to leave her to go on some manner of dangerous mission to find Charles Mace.

If anything should happen to him tonight... No, she would not think it. Could not bear to.

Arianna frowned, wishing he were not so cavalier about the peril he faced. "Doing what?"

"Wringing your hands and nibbling on your lower lip as you do whenever you are fretting about something." He drew her to him for a kiss that was far too short. "You needn't worry, beautiful. All will be well."

"If all will be well, then why am I here?" she asked again, gesturing to the elegant room around her.

It was a guest bedchamber in the Duke of Ridgely's astoundingly large and elegant Mayfair manse. Just how Logan was acquainted with the notorious duke remained a mystery to Arianna, but she was accustomed to the secrets her husband was forced to keep. Ridgely traveled in a fast set, and he was a third son who had unexpectedly inherited the dukedom the previous year. His reputation was black as the night.

"Because I need to be certain you're safe," Logan told her urgently, caressing her with his warm, callused hand. "This mission is going to require all my concentration, and knowing you are out of harm's way is essential."

"But as a guest of the Duke of Ridgely," she said. "I scarcely even know the man. What can be the harm in remaining at your rooms?"

"The place where Mace is hiding is far too near to my rooms for my liking," he explained patiently. "Should he escape again, there is no telling where he will go or what the bastard will do. Here with Ridgely and his ward, you are safe. I'm not taking any chances with you."

She clasped handfuls of his coat. "But what of the chances you take with yourself?"

When she had passed on the information from her father concerning Mace's whereabouts, she had—and quite naively, she understood now—failed to imagine Logan would be taking part in the mission to capture him.

"I know how to take care of myself," he told her softly. "I'll come back to you, beautiful."

Unshed tears burned her eyes. They were still newly wed. It had been glorious, waking in his arms every morning, making love with him each night. She did not recall ever having been so happy.

Until now.

She wished the Guild to the devil in that moment.

"You must come back to me," she told him sternly, a hitch in her voice.

"Always," he promised.

But she knew, as she searched the shadows in his hazel eyes, that he could not offer this promise with certainty. Rather, he was telling her what she wished to hear. Trying to comfort her.

The tears slipped down in earnest now as she pulled on his coat and rose on her toes to kiss him again. The salt of her sorrow mingled with the taste of him as she kissed him and kissed him, inhaling deeply of his scent. She could not lose this man.

Logan was kissing the corners of her lips, then her cheek, cupping her face in one hand as he reached her ear.

"You mustn't weep," he murmured.

She shivered, and not from cold or desire, but from fear. "When will you return?"

"As soon as I'm able." He embraced her tightly, their bodies flush, and she thought this must be how it felt when soldiers prepared to leave for battle. Their loved ones holding on until the very last second, despairing to send them into the uncertain abyss of the future.

"Not soon enough," she whispered.

"I want you to promise me you'll stay here until I return, or until Ridgely tells you otherwise," Logan said firmly. "Promise me you will."

She knew what the *or* truly signified in Logan's command. He was telling her that she must remain at the duke's residence either until he came back for her, or until the duke informed her of Logan's death. Her stomach felt as if it were upending, bile clawing up her throat. Why had she not kept Father's information to herself? She ought to have never said a word.

But she knew why. It was because she had wanted him free of the Guild so that they could begin their life together. In her own selfish desire to have him safe and all to herself, she had unwittingly put him at grave peril. She would not forgive herself if anything happened to him this night.

"Arianna," he prodded at her silence.

"I promise to stay," she managed, though it pained her greatly.

"Good." His lips found hers for another kiss, this one longer than the last. "I must go, love."

No. These were not the words she wanted to hear. Nor was it the outcome she wished. What she wanted more than anything was to be back at Logan's rooms, naked and in his bed.

"Can you not linger another few minutes?" she asked, so very reluctant to let go of him.

He shook his head. "I'm afraid not." One more kiss. "Whatever happens this night, never doubt that I love you, Arianna Sutton. I love you with everything in me."

"Oh, my darling man." She bit her lip to stave off a fresh rush of tears. "I love you, too."

But if there was anything she had learned in this life, it was that sometimes, not even love could prove enough.

CHAPTER 19

The derelict tenement where Charles Mace was said to be hiding now loomed in the darkness of the night. After the last debacle with Whitehall and Mace's subsequent escape, Tierney had chosen not to involve Home Office in the evening's attempt to capture Mace. Logan agreed with the reasons why, but he couldn't say he faced what lay ahead without more than his fair share of misgiving.

"First," Tierney had said when they had been formulating their plan, "we don't know whether or not the information provided by Viscount Inglesby is accurate. He may have been provided false information, or he may be willingly making fools of us."

Logan hadn't argued the points—either situation could prove equally accurate.

"Second," Tierney had added, his face going dark with barely suppressed anger, "we don't want to take a chance that Mace escapes this time. Whitehall had their chance, and they failed. Now, it's our turn, and we'll do this the right bloody way. We'll go in under the cover of darkness, when he's likely to be asleep, and take him without a fight."

Still, to call the mission ahead of them dangerous was an understatement if ever he'd heard one. For if Mace wasn't sleeping, or if he woke at an inopportune moment, the fury of hell would break loose. Desperate men committed desperate deeds, and Logan didn't doubt Mace would be any different than the countless others he'd dealt with during his time with the Guild.

At least this would be his last mission.

One more, and then, *finis*.

Arianna's face flashed before his mind. Lovely and pale, the tracks of tears glistening on her silken skin. She hadn't wanted him to do what he was about to do, and he couldn't blame her. But there would be no future for them, no rest, until Charles Mace was in prison where he belonged. If he roamed free, a pall of doubt would forever hang over Logan and Arianna like a death shroud. Or worse.

"Are you ready?" Tierney quietly asked at Logan's side.

Logan nodded. "As ready as I'll be."

Tierney's teeth flashed white in the darkness. "I'll be waiting with my men. If anything goes amiss, raise the cry and we'll come inside."

He knew how this went. They'd done it before at least a dozen times, if not more. But on those previous occasions, he hadn't had a wife waiting for him, a woman he loved and would surrender his bloody, still-beating heart to protect.

"Let's pray it doesn't come to that," he said wryly, for he had no intention of needing to raise a cry.

If he did, that meant he was in trouble.

And if he was in trouble, there was a chance he couldn't return to Arianna.

And that, more than anything else, was bleeding unthinkable.

"Are you certain you only want two men?" Tierney probed. "Three might be a better number."

For a selfish moment, he wished he had Chapman here with him, but he hadn't wanted to take the risk of the older man getting injured, or worse. He had become something like a father to Logan over the time they had known each other. Instead, Chapman was back at Logan's rooms, making certain Arianna didn't somehow manage to slip away from Mayfair and return despite his orders, stubborn, headstrong woman that she was.

Instead, he had relatively fresh Guild recruits to aid him. But they were young and strong, and they'd be nimble in a pinch, even if he didn't like taking green bucks as his protection.

"Two is sufficient," he told Tierney. "Any more, and there will be confusion in the darkness. This needs to proceed smoothly if we're to succeed."

Aye, it would need to go smoothly indeed.

Tierney nodded. "Be safe, Logan."

It was the closest Tierney had come, in all the time Logan had been a member of the Guild, to showing true emotion. But he couldn't afford it to affect him, for he had a traitor to apprehend.

"You as well," he said, before nodding to the two men who were to accompany him.

John and Ambrose accompanied him to the door of the tenement. The plan was simple and had been laid out at Guild headquarters earlier. They would break open the door as quietly as possible and then silently travel through each room separately until they found Mace, hopefully abed. It was times such as these that having aided his brother Wolf as a cracksman in his youth proved endlessly convenient. He knew how to find his way through any door in the city. A crow and a false key later, and they were inside, moving into the shadows.

The stench of the tenement, far worse than that of the

alleyway, even, hit him. Cooked food, stale sweat, piss, and unwashed linen. It was the scent of his younger years, laden with memories he couldn't afford to indulge. Not when he was hunting a dangerous man.

They passed through the first room unencumbered and parted ways as planned, John taking the stairs and Ambrose moving into a second chamber while Logan prowled the hall. The layout of the building was no different from a hundred others in the city, easily spanned and searched.

He moved with care, opening doors and finding two rooms silent and empty. The building had appeared abandoned, and yet, the smells within suggested it was very much lived in, and there was no telling who else they might find aside from Mace. Logan didn't want any innocents getting hurt.

The creak of a floorboard as he entered a new room suggested he wasn't alone. The hackles rose on the back of Logan's neck as he kept his pistol before him in a tight grip.

A sudden rush of movement behind him took him by surprise. Logan began turning toward the source, blinded by the lack of light, but something heavy crashed down on the back of his head. There was the sear of pain, a flash of white like lightning, and then he knew nothing more.

∼

"Just where the devil do you think you're going, madam?"

The sharp, commanding voice of the Duke of Ridgely at Arianna's back made her pause, heart pounding with so much ferocity, she vowed he could likely hear it.

She turned to face him as he approached down the hall, a flickering taper in hand that cast an eerie glow around him, making him look even larger than he was. While he moved with an indolent grace and watched the world with a carefree nonchalance that suggested he was merely awaiting his next scandal, she had seen past his mask at dinner the night before. His affectations hid a clever mind and a sharp wit. He wanted the world to see him as a rakehell and a ne'er-do-well. His association with Logan, however, suggested otherwise.

"Forgive me for wandering in your home at such an early hour," she attempted to appease him, pretending as if she hadn't just been determined to escape and try to find Logan.

Hours had passed, and then almost all the night, and still, he had yet to return. She hadn't been able to sleep, and had spent the time alternately pacing the floor, rushing to the window that overlooked the street below in the hope she would see Logan returning at last, and casting up fervent, desperate prayers. As the faint strains of dawn had begun to paint the sky, she'd known that she could not wait any longer.

Remaining here, as a guest to the duke, was futile and foolish. She could not shake the awful premonition that Logan was in terrible danger, that perhaps something had happened to him. For why else had he not returned? And yet, here she was, a world away, of no use to him at all. She needed to find him.

"I'm quite familiar with roaming the halls at late hours," the duke drawled as he sauntered nearer. "However, as an expert in such matters, I can assure you that one doesn't go flitting about the halls before dawn whilst dressed for the night air. A dressing gown, perhaps, in the name of modesty. But a pelisse? I think not."

"I was chilled," she lied.

Yes, she was dressed to flee, it was true. He had been adamant about her remaining precisely where she was the night before and had told her he took his promise to her husband very seriously. She had taken care not to make any noise, but the hallway possessed a great deal of irritating creaks she hadn't been able to avoid. The duke's state of dress suggested he'd already been awake despite the hour. Was he as concerned about Logan's failure to return as she was, then?

"You were going to leave," Ridgely corrected her gently. "And that, I cannot allow, madam. I am under the strictest of orders to keep you here until your husband fetches you or…"

His words trailed off as he apparently thought better of telling her everything. But it was too late. She'd heard the implication, and it made an invisible fist close on her heart in a bruising grip.

"Or what, Your Grace?" she asked, dreading the answer, and yet needing to hear it.

"Whatever are the two of you discussing at such a late hour?" asked a female voice.

Beyond the duke, the shadowy figure of his ward, Lady Virtue, could be seen, resembling nothing so much as a wraith as she floated forward, clad in a dressing gown, her hair unbound and tumbling around her shoulders. Lady Virtue, it would seem, had been abed.

"Why are you awake?" the duke grumbled crossly, turning toward his ward. "Is this not the time for babes to be off visiting Queen Mab?"

"I am hardly a babe, Your Grace," Lady Virtue returned, her tone arch. "Indeed, I am the furthest from it. I dare say that some of the amusements that interest me would even put *you* to the blush."

"What amusements, curse you?" the duke demanded of his ward. "Why must you persist in being so much trouble? And why are you wandering about the halls in nothing more than a dressing gown?"

Arianna would have been amused, perhaps even intrigued, by the interesting dynamic between the duke and his ward. But the man she loved was somewhere in London, attempting to capture a dangerous madman. He'd been gone for hours now.

And she was not inclined to think of anything other than him.

"Forgive me," she interrupted them, feeling the urge to run. Would either the duke or his ward give chase? She thought not. Perhaps she ought to test her theory. "I am feeling unwell and supposed to return to my own home."

"You cannot," the duke said, turning back to her. "I'm sorry, my dear, but you're to remain here, and that's the way of it."

Frustration had her shoulders stiffening. "Says who?"

"Says your husband," came Ridgely's stern response.

"Interesting, your respect for a husband," Lady Virtue said, her tone rather snide. "When ordinarily you are making them cuckolds."

Ridgely turned back toward Lady Virtue. "My lady, you will hold your uncivil tongue."

Lady Virtue merely smiled. "Is it a sin to speak truth?"

"Hoyden," he said, but there was not any sting in his voice. "I ought to turn you over my knee and give you a thorough spank for your willfulness."

"I welcome you to try." His ward shrugged. "You'd have to catch me first, and given your advanced age, I very much doubt you could."

"By God," the duke muttered.

Arianna took advantage of the duke's distraction to quietly back away. As Ridgely and his ward continued to bicker, she slipped down the hall. And when she heard the duke call after her, she grasped her skirts in both hands and took off into a run.

DESPERATION PROPELLED Logan and Tierney through the predawn streets. Logan held the reins in a tight grip as he directed the curricle onto a narrow alley, his hands damp with perspiration, heart hammering a hard rhythm to match the frantic clop of the horse's hooves.

"I'm going to kill the bastard," Logan vowed. "When I find 'im, there ain't going to be a chance to deliver Mace to Whitehall. Because I'm going to gut him like a fish."

"If you don't kill him, I will," Tierney returned, his voice clipped and cold, laden with scarcely suppressed rage.

And there was more than good reason for it. Tonight had been an ambush. Although Logan had been the intended target, Tierney and other loyal Guild men had been injured in the fray. He'd come into the abandoned tenement to find Tierney and his men locked in a battle with Mace, Ambrose, John, and another cove who had been laying in wait to attack him in the darkened room.

The latter two had been killed in the ensuing melee.

Ambrose had lived. Mace had escaped.

Logan and Tierney had interrogated Ambrose for most of the night. They'd finally resorted to torture, forcing the truth from him. And that was when Ambrose had revealed that Mace had orchestrated the entire affair. He wanted Logan dead, and he wanted Arianna dead as well, in retaliation for what had happened to his brother. In a cruel, terrifying act of selfishness, Inglesby had sold his own daughter's safety to the Society.

Mace had never been hiding at the tenement. It had been a ruse to lure Logan and other Guild men inside to attack them. The plan had been to burn the derelict building to the ground afterward.

"You don't think he knows where my rooms are, do you?" Logan bit out.

"Fucking hell." Tierney's voice was uncharacteristically

thick with emotion. "I don't know what to think at this juncture. I believed we were two steps ahead of the devil, and he nearly had us all butchered today."

A shiver passed down Logan's spine at the reminder of how close they had all come to death. He well understood his superior's disgusted frustration and anger. They had learned from Ambrose that the London Reform Society was being funded by a group of wealthy merchants who hoped to obtain a greater stake in the government should the Society succeed in the revolution they were planning and attempting to orchestrate. The Society was flush with funds, so much so that they had begun to successfully infiltrate the Guild. Every action had been taken with the goal of undermining the Guild, Whitehall, and—ultimately—the Crown.

But the information which had led to tonight's near-decimation had been different. It hadn't been an aim of the Society. It had been purely and solely Charles Mace's attempt at gaining revenge. He'd intended for Logan, Tierney, and the rest to be killed at the tenement where they'd been led like lambs to the slaughter. But Mace himself had slipped away in the intervening fury which had been unleashed.

And now, they once again didn't know where the hell he had gone. Logan suspected he knew. Charles Mace's objective had been more than apparent. He wanted vengeance. Having lost the battle against Logan, Tierney, and their loyal men, he'd fled. There was one logical place for him to go.

Logan's rooms.

He very much feared the bastard would be looking for Arianna next. At least she was safe—as safe as she could be— far away in Mayfair. The Duke of Ridgely was no savior, and nor was he a man who Logan would ordinarily entrust with his wife. However, Logan had been admittedly desperate, and he hadn't had a better option. Ridgely's membership in the

Guild had, quite naturally, lessened since he'd unexpectedly inherited both his title and a ward in fairly rapid succession.

At long last, the familiar stretch of road came into view, Logan's humble lodgings looming. Everything unfurled next in a blur of color and sound. He pulled to a halt before his rooms and instantly knew something was wrong. The door was ajar.

"Jesus," he bit out, heart hammering harder as he prayed that Arianna had not somehow returned and that Chapman was safe.

"Slowly," Tierney cautioned with a staying hand on his arm. "If Mace is within, it won't go well."

"I'll kill him with my bare fucking hands," Logan growled as he passed the reins to Tierney and leapt from the curricle.

Ignoring Tierney's angry shouts, he landed on his heels before racing forward, pistol withdrawn, out of his mind with worry and fear and the need to protect and defend anyone close to him. Head pounding, body weary after the hell he'd been through, he didn't stop.

Not even when he reached the pool of blood seeping under the door.

He ran past it, dropping to his knees alongside Chapman, who lay on his back, gasping for breath.

Logan forgot Guild rules. Forgot everything.

He fell to his knees at his friend's side. "Sweet Christ, Chapman, no. Who did this to you?"

"Don't...know...who." Chapman grasped at Logan with rust-stained fingers, a trail of blood trickling from the corner of his mouth. "Was...looking...for...your woman."

They'd come for Arianna.

Desperation seized him.

"She wasn't here, was she?"

"No," Chapman mouthed, sputtering and coughing, his labored breaths growing harsher.

"Thank Christ," he breathed. "Don't say anything."

Logan attempted to assess the injuries his aide had sustained. The vicious-looking wound in his guts stole his breath. For he knew from the placement and the amount of blood present that it was a deadly wound. Chapman would die.

"Need…to…tell you," Chapman rasped. "They took…her."

New fear seized him. Perhaps Chapman was out of his head. Her? Arianna? What the hell? She was meant to be safe with Ridgely. Far away from here in Mayfair where he had left her. Had she somehow been taken by Mace?

Bile rose in his throat.

"Who did they take?" he asked urgently, noting the pallor of his aide, the breaths growing ever more labored and difficult.

"Said she was…your sister," Chapman said. "Lily was…her…name. They…thought she was…Mrs. Martin."

Lily. Saints above. His youngest sister Lily had somehow been taken by Mace. And Mace had fatally wounded Chapman in the process. Because he'd believed he was taking Arianna. Ice-cold fear skated down his spine.

"Fucking hell." Tierney was at Logan's side now, pistol raised. "What has happened?"

"Mace was here," Logan choked out. "He stabbed Chapman, and he's taken my sister."

"Sister?" Tierney repeated, incredulous.

"Logan!"

The sharp cry of his name in the familiar, beloved voice had Logan turning back to the street where a carriage had rolled to a halt, bearing the Ridgely ducal crest. The door of the conveyance was open, and Arianna had clearly thrown herself from it in much the same fashion Logan had from the curricle moments earlier, running to him in a swirl of petticoats and pelisse.

Tierney cursed beneath his breath.

Chapman coughed, his breathing increasingly labored and difficult.

And Arianna was running toward them. Safe, thank Christ. But Lily wasn't. And Chapman wasn't going to live. Yesterday's hell was seeping into today, with no sign of ending.

He was weary to the bone and devastated, though relieved beyond measure to see the woman he loved running to him.

"Chapman?" Arianna fell at his side, weeping fully, tears coating her cheeks. "No! Please, no. You cannot die. You must live."

Chapman choked on his own blood, He reached for Arianna with a blood-soaked hand. "Take...care...of...him...my lady."

Arianna accepted the hand, heedless of the blood. "Always," she promised.

"I'll avenge you," Logan vowed to his loyal aide. "I swear to you that I will avenge you."

"God...go...with you," Chapman said, and then the life fled from him as Logan watched.

CHAPTER 20

Logan rapped on the door of The Sinner's Palace and waited, desperation seizing him in an iron grip. He'd left Arianna safe with Ridgely once more, with her tearful promise she'd not go anywhere until he returned. Tierney, meanwhile, had beaten the location of Mace's hiding place from Ambrose. They'd formed a frantic plan to rescue Lily, but with so much betrayal in the ranks of the Guild, they needed men they could trust to get to Lily before it was too late.

They needed Suttons.

A small door within the larger portal slid open to reveal a pair of eyes. "Hell's bleeding closed today."

The door snapped shut.

Logan rapped again, with greater insistence. "I'm not here to gamble. I need to speak with Jasper."

The door slid halfway open. "Tradesmen round the back, but he ain't seeing tradesmen today. Come again tomorrow."

"Damn you, I'm not a tradesman," Logan snarled, losing his patience. "I'm his goddamned brother. He'll want to see me."

"All the brothers are within," said the voice of the guard.

Logan was tall, and it wasn't difficult to peer into the viewing slot. "Randall, is that you?" He tore off the hat that had been shielding his face. "It's me, Logan."

The large door swung open with a creak.

"You're bloody," the guard observed, lip curled. "You been hushing culls?"

Not a warm welcome from one of the family's most trusted men, then. Fair enough. He deserved no less, especially for the peril he had brought to Lily.

"Not today," he told Randall honestly. "Where are my brothers? I need to see them. It's concerning Lily."

"Miss Lily?" Randall's eyes narrowed. "No one's been able to find 'er all morning. Missing, she is. What do you know of where she's gone?"

Far more than he should. If anything happened to her, he would never forgive himself. The fault would be his, and his alone.

"I don't answer to you," Logan reminded the guard sharply. "Take me to Jasper, or I'll find him myself."

He moved to skirt the stubborn guard, knowing that every moment wasted was another that could be his sister's last.

"Aye." Randall nodded, his tone steeped in reluctance. "Follow me, then."

The guard led him down the familiar hall to the family parlor. Randall paused to knock, and Logan recognized Jasper's voice.

"Come," he barked, sounding tense.

Logan pushed past the guard, throwing open the door to the room, stopping on the threshold. Within, his brothers had gathered. Jasper, Rafe, Hart, and Wolf. And another man, one he realized belatedly as a cove who had come to Tierney for funds. Logan had been concealed in Tierney's office, hiding behind a panel in the wall, when Tarquin Bellingham had arrived. He wondered for a fleeting moment what Bellingham was doing within, what his connection was to the Suttons.

"Loge?" Jasper asked, frowning. "What the devil are you doing 'ere?"

"And why are you soaked in blood?" Rafe asked grimly.

"One of my men was killed this morning," Logan explained, his voice rough with emotion he could not quite conceal—grief for Chapman, fear for Lily, so many regrets. "He was stabbed in the guts. I found him as he lay dying, and he told me they'd taken a woman who said she was my sister. He heard her tell them her name was Lily."

Mace would stop at nothing to destroy him in the twisted name of vengeance, and he would not stop at harming a woman. Especially not if he believed she was Logan's wife.

"Lily." Bellingham went pale, looking as if he'd been stabbed himself. "Who has taken her?"

"An enemy of mine," Logan explained grimly. "One who wants me dead."

"Why would she 'ave been taken?" Jasper asked, urgency creeping into his voice as it lashed out like a whip.

"Because they mistook her for my wife," he answered.

Thank the Lord Arianna was safe. But Lily was not. His sister was innocent, and she did not deserve to die.

"Wife?" Hart repeated. "You've wed?"

"I'll not speak of it," Logan said curtly, for there wasn't sufficient time to explain; every moment they tarried was one in which Mace could be harming their sister. "It ain't important. What matters is finding Lily before it's too late."

"Why should we trust you?" Wolf demanded, speaking for the first time since Logan had entered the room.

Logan deserved his brother's scorn, his mistrust. Once, he and Wolf had been inseparable.

"Because you want our sister to live," Logan said, holding his gaze. "Time ain't on our side. If we want to find Lily before it's too late, you're all going to have to trust me."

"He's right," Jasper said grimly. "We've gathered to form a plan, to find Lily. And no matter what the arsehole says, Logan's got Sutton blood running through those veins."

The acknowledgment sent an odd rush of relief through Logan. He hadn't considered himself anything other than a member of the Guild for so long now. It felt good to be a Sutton.

It felt *right*.

Logan nodded to his oldest brother. "We'll need all the men we can get. And we'll need to act fast."

―

"Tell us where to find Mace and the lady, or I'll put my bullet between your eyes," Logan said to the man who had been guarding the dilapidated building where they believed Lily was being held.

Jasper and Wolf held each of the man's arms, incapacitating him. But it was Logan's pistol, the barrel pressed to the wide-eyed cove's temple, which had rendered him utterly still.

"Don't kill me, please," the man begged. "I don't want to die."

"Then squeak," Logan ground out.

"The b-back room," the man said, stumbling over his words in his apparent fear. "The door is closed, b-but you'll find them w-within."

"Hold him here," Tierney told Jasper and Wolf, meeting Logan's gaze and tipping his chin toward the squalid hall which led to the room in question. "Come."

They moved down the hall as quietly as possible, careful

to keep their booted feet from giving them away. One wrong move could cost them everything.

As they approached the door, Logan turned to his superior. "I'll go in," he mouthed.

Tierney nodded his permission.

With Tierney at his back, Logan kicked open the door, pistol before him. Mace was inside, doubled over and breathing heavily, along with a tied-up and bruised Lily. Relief washed over him. She was alive. And not only that, but it appeared that his sister had been defending herself against the bastard.

Thank God.

"Stay where you are," Logan warned Mace sharply, fearful the bastard would try to further harm Lily.

But it wasn't Lily Mace wanted to attack now. With an inhuman growl, Mace lunged toward Logan. His response was instant and instinctive. He had no other choice, no time for thought. Logan pulled the trigger, the report of his pistol echoing through the room.

Mace fell forward, slumping to the floor, struggling for breath.

"You… bastard," he gasped out, blood trickling from his lips. "I should've…killed you…when I had…the chance."

Logan recalled the day Clifford Mace had been killed all too well. The sound of the bullet whizzing through the air near his head. He hadn't died that day, and he knew it was because he'd been meant to live. To seize the life awaiting him with Arianna at his side.

And it was for Arianna's sake, along with Lily's and everyone else Charles Mace had harmed, that Logan took action now. He stalked into the room, determined to put an end to Mace before he could hurt anyone else.

"But you didn't, did you?" He stopped before Mace, and took aim again.

Another deafening report, and Mace went silent and still. It was over.

At bleeding last.

Logan moved to where Lily cowered on the dirty floor, trembling violently. He wrapped his arms around his sister, trying to offer comfort. "Hush. It's me, Lil. You're safe now."

He knew then, as he cut Lily's bonds and took her into his arms, that he could never walk away from his family again. His time in the Guild was done.

~

HE LOOKED as if he were about to faint away from exhaustion. But Arianna threw herself into Logan's arms anyway, not caring that the Duke of Ridgely and his ward were their audience in the duke's drawing room.

"You're safe," she murmured into his ear, realizing she was trembling from the intensity of her relief.

He had changed from his blood-soaked garments, and she was glad of it as she clung to him, holding as tightly as she could, breathing in his familiar scent of musk with a hint of leather.

Logan lifted her so that her feet were dangling from the duke's Aubusson. "And so are you," he said, his arms wrapped around her in near-bruising force, as if he feared she would disappear if he let go.

"What of your sister?" she asked hastily. "Did you find her?"

"Aye, we found her," Logan said grimly. "She was battered and bruised but will heal. Mace, on the other hand, ain't going to be so fortunate."

"Thank heavens your sister is alive," Arianna said.

"Mace is dead?" Ridgely asked, his countenance solemn from where he stood across the room.

"Gone to Rothisbones," Logan confirmed, his voice emotionless.

Sadness joined the relief. Arianna was happy to know Mace could no longer harm anyone else, but she hated the violent end the man had come to.

She tipped her head back, searching her husband's expression. "Did you…"

Arianna allowed her words to trail off, not wanting to complete the question.

Logan gave a short, jerky nod as he set her back on her feet. "Aye."

There was sorrow in his voice, in the harsh set of his mouth. The task had clearly brought him no pleasure.

"You promised Chapman that you would avenge him," she said softly. "And you did."

The memory of the kindhearted older man lying in a pool of his own blood, breathing his last, would haunt Arianna to her dying day, she knew. She could not fathom its impact upon Logan, and nor did she miss the sheen of tears in his hazel eyes now.

"It's my fault he's gone," Logan said wearily.

"You couldn't have known what would happen," Arianna reassured him. "You were doing everything in your power to see Mace captured."

And in the end, Logan had prevailed, even if it had been too late to save Chapman's life. At least his sister had been spared. Still, her heart ached for Logan and for the loss of Chapman both.

The duke spoke again then. "Lady Virtue and I will leave you in privacy."

Logan gave a curt bow toward Ridgely in response. "My gratitude for keeping my wife safe."

"As safe as she allowed," the duke said pointedly, before looking to his ward. "Come, my lady."

"Of course, Your Grace," Lady Virtue murmured with a notable lack of her customary insolence.

With a bow and curtsy, the two removed themselves from the drawing room, leaving Logan and Arianna alone.

Logan hauled her into his arms again, holding her even more tightly than his first embrace as he buried his face in her hair. "I was so damned afraid I wouldn't be able to come home to you."

"As was I." Hot tears seeped from the corners of her eyes.

So much danger, so much loss, and neither of them had slept. But she was incredibly grateful to have him alive in her arms.

"There's something I must tell you," he said, kissing her crown.

She tilted her head back to search his gaze. "What else can it be?"

"It's your father," Logan explained gently. "He was far more involved in the Society than we knew. The information he provided you last was intentionally wrong—it was meant to be an ambush, but Tierney and I lived. We've been questioning Mace's surviving men, and they've told us that Inglesby was helping Mace to save himself. After his brother's death, Mace wanted revenge on the Guild and anyone associated with it. Mace took Lily captive, mistaking her for you."

"My God." Full realization hit Arianna then, and the world seemed to tilt, threatening to send her sprawling. "My father was responsible for all this."

Responsible for Logan's life being imperiled.

Responsible for Chapman's death.

Responsible for Lily Sutton's kidnapping.

And responsible for putting Arianna in danger, too.

"I can't protect him, even if I wanted to," Logan told her.

"He'll be sent to prison for his crimes, along with a group of wealthy merchants who were funding the Society."

Had she ever truly known her father?

Arianna reeled.

"Say something, love."

Logan's face was fraught with worry. After everything he had just endured, he was concerned for her.

"He doesn't deserve protection," she managed past lips that had gone numb with shock. "Not from you, nor from anyone. He must pay for his crimes."

"And he will," Logan agreed, taking her hands in his. "As will the others."

"I am so very sorry for everything that has happened, Logan," she managed, heartsick. "I hope you can forgive me."

He tugged her into his chest, and she went willingly, twining her arms around his neck. "Floating hell, there's nothing to forgive. Just love me. That's all I ask."

"Always and forever," she promised through her tears. "I love you, Logan Sutton."

How good it felt, using his true name. No more secrets or danger. They would heal together, she knew.

He lowered his forehead to hers. "And I love you, Mrs. Logan Sutton."

EPILOGUE

Logan's heart was full as he took in the smiling faces of his siblings and their spouses, seated around the table. The first dinner he and Arianna had hosted at their town house had been a resounding success. Every Sutton was in attendance.

There was his eldest brother Jasper and his wife, Lady Octavia, a matched pair with their dark hair. At Lady Octavia's side was his sister Caro flanked by her husband, the famed prizefighter Gavin Winter. To their right was his brother Rafe and his wife Lady Persephone. Next to them was seated his sister Pen and her husband, Viscount Lindsey —or, as Pen sometimes teasingly called him, Lord Lordly. Then, there was his brother Hart, with his wife Lady Emma at his side, followed by his brother Wolf and his wife, Lady Portia. At Lady Portia's side was his sister Lily, seated with her husband, Tarquin Bellingham, and the circle was complete with Arianna at Logan's side.

The Suttons had indeed been reunited.

"Arianna and I are so very thankful you were all able to

join us this evening," Logan said, raising his glass of wine to the table.

"There's nowhere else we'd prefer to be, brother," Jasper told him with a warm smile.

Being a married man, settled down with children and the calming influence of his wife, suited him. The Sinner's Palace and The Sinner's Palace II were both thriving. As was Lady Octavia's gossip journal, *Tales About Town*. The rest of his siblings, from Lily and Tarquin, to Caro and Gavin, were equally settled, every bit as happy and content in their lives.

Not so very long ago, he wouldn't have dreamed this dinner possible. But with Mace dead, and the remaining colluders imprisoned, Logan was free to live as he wished. Free to return to his family without fear of reprisal or danger. And most importantly of all, free to start a family of his own with his beloved wife.

They had spent many nights—and quite a few days as well—working toward that goal. He hoped that one day soon, their efforts would prove successful and they'd have a babe of their own on the way.

"Thank you for welcoming me into your family," Arianna added, lacing her fingers through Logan's atop the table. "You are the family I have always wished for myself."

Arianna's father had ended his own life rather than face imprisonment or hanging for his involvement with the Society. They had managed to keep the true origin of his death hushed, to keep the scandal from affecting Arianna's sister, Juliet, who had married Lord Newbury and promptly hidden herself away in the countryside.

"We are the family you deserve, my love," Logan told his beloved wife softly.

"To the Suttons," Rafe declared, raising his own glass in a toast.

Everyone raised their glasses. "To the Suttons," they echoed.

~

"Tell me something that only you know," Arianna murmured to Logan that night when they were alone in the privacy of their chamber.

She was on her stomach, draped over his bare chest in the bed, delightfully sated. But she also had news she wished to impart. And she had chosen this evening—the first dinner they had hosted at their new home, all the Suttons in attendance—to tell him.

Of course, when her husband had first come into the room and kissed her breathless, she had grown understandably distracted. They'd made love in unhurried fashion, worshiping each other with their hands and mouths.

"Our old game," he said, a smile in his voice as his hand passed up and down her spine, then sifted through her unbound hair.

"Yes." She kissed his chest. "We haven't played it in some time now."

"Hmm." He lifted a curl, then let it fall over her shoulder blade. "Do you know, that I cannot think of a single secret to tell? I fear I've grown quite boring now that I've retired from the Guild. You know everything there is to know."

In the wake of the awful day Chapman had been killed and Lily had been kidnapped, the Guild had been disbanded. Logan and some of the other members had formed a new venture, offering their services for hire. She was abundantly grateful that he was no longer involved in such dangerous work and that he had found a way to spend his days that fulfilled him and provided a handsome income.

"Surely you must have one secret remaining," she said, nibbling on her lower lip.

"That I love you desperately?" he asked, caressing her nape beneath the curtain of her hair.

She kissed his bare skin again. "Hardly a secret, husband."

"That I love the breathy little moans you make when I lick your pretty cunny?"

His wicked words sent a wanton rush of heat to her core. "You shall make me blush."

"And make you wet, I hope," he growled, kissing the top of her head.

"Logan," she chastised without heat, still smiling, stroking his chest. "You are scandalous."

"Aye," he said without shame. "I am; 'tis a family trait, I fear. But now I suppose I must return the favor. I've told you all I can think of, having no secrets from my beloved wife. Your turn, Mrs. Sutton. Tell me something that only you know."

At last. She smiled and tilted her head back so she could see his face as she caressed higher, her hand coasting along his neck until she cupped his jaw. Their gazes met.

"I am going to have your babe," she said.

His lips parted, the wonder in his expression filling her heart with searing warmth. "You're going to have our babe?"

Tears blurred her eyes and she blinked furiously to clear them. "Yes."

With an exuberant cry, he rolled them as one, so that she was on her back and he was settled between her thighs. He braced himself over her, careful to keep his weight from crushing her belly, and lowered his head until his lips feathered over hers in a slow, gentle kiss.

"That calls for a celebration, beautiful," he said against her mouth.

"What manner of celebration?" she teased, feeling his hardness against where she ached for him the most.

"Patience, my love, and you'll see."

Logan's lips settled over hers, and Arianna held him to her, her beloved spy from the wrong side of London, who had taught her to never accept any less than what she deserved: his love and a lifetime of happiness.

∼

Thank you for reading Logan and Arianna's love story! I hope you loved their happily ever after as much as I loved writing it. There will be more to come from some of the characters you've met between these pages, including Archer Tierney and the Duke of Ridgely! Keep reading for a special sneak peek at the first book in the Rogue's Guild series, *Her Ruthless Duke,* available here. The very best way to find out what I'm writing next is to sign up for my newsletter here:
http://eepurl.com/dyJSar

Looking for more deliciously wicked historical romance? Turn the page for a list of my books.

∼

Her Ruthless Duke
Rogue's Guild
Book One

CONSCIENCELESS SEDUCER, cunning spy, confident scoundrel. Trevor Hunt, the Duke of Ridgely, has been called many things, most of which are true. Reviled by his family, hated by many, he's earned his reputation in the seedy streets of London and in more than his fair share of bed chambers. But battling deadly foes and irate husbands failed to prepare the duke for the most troublesome role he's played yet: guardian to one maddening hoyden.

Lady Virtue Walcot has spent most of her life abandoned, ignored, and forgotten. She's used her unfortunate circumstances to her advantage, filling her time with books and knowledge, yearning to build an independent life for herself. When her father's sudden death leaves her the ward of a ruthless former spy, her world is instantly upended.

An innocent ward is a burden Ridgely never asked for, and he'll do everything he can to see the chit wedded and his duties happily ended. There's just one small problem. He can't stop thinking of ways he might put the luscious Lady Virtue's sharp tongue to better use than pointed barbs in his direction. And then there's the matter of the unknown villain who's trying to kill him. Best make that *two* small problems, one deuced enticing and the other downright dangerous…

Chapter One

TREVOR HUNT, sixth Duke of Ridgely, Marquess of Northrop, Baron Grantworth, glared at the menace who had invaded his home a fortnight ago, doing his utmost not to take note of the tempting ankles peeping from beneath the hems of her gown and petticoats. A damned difficult task indeed when the menace in question loomed above him from the top rung of the ladder in his library. There was nowhere to look but up her skirts.

In his time as a spy working for the Guild, reporting directly to Whitehall, he'd faced fearsome enemies and would-be assassins. He'd been shot at, stabbed, and nearly trampled by a carriage. But all that rather paled in comparison to the full force of Lady Virtue Walcot, daughter of his late friend the Marquess of Pemberton, Trevor's unexpected and unwanted ward, and minion of Beelzebub sent fresh from Hades to destroy him.

"Come down before you break your neck, infant," he ordered her.

He hadn't a conscience, but he had no intention of beginning his day by witnessing the chit tumbling to her doom. He had yet to take his breakfast, after all.

"I am not an infant," she announced, defiance making her tone sharp as a whip from her lofty perch.

The minx hadn't even bothered to cast a glance in his direction for her response.

No, indeed. Instead, she continued thumbing through the dusty tomes lining the shelves overhead, relics from the fifth Duke of Ridgely. Likely, the duke had wanted to impress his mistress of the moment. Trevor strongly doubted his sire had ever read a word on their pages. *Hmm.* When he had an opportunity, he'd do away with the lot of them. He'd quite forgotten they were there.

"Child, then," he allowed, crossing his arms over his chest and keeping his gaze studiously trained on the shelves instead of the tempting curve of her rump overhead. "For a woman fully grown would never go climbing about in her guardian's library, putting her welfare in peril."

"She would if she were looking for something to occupy her mind, aside from the tedium her guardian has arranged for her."

Lady Virtue was, no doubt, referring to the social whirlwind he had arranged with the help of his sister, all in the name of seeing the vexing chit wedded, etcetera, and blessedly out of his life.

"Ladies love balls," he countered, uncrossing his arms and settling his hands on his hips instead.

Lady Virtue made him itchy. Whenever she was within arm's reach, he found himself wanting to touch her, which made absolutely no sense, given that she was an innocent, and he didn't bloody well *like* the chit.

"Not this lady," she called from above.

Trevor was certain she was disagreeing with him merely for the sport of quarreling. "Ladies adore those terribly boring affairs with musicians."

"Musicales, you mean?" She sniffed. "I despise them."

"A tragedy, that," he quipped. "In order for you to find yourself happily married, you need to attend society events."

Another disdainful sniff floated down from above. "I have no wish to be married, happily or otherwise."

So she had claimed on numerous occasions. Lady Virtue Walcot was as outspoken as she was maddening. But she remained his burden for the year until she reached her majority and was no longer his ward. Those twelve months loomed before him like a bloody eternity. The only escape was finding her a husband, which he intended for his sister to do.

Clearly, Pamela was going to have to work harder at her task.

He caught another glimpse of Lady Virtue's ankles and then cursed himself as his cock leapt to attention. He'd always had a weakness for a woman's legs. Too damned bad these legs belonged to *her*.

He cleared his throat. "You'll change your mind."

"I won't." She pulled a book from the shelf. *"The Tale of Love."*

Oh, Christ. He knew the title. Knew the contents within. Despicably, deliciously bawdy, that book. Decidedly not the sort of tome she ought to be reading. If anyone corrupted her, it wasn't going to be Trevor.

Unfortunately.

"That's not for the eyes of innocent lambs," he said. "Put it back on the shelf."

"I never claimed to be an innocent lamb." The unmistakable sound of her turning the pages reached him. "Why, it's an epistolary. There can hardly be any harm in that, can there?"

He ground his molars and glared at the spines of books before him, surrendering to the need to touch something and settling on the ladder. At least it wouldn't go tumbling over with him acting as anchor.

"Don't read it, infant," he called curtly. "That is a command."

"I'm not that much younger than you are, you know." More page turning sounded above. "*Oh*! Good heavens…"

"Damn it, I told you not to read the book." He gripped the ladder so tightly, he feared it would snap in two. "If you don't get down here this moment, I'll have no choice but to come after you and bring you down myself."

"Don't be silly. The two of us will never fit on this ladder, and your head would be nearly up my skirts."

Yes, precisely.

And he wouldn't hate it, either.

"Down, or I go up," he countered grimly. "You have until the count of five. One, two, three…"

Want more? Get *Her Ruthless Duke* now here!

DON'T MISS SCARLETT'S OTHER ROMANCES!

Complete Book List
HISTORICAL ROMANCE

Heart's Temptation
A Mad Passion (Book One)
Rebel Love (Book Two)
Reckless Need (Book Three)
Sweet Scandal (Book Four)
Restless Rake (Book Five)
Darling Duke (Book Six)
The Night Before Scandal (Book Seven)

Wicked Husbands
Her Errant Earl (Book One)
Her Lovestruck Lord (Book Two)
Her Reformed Rake (Book Three)
Her Deceptive Duke (Book Four)
Her Missing Marquess (Book Five)
Her Virtuous Viscount (Book Six)

League of Dukes
Nobody's Duke (Book One)
Heartless Duke (Book Two)
Dangerous Duke (Book Three)
Shameless Duke (Book Four)
Scandalous Duke (Book Five)
Fearless Duke (Book Six)

Notorious Ladies of London
Lady Ruthless (Book One)
Lady Wallflower (Book Two)
Lady Reckless (Book Three)
Lady Wicked (Book Four)
Lady Lawless (Book Five)
Lady Brazen (Book 6)

Unexpected Lords
The Detective Duke (Book One)
The Playboy Peer (Book Two)
The Millionaire Marquess (Book Three)
The Goodbye Governess (Book Four)

The Wicked Winters
Wicked in Winter (Book One)
Wedded in Winter (Book Two)
Wanton in Winter (Book Three)
Wishes in Winter (Book 3.5)
Willful in Winter (Book Four)
Wagered in Winter (Book Five)
Wild in Winter (Book Six)
Wooed in Winter (Book Seven)
Winter's Wallflower (Book Eight)
Winter's Woman (Book Nine)
Winter's Whispers (Book Ten)

Winter's Waltz (Book Eleven)
Winter's Widow (Book Twelve)
Winter's Warrior (Book Thirteen)
A Merry Wicked Winter (Book Fourteen)

The Sinful Suttons
Sutton's Spinster (Book One)
Sutton's Sins (Book Two)
Sutton's Surrender (Book Three)
Sutton's Seduction (Book Four)
Sutton's Scoundrel (Book Five)
Sutton's Scandal (Book Six)
Sutton's Secrets (Book Seven)

Rogue's Guild
Her Ruthless Duke (Book One)

Sins and Scoundrels
Duke of Depravity
Prince of Persuasion
Marquess of Mayhem
Sarah
Earl of Every Sin
Duke of Debauchery
Viscount of Villainy

The Wicked Winters Box Set Collections
Collection 1
Collection 2
Collection 3
Collection 4

Stand-alone Novella
Lord of Pirates

CONTEMPORARY ROMANCE
Love's Second Chance
Reprieve (Book One)
Perfect Persuasion (Book Two)
Win My Love (Book Three)

Coastal Heat
Loved Up (Book One)

AUTHOR'S NOTE ON HISTORICAL ACCURACY

Spies in Regency England? Secret plots to overthrow the government? Plots against the Tower of London? Yes, indeed. The events in this book are based on real-life happenings. The London Reform Society, while a product of my imagination, is based on reform groups of the era, such as the London Corresponding Society and the Sheffield Society for Constitutional Information. It's important to note that few of the members of such organizations espoused violence in the name of their cause, but some, like my fictional Mace brothers, did.

This was a time of unrest, fueled by the French Revolution and the Napoleonic Wars, with great disparity between the ruling class and the working class. It created the perfect breeding ground for unrest, a call for reform, and political intrigue. There was a pervading sense of fear surrounding reform movements, particularly on the part of the Crown. Outspoken reformers and revolutionaries were regularly arrested, tried for sedition, and transported or hanged.

During this period, there were spies and informants working through Bow Street and Whitehall, seeking to temper large-scale movements just as my fictional Guild was doing, many of them being paid to do so. During the Spa Fields Riot of 1816, there was a plot to take the Tower of London and the Bank of England and seize government control. The plot failed. Five-hundred-pound rewards were offered for the capture of conspirators who had gone into hiding, like Jem Watson and Arthur Thistlewood.

In all, it was an environment ripe for informants, double agents, and danger. I hope you enjoyed my fictional foray into the fascinating fabric of Regency England's underbelly.

As always throughout this series, the cant speech used by the Suttons has been sourced mostly from *The Memoirs of James Hardy Vaux* (1819) and Grose's *Dictionary of the Vulgar Tongue* (1811).

ABOUT THE AUTHOR

USA Today and Amazon bestselling author Scarlett Scott writes steamy Victorian and Regency romance with strong, intelligent heroines and sexy alpha heroes. She lives in Pennsylvania and Maryland with her Canadian husband, adorable identical twins, and two dogs.

A self-professed literary junkie and nerd, she loves reading anything, but especially romance novels, poetry, and Middle English verse. Catch up with her on her website https://scarlettscottauthor.com. Hearing from readers never fails to make her day.

Scarlett's complete book list and information about upcoming releases can be found at https://scarlettscottauthor.com.

Connect with Scarlett! You can find her here:
Join Scarlett Scott's reader group on Facebook for early excerpts, giveaways, and a whole lot of fun!
Sign up for her newsletter here
https://www.tiktok.com/@authorscarlettscott

- facebook.com/AuthorScarlettScott
- twitter.com/scarscoromance
- instagram.com/scarlettscottauthor
- bookbub.com/authors/scarlett-scott
- amazon.com/Scarlett-Scott/e/B004NW8N2I
- pinterest.com/scarlettscott

Printed in Dunstable, United Kingdom